BIRDY

JESS VALLANCE

HOT
KEY
BOOKS

First published in Great Britain in 2015 by Hot Key Books
Northburgh House, 10 Northburgh Street, London EC1V 0AT

A CIP catalogue record for this book is available from the British Library.

ISBN: 978-1-4714-0466-5

1

This book is typeset in 10.5 Berling LT Std using Atomik ePublisher

Printed and bound by Clays Ltd, St Ives Plc

FIFE COUNCIL	
97487	
PETERS	29-Mar-2016
TF	£7.99
TEEN	FIFE

Hot Key Books is part of the Bonnier Publishing Group
www.bonnierpublishing.com

1

It's 7.42 p.m. right now and I've been trying to get this started since three o'clock so I'm just going to have to get on with it. I've just been struggling with the perfect moment to step into the story, you know? Trying to work out how much you need to know about me, and about Bert, to understand how it all happened. Whenever I ask anyone what to include they always just say, 'Everything. Anything that's important.' And if they really want to know *everything* then I suppose I should start with the day I first found out about Bert. That was the very beginning, after all.

It's funny, isn't it, when you think back to something like that – some completely normal afternoon when nothing very important or memorable seemed to happen but when someone told you something that later turned out to be the thing to change your life forever. I wonder if I would've acted differently, in that conversation, if I'd had even half a clue of what it was going to lead to. Maybe I would've listened a bit harder, remembered a few more of the details. In all honesty though, I don't think my answer would've been any different. I would've still said yes.

* * *

It was a Wednesday afternoon that started this whole story off. The first Wednesday of Year Ten, in fact. It was the end of registration and it was boiling in the classroom – that sticky kind of heat that makes everyone all restless and irritable. All the boys had their shirts undone to halfway down their chests and people were fanning themselves with exercise books. Everything stank like onions.

Mr Hurst – he was our form tutor that year – finished the register and closed it up with a noisy yawn. He read out a notice about the toilets in Red Block being out of order, then shooed us off to our afternoon lessons, calling, 'Ties, folks. Ties . . .' in his usual bored voice. Everyone drifted towards the door but as I passed his desk, he looked up at me.

'Actually, Frances,' he said, in a low voice. 'Could I borrow you for a minute?'

I shrugged and nodded, feeling that funny mixture of curiosity and trepidation you always get when a teacher asks you for a private word. That's the feeling I always got anyway. I suppose if you were Jac Dubois or Megan Brebner and you were used to getting hassled by teachers, those chats just made you feel bored. Or defiant or something. But for me, someone who was basically ignored by everyone, it was kind of exciting to be summoned like that.

We watched the last of the class leave the room.

'Close the door please, Dan,' Mr Hurst said.

Daniel Greengrass replied by slamming it behind him, making the windows rattle. Mr Hurst rolled his eyes and sighed, which was about as close as he ever got to blowing a fuse.

There was always something very weary about Mr Hurst.

2

He huffed and puffed his way through every day, checking the clock on the wall every two and a half minutes. I think he spent the whole day just counting down the seconds to home time. Afternoons were definitely the worst for him. Sometimes he could hardly be bothered to finish his sentences.

Mr Hurst leant back in his chair and ran his hand through his straggly grey hair. I hovered in front of him, picking at the label on my history folder, and waited for him to start talking.

'Frances, I have a favour to ask.'

He clasped his hands behind his head, showing two dark circles of sweat on the armpits of his shirt. He must've seen me looking because he quickly put his arms down again and rested his fingers on the edge of his desk, tapping them a bit.

'Oh yeah?' I said, looking down and fiddling with a ripped nail on my thumb.

I was interested in what he was going to say, but I knew it was important not to let that show too much. There was no telling what errands you might get roped into if you were seen as too amenable at times like these.

'The thing is,' Mr Hurst went on, 'I've just this lunchtime been informed that we're to have a new member join our tutor group. Tomorrow. A girl called . . .' he checked a note on his desk, 'Alberta. Alberta Fitzroy-Black.'

Two surnames, I thought straight away. A posh one. I wondered if there was some kind of story there. Posh kids didn't come to Whistle Down Academy, as a general rule.

'She's going to be in this class, as I say, and looking at her sets and options, it looks like you two have the same timetable, so I wondered if you would help me out – help *her* out – and take her under your wing for a few days? Just until she finds her feet?'

'How do you mean?' I said. 'What do I have to do?'

The thought of being in charge of someone else, someone who'd look to me for guidance, made me a bit nervous. Who was I to be giving advice on how to do things? I was hardly a shining example. Of anything.

Mr Hurst waved his hand in a vague, non-committal kind of way. 'Oh you know. Show her the toilets. Explain how the canteen works. Make sure she doesn't get lost. Nothing too arduous. It won't be for long, I'm sure . . . and well, you never know. You might get something out of it. It might be nice for you to . . . to make a friend.'

I gave Mr Hurst a little offended frown. I didn't really like the way he was hinting that I was somehow lacking in the friendship department. I mean, I was of course, but there was no need for him to bring it up. Being lonely is hard enough without people embarrassing you by pointing it out. Also the idea that I'd see any new acquaintance as a potential best friend was a bit hurtful, I thought. Why do people always think that just because someone's on their own a lot that they haven't got any standards? If anything, it should be seen as the opposite – evidence of a bit of discernment. Other people might be happy saddling themselves to the first person to look at them twice in maths, but maybe I wanted more than some meaningless union of convenience formed around the need to share a calculator. People never thought of it like that, did they?

Mr Hurst obviously realised he was heading down a dead end with that line of persuasion and quickly changed tack. 'Look, Frances. I could just really do with a sensible girl like you giving her a positive first impression of Whistle Down. Help me out here, would you?'

I thought for a moment. I figured it might be something interesting to do for a couple of days, a bit of a distraction from the usual monotonous regime of lessons, lessons, lunch, lessons, home. Why not, I thought. No harm in it.

'OK,' I sighed. 'Fine. But I'm only doing it for a day or two. After that, she's on her own.'

I often found myself slipping into this persona – frosty, aloof. It wasn't deliberate usually, but I suppose it made sense. It's the only way to really cope with being an outsider in the long run – convince yourself and everyone around you that you don't want anyone anyway. I suppose at this point I was also setting myself up for the very real possibility that this new girl would ditch me as soon as she got the measure of me anyway. I guess I just wanted to make it clear that I wasn't seeing this as a long-term alliance so that when it all fell apart it was on the record that I'd planned to drop her first.

Mr Hurst looked like he was going to argue about that but I guess he just couldn't be bothered. 'Fine . . . Fine,' he said absently, then he opened a file on his desk and I took that as my signal to leave.

'Oh, Frances,' Mr Hurst called, as I headed for the door. 'One other thing . . .'

I turned back, my hand on the handle.

'I understand Alberta's had a pretty difficult time of it lately so . . . be gentle with her, won't you?'

I didn't ask about what he meant. I just nodded. And then I left and that was it. That was how it started.

2

In a way, I'd been waiting for something big to happen for ages. I didn't know what exactly, but I'd always had a feeling like I was just hanging on for something to come along and make things different. I felt a bit like I was in a waiting room – my real life, the one I was supposed to have, hadn't started yet.

For years, I'd been looking ahead to any little milestone that was coming up, and every time I'd think, This'll be it this time, if I can just get there – to the next year at school, to a particular school trip, whatever – then that's when it'll happen. I'll meet some new people. I'll find some girls like me who are never going to be the cool and popular ones but who are quirky and interesting and we'll form a solid little gang where we'll talk about books and watch unusual Japanese films and learn a martial art together. But then the milestones would come and nothing would change. And by this point I'd just about given up hope that it ever would. I certainly didn't realise that *this* was it. Not that day in the classroom with Mr Hurst anyway.

I'm not meaning to present all this as a sob story, by the way. I do realise that being a bit of a loner isn't the worst thing that's ever happened to a person. But it's important that you know the background, I think. I know people will wonder about some of the things that happened that year, about how I could've been so sucked in by Bert and why I made some of the decisions I did, but you need to understand how things were for me at the time she came into my life. I do realise I'm not completely blameless in this story, but maybe if I hadn't been so fed up I would've been a bit more guarded, wouldn't have put so much energy into her. Maybe. But who can really say for sure how they'd act if they got the chance to go back?

The main thing to say is that if they want to know all about that year – about what Bert did – they'd be best off just asking her themselves. They have already, I suppose. But these people love going over the same ground, again and again and again. And actually, the more I think about it, the more I like the idea of having my say. I like the idea of getting it all down on paper. I've never been one for writing in a diary – it's not like I would've had much to put in it before Bert – but that year is something I'd like to have a record of. Not just for them, but for myself too. And also for anyone else who asks. The last thing I want to happen is for the whole story to get all Chinese-whispered and people to start inventing details about Bert's personality and what she did and everything else that happened. I hate that kind of unfairness. I suppose I can't really stop that happening but at least this way there'll be an official version for people to refer back to.

Other people have started telling their own versions of the story already actually. The media especially. It's usually the same old crap, focusing on all the wrong details and missing the point entirely. I did read one interesting article on it all though. It was in one of those pseudo-scientific magazines – the kind that like to write about holistic nutrition and acupuncture and the nurturing of the 'self'. They called the whole thing 'the tragic unravelling of one damaged teen's psyche' and as these things always do, went on about the 'numerous failings and missed opportunities of the agencies involved'. All total rubbish of course – who could've predicted what was going to happen? – but at least that version was a bit more sympathetic than the spiteful, sensationalist stuff the tabloids like to churn out. They're all adamant that this should be my account. My observations on the year. It does make sense to ask me, I suppose. I was there after all, right in the middle of everything. And the truth of it is, I'll probably be able to give them a much more accurate summary than Bert ever would.

The thing is, for all Bert's lovely qualities – and there were lots of those, whatever she did in the end – she was never really any good at the kind of clear thinking that's needed to get through this kind of thing. I mean, she wasn't stupid by any means and I'm not saying that to make you think badly of her. I just really want this to be a totally fair, impartial account and the truth is she was always just so easily distracted and emotional that I don't honestly know if she could sit down quietly for long enough to get the whole story down on paper. She'd probably get bored of the project halfway through and start turning pages into origami frogs or something.

That was always the interesting thing really, with Bert and me. We were both total misfits obviously but apart from that we were actually complete opposites in lots of ways. And that was a good thing, I think. It seems funny to me now, the way people always talk about what they've got in common with someone, as if that counts for anything. If my time with Bert taught me anything, it's that it's the differences that are important. It's like a jigsaw, I suppose. To fit together you've got to be different. If you got two jigsaw pieces that were exactly the same, they'd bump up against each other and never sit comfortably at all. It was like that with Bert and me. I was the logical one, the thinker. She was the creative one. The entertainer. And we slotted together very neatly indeed. Most of the time.

Anyway. I suppose what they're looking for here is a straightforward report. That's what I'm aiming for anyway – a clear rundown of events, exactly as they happened. I think I've done enough of an introduction now so here I go with the proper story:

My name is Frances Bird. I'm fifteen. This is the story of what happened last year. The year I finally found my best friend and the year she betrayed me.

3

I thought about what Mr Hurst had said all the way home. 'A difficult time of it,' he'd said. What could that mean?

The important thing, I thought, was whether the phrase 'difficult time' had come from the new girl herself or from Mr Hurst. If it was from the girl or her family, it could mean anything. It could mean nothing. Some people announced they were having a difficult time if they'd got behind with their homework or if they'd had an unfortunate haircut. Mr Hurst, though . . . he didn't really go in for melodrama. He probably wouldn't call it a 'difficult time' unless you'd been sentenced to life in prison for an offence you didn't commit or had had at least two limbs amputated. In a way, I hoped the words had come from him. It would be good to meet someone with a bit of mystery and intrigue about them. Someone who would make me look like the normal one.

When I got home that afternoon, I found my grandparents exactly where I found them every day: Nan in the kitchen standing at her ironing board, occasionally turning to the stove to stir a bubbling pot of some kind of sludgy stew, Granddad in the living room, sitting bolt upright in his beige armchair listening to the cricket. As usual, he was wearing a proper shirt and tie, shoes shined to perfection, white hair combed backwards.

I went into the lounge and put a crossword on the arm of Granddad's chair. I'd nicked it from history I think – it was a photocopied thing, all the clues describing different twentieth-century world leaders or stages to war or something.

'Here you go, Granddad. Got this for you. It's a tricky one!'

Granddad looked up at me and smiled, but he didn't say anything so I just picked his pen up from where it'd rolled on the floor and gave his hand a squeeze. Just when I was going to take my hand away he put his other hand on top and we stayed like that for a minute, in a hand sandwich. Until I slid mine out and then Granddad just smiled again, but in a bit of a sad way perhaps.

Granddad loved doing puzzles, especially crosswords. Nan encouraged it – she said it kept his mind sharp. I didn't see the point of bringing up the fact that if you looked at one of his completed grids for more than a second or two, you'd quickly see he'd just filled it in with any words that would fit the squares. In fact, by this point, I think he was just sticking any old letters in there. Looking back now, I think Nan knew this really. It just wasn't something anyone wanted to acknowledge. All my life Granddad had been there, always so capable, fixing things, not talking a lot but always offering a few wise words of advice and a kind smile any time I was down in the dumps. I hated to think about what was happening to him, about that clever old brain of his slowly crumbling away. I suppose Nan felt the same, although she'd never say so. It wasn't really

Nan's style to talk about all the parts of our lives that had gone wrong. Which is probably why she ended up not saying very much at all.

I went upstairs to my bedroom and tucked the copy of *Brave New World* that I'd picked up from the school library under my mattress. I was a big reader. I could spend whole days absorbed in a book, whole weekends in the library or the park, completely oblivious to my surroundings. 'Escapism', I suppose they'd call it, but I never really liked that term much myself. I mean, who is it exactly who gets to decide which parts of your life are real and which parts are only allowed to count as an escape from that reality? I preferred to think that good books *were* my real life and all the other stuff – school, chores, all the rest of it – was just an interruption. I was quite into dystopias at this point. I'd already worked my way through *1984* and *Fahrenheit 451*. It fascinated me, the idea of these awful oppressive societies. I suppose it was just nice to read about people whose lives were more depressing than my own. Helped keep my spirits up, really. I was pretty sure Nan wouldn't share my captivation though.

There were at least ten books under my mattress at this point which was on account of the fact that Nan had very strict ideas about which books were 'suitable' and which might lead me astray in some unspecified way. Nan categorised most books, TV, clothes, people – most *things* – in the second category. Along a single shelf above my bed were the things that Nan had decided were acceptable: a copy of the Bible, a small selection of Enid Blyton books, *Pride and Prejudice*, a jigsaw puzzle showing an oil painting of Lake Windermere and an atlas. I'm fairly sure that Nan had never read *Pride and Prejudice* any more than she'd read *1984*, but that didn't matter. Nan's verdicts of unsuitability never had much to do with logical reasoning.

I'd lived with my grandparents since I was two and a half. Since the day my alcoholic mum decided that living with me was too much to cope with and swallowed eighty-four sleeping pills, which turned out to be just enough to send her into that special kind of sleep from which you never wake up. I was left to shiver in a disintegrating nappy and forage for food in the bin. Apparently it was four days until anyone found me. What with all the drinking and the drug-taking to be doing, not to mention the odd bit of shoplifting to pay for it all, Mum didn't have much time for friends and she hadn't bothered to keep Nan and Granddad posted on her whereabouts so they were rather surprised to find out I existed at all. I suppose there must've been a funeral although I don't know who would've gone to it. I'm pretty sure I didn't. Who knows where my dad was. Who knows *who* he was, come to that.

Before you start feeling all sorry for me at this point – don't bother. I don't feel sad about my parents. If I had to put an emotion to it, I'd say angry would be the most accurate choice. Angry at how Mum could've done that to Nan and Granddad. I wonder what they would've been like if she hadn't. I wonder if Granddad would still be well if she was still alive. But even so, it's just not a big deal for me. You're just going to have to take my word for that.

Dinner was at six-thirty sharp, just as it had been every day for the last twelve years. Wednesday meant beef stew and carrots. Having specific meals on set days was important, Nan always said. Made sure we were 'balanced'. Mealtimes in our house were quiet. Nan didn't believe in having the radio on when we were eating, so usually the only sounds would be our cutlery scraping on our plates and the kitchen clock ticking loudly on the wall above the door. I don't know if there's a more depressing sound on earth than a ticking clock.

'How's the cricket?' Nan asked Granddad after a while.

Granddad nodded and chewed slowly. 'Good,' he replied. 'Fine.'

Nan knew better than to ask about the score or runs or batters or anything. Neither of us wanted to watch Granddad frown as he searched his mind for the details of the match, only to shake his head, defeated, when nothing came to him.

We were quiet again.

'How was school?' Nan said.

'OK,' I said, pushing my meat around my plate.

We couldn't afford the good bits of a cow, so we always had the stuff everyone else would probably have thrown away. Chewy, gristly stuff. Ears. Nostrils. Arseholes, probably. I'd rather have gone vegetarian but there'd have been no way Nan would've stood for that kind of 'new age, hippy claptrap'.

At dinnertimes I always tried to think of jolly, upbeat anecdotes I could tell them about my day, anything to try to make the room feel less gloomy, but the truth was, nothing very jolly or upbeat ever really happened to me. I didn't mind making things up from time to time but it was a bit of a creative challenge, inventing new stories every evening. At least today I had my little chat with Mr Hurst to tell them about.

'There's a new girl coming,' I said. 'Tomorrow. I've got to look after her. Mr Hurst said I'd been especially picked to show her around and things, you know – because they think I'm a good advert for the school.'

'Don't play with your food,' Nan replied.

Then after a pause she added, 'What do you mean, new? Who is she?' Nan peered at me suspiciously, no doubt already deciding that this new girl was likely to be unsuitable.

I shrugged. 'I don't know. Alberta Fitzroy-Black is her name. That's all I know. But I'll have to look after her and help her settle in and everything. It's quite a big responsibility really.' I decided it wasn't a good idea to mention the difficult time she'd had. That was bound to be seen as evidence of unsuitability.

Nan crinkled her nose. 'Funny name,' she said. 'Never understood why people feel the need to double-barrel themselves like that. What makes them think they're so bloody special, that's what I want to know. She'll be stuck up, that one. Mark my words.'

I nodded and we finished our meal in silence.

The thing about not having much in the way of excitement in your life is that anything out of the ordinary suddenly seems very big indeed. Almost too big sometimes. I felt like this about the arrival of the new girl. Although initially I'd been a bit excited about being singled out to look after her, the more I stewed about Alberta Fitzroy-Black, the more it seemed like a bad idea that she should be handed over to me. As I walked to school the next morning, I used the tiny nuggets of information I had to build up quite a picture of her:

She was posh, obviously, and Nan was right – that'd mean she'd think she was too good for Whistle Down. Her 'difficult time' would've been some falling out with another posh girl at an exclusive private school. Her parents would dote on her and would've assured her that the whole thing was all the other, *nasty* girl's fault, so she'd be all full of angst but she'd have that righteous way about her that people get when they feel they've been wronged. And she definitely wouldn't like me, of course. She'd ditch me at the first opportunity and be off with Megan or someone, laughing at how ridiculous it was that they'd tried to partner her up with a loser like me in the first place. No, I decided. I didn't want anything to do with her. I'd find Mr Hurst and ask him to buddy her up with someone else. They were welcome to her.

But as I headed up to the staffroom, hoping to catch Mr Hurst before the bell, I bumped into him coming the opposite way.

'Ah, Frances!' he called when he saw me. 'Good, there you are. She's here already. Alberta. Come and meet her.'

4

She was sitting in reception, on one of the cracked leather chairs that were arranged in a semicircle around a coffee table. She was sitting upright, her hands folded in her lap, but she didn't look nervous as such. More just alert. Keen, I suppose.

'Alberta!' Mr Hurst called as we approached.

She turned to look at us. Her expressions seemed exaggerated – wide, surprised eyes, then breaking into a huge, delighted smile. She stood up.

'Hello!' she said, and she actually waved. I wanted to laugh.

She seemed so grown up. That was the first thing I thought. Almost like an adult. She was big. Not fat, not at all, but tall-ish. Five foot nine, she'd later tell me. A good half a foot taller than me. She wasn't lanky though, she didn't stoop like lots of the tall ones do. She looked sturdy. Solid. Her skin was tanned and her hair was flecked with blonde like she'd been in the sun. She looked clean and wholesome. Everything about her glowed with health.

She stood and looked at us, holding her bag in both hands, letting it dangle around her knees. Even if I hadn't already known, her uniform would've automatically given her away as a new girl.

The uniform at Whistle Down was black and white. The boys had to wear a tie, but the best the teachers could get out of most of the girls was black trousers and some kind of white top. Some of us – me included – wore the official school sweatshirt, which showed the school's leaf logo embroidered in blue in the corner, but that's about as smart as we got. Bert, however, was sporting the full works: pleated black skirt, white shirt with proper collar and tie and – this was the real giveaway – black Whistle Down blazer complete with light blue logo and dark blue trim. I didn't think I'd seen that on anyone older than Year Seven before. The thing was though, she actually didn't look bad. Somehow, she made the whole thing seem rather stylish.

Mr Hurst extended his hand as if going to shake Bert's, but he seemed to think better of it at the last moment and gave her an awkward pat on the upper arm instead.

'Welcome, welcome!' he said. 'Welcome to Whistle Down Academy. I'm Mr Hurst, your form tutor, so I'm afraid you'll be seeing me twice a day, for this year at least.' He did a nervous laugh and Bert beamed back and nodded.

'And this,' Mr Hurst went on, 'is Frances. She's in your tutor group – 10KH that is – and she'll be looking after you for a few days.'

'Hey,' I said, giving her a wide smile that I hoped said 'welcome' rather than 'I'm mental'.

'Hi, Frances!' Bert said, turning her attention to me. I noticed straight away that Bert had this way of gazing at you when she was talking to you, like she thought you were quite important. 'I love that name. Do you know, I met a family in Brazil once who called every one of their children Frances. Two girls, and then Francis with an i for the three boys. "It's our favourite name," the parents said when we asked about it. That was all there was to it as far as they were concerned. How brilliant is that?'

I blinked, slightly overwhelmed by this onslaught of information. 'Uh, yes. Brilliant.'

Her voice interested me. There was something very clear about it. A little bit posh, but not very. She just sounded very, very English.

Bert laughed. 'They had to have nicknames,' she went on. 'The Franceses I mean. To tell them apart. I can't remember them all now though . . .' She frowned as she thought about it.

'Well, anyway, shall we –' Mr Hurst said, starting to turn back towards the main school building.

'Criceto!' Bert said suddenly, her frown clearing and her smile back, brighter than ever. 'That was one of them. Criceto. It means hamster, in Portuguese. He was little, that one. *Ginormous* teeth though. Perfect name for him, really.'

Bert laughed, poking her own front teeth over her bottom lip and scrunching up her nose.

I just stared at her. I wasn't really sure what to make of it all, of this tall, tanned, slightly posh girl I'd only just met, standing in reception in a shirt and tie, doing an impression of a Brazilian hamster.

I think Mr Hurst could tell he was going to have to be more decisive if he was going to move things on. 'Right, yes,' he said briskly. 'Very good. Let's get to our tutor room now though, shall we? So there's time for you to meet everyone before lessons begin.'

'Oh yes,' Bert said, nodding. 'Terrific. Let's.'

Bert followed us back to registration, the whole time gazing around with her mouth slightly open, as if we were leading her through a mythical land. On the way we passed the girls' toilets and I wondered if I should point them out to Bert, but I chickened out. I felt self-conscious starting my tour with Mr Hurst there. I decided to wait till I had Bert to myself.

Mr Hurst was a geography teacher so our tutor room was in the humanities area of the school – Green Block. All the areas of the school were named in this way – Blue Block for science, Red Block for arts and so on. The school wasn't really divided into blocks at all though, it was just a spiral of corridors arranged around the main hall so who knows why they decided to call everything a block. I always thought it made the place sound like a prison. Maybe that was the idea.

When we got to the classroom, most of the rest of our tutor group were already there, slouching across the chairs, their feet up on the desks.

Gary Chester and Jac Dubois were tossing a mini rugby ball between them. As we came in, it bounced off the wall and hit Megan Brebner on the back of the head just as she was applying her lip gloss. The stick shot off to the side, painting a bright pink line across her cheek. Megan's mouth hung open, and she blinked a few times. Then she got up and thumped Gary on the arm.

'You're such a *dick*,' she said. She bent down to use the bottom of Gary's shirt to wipe her cheek clean and the whole class laughed.

I didn't join in the laughing though. It wasn't because I didn't find it funny so much, just because it wasn't my place.

It's like when you're on the bus and some people behind you are sharing a funny story. You don't join in, do you? You don't sit there giggling. You just accept that you're not part of it and mind your own business.

'That's enough!' Mr Hurst called, clapping his hands. 'Gary, Jac, sit down now. Put your toys away. Megan, you know the rules about make-up. If you're going to break them at least be subtle about it. Everybody, quiet please.'

I took my own seat at the front of the class and there was the sound of shuffling and scraping chairs as people settled into their places. A few people were looking at Bert now, noticing her for the first time.

'Everyone,' Mr Hurst called. 'I'd like to introduce Alberta. She's joining this tutor group today. I'm sure you'll all make her very welcome.' He sat down at his desk and turned to Bert. 'Uh, Alberta? Would you like to . . . say a few words, introduce yourself?'

God, I thought, what an awful thing to make her do – surely no new person wants to stand at the front and introduce themselves. Bert seemed unfazed though.

She smiled around at everyone. 'Hello!' she said, in her loud, clear voice. 'I'm named after the place, Alberta. Not the big one in Canada, the little one in Virginia. It's tiny actually – only about a hundred people live there. Mum and Dad were driving across America when Mum started to get terribly sick so they stopped at the chemist there – you know, for the pregnancy test – and so that's where they were when they found out I was on the way: Alberta, Virginia. I suppose they might've decided to call me Virginia but I must say on balance I think

I prefer Alberta. There's something rather austere about the name Virginia, I always think.' Then she stopped herself, her eyes wide again. 'Oh sorry,' she said. 'I mean, if anyone's name is Virginia or anything. It is a lovely name still, just wouldn't really suit *me* I don't think.'

We all just stared at her for a moment, fascinated by the unusual creature before us. You didn't really come across people like Bert at Whistle Down.

'Anyway, I'd best sit down,' she said to Mr Hurst. 'Shall I sit next to Frances?'

'Uh, yes. Yes, good idea,' Mr Hurst said, clearly as taken aback as the rest of us.

As Bert headed to her seat, Jac Dubois lifted his arm and held up one index finger high above his head. Over the other side of the room, Gary caught sight of the gesture and laughed.

'No way, man! You can't be serious.' He shook his head. 'You got no standards, mate.'

Jac just shrugged and smirked, and a few of the other boys laughed.

Bert looked between them, confused, her smile fading for the first time. Then she slipped into the chair next to me. I could smell her shampoo, I think. Or maybe it was the soap her clothes had been washed in. She smelt like apples and cut grass. A sunny sort of smell.

'That's enough, Jac!' Mr Hurst said, managing to raise his voice at last.

Jac smirked again and lowered his hand. 'What did he mean, that boy?' Bert whispered to me as Mr Hurst began the register. 'Why did he put his finger up like that?'

'Nothing,' I whispered back. 'They're morons. Don't worry about it.'

Bert frowned but she didn't say anything else. Instead she opened her bag and took out a whole selection of items – a brown leather pencil case, a long metal ruler, an A4 notebook, a calculator and, for some reason, a bag of cherries. I watched her, wondering what she was up to.

She saw me looking and misread my expression. She held the bag of fruit out to me. 'Sorry,' she whispered. 'Would you like one?'

I shook my head. 'No, I'm all right thanks. But . . . you know, you don't really need any stuff at the moment. This is just registration. We'll be moving for first period.'

Bert nodded. 'Ah. OK,' she said. 'Say no more.' She slid her things back into her bag, then she turned to me again. 'What's registration?'

I looked at her, wondering if she was for real. I decided at this early stage in the game I was going to have to humour her.

'Well, it's this bit,' I said. 'Where Mr Hurst takes the register. To check who's here. Then we'll go to lessons after that.'

Bert nodded, but she had the slightest crinkle between her eyebrows. 'I see. Jolly good.'

Bert obviously hadn't forgotten Jac Dubois and his finger because as soon as Mr Hurst closed the register, she brought it up again. 'Tell me, please,' she said, her blue eyes wide. 'Was it about me?'

I sighed. 'It just means one,' I said. 'Out of ten.'

Bert frowned and she looked upwards, trying to work it out. 'One out of ten? Well that can't be a good thing, whatever it is. One seems ever so low.'

I tried to think of something I could say to gloss over the matter but nothing came to me.

I sighed again. 'It means out of ten, he'd give you *one*.'

I cringed at the sound of it. I wished I could've thought of some other explanation instead. But it didn't really matter because Bert still wasn't getting it.

'But why? Based on what? What have I done to deserve such an abysmal rating?' She didn't seem annoyed, just genuinely concerned.

'No, it means . . .'

I hesitated, not sure how to explain it any more explicitly than I already had. I was having a hard time making an assessment of Bert. I wasn't sure what she'd be more offended by – the truth of what Jac meant or if I left her thinking she'd got a low score for some reason. The last thing I wanted to do was upset or embarrass the girl when she'd only been at school five minutes. I was annoyed with Jac Dubois. Why did he have to be such an idiot?

'It just means he'd like to . . . kiss you,' I said eventually. 'He'd like to give you *one* kiss.' That would do – not quite as pervy as the truth but at least she'd know she hadn't done anything wrong.

'Oh!' Bert said, blinking. 'Oh, OK.' She frowned again but she didn't say anything else on the subject.

I hoped I'd done the right thing.

5

Bert seemed to find the whole notion of moving from one classroom to another each time we changed lessons a bit baffling. Every time the teacher dismissed us and people began noisily packing up their bags and scraping their chairs back, Bert looked around, her mouth open, as if to say, 'What, not again, surely?'

When I asked how she was finding that aspect of things – it was true that battling through the crowds every hour was a bit of a pain and perhaps her last school had been smaller, less hectic – she put her head on one side and said, 'Well, it's just that it seems ever so inefficient, doesn't it? To keep spending all this time charging about the place, standing up and sitting down, packing and unpacking. I suppose I'd rather thought the teachers would come to us.'

'Was that how it was in your old school?' I asked.

'Oh no,' she said, seemingly surprised by the question. 'I've never been to school before.'

So that was a bit of a bombshell.

Annoyingly, Bert delivered it just as we were sitting down to begin a maths test so I couldn't question her until lunchtime when, as per Mr Hurst's instructions, I'd planned to help her get to grips with the canteen.

I thought I'd better let Bert eat before I started grilling her on her previous educational experience so we collected our trays and joined the back of the queue.

Bert kept standing on tiptoes, trying to peer over people's heads to see what was on offer. I had a bad feeling that she was going to be disappointed when she saw the greasy junk she had to choose from. I shouldn't have worried though. When we got to the front of the queue, Bert surveyed the steaming vats and trays, her eyes shining.

'Chips!' she said. 'Oh how I love chips! And pizza! Oh my, sausage *rolls*! You know, normally I only get to eat this sort of food on special occasions. Is it always this brilliant?'

'Uh, yeah. I guess.'

Bert piled her plate very high indeed. A whole dish of chips. A slice of pizza, two sausage rolls, a cheese burger and a flapjack. You don't like to say anything, do you, about how much someone eats, especially not when you've only known them a few hours, so I just waited patiently while she made her selections. When she was done, she headed to a spare table in the corner, walking straight past the till.

'Uh, Alberta?' I called after her. 'You have to . . . you know. Pay.'

'Oh!' Bert looked down at her tray and then over to the till. 'Oh!' she said again. 'I'd rather thought it was . . . free. You know, like the exercise books and paper and whatnot. I thought it was a sort of . . . all-inclusive deal, as it were.'

'Uh . . . no,' I said. 'It's not.'

I started to panic that Bert wasn't going to have any money on her and that she'd have to put everything back. She'd be so embarrassed, with people in the queue complaining and tutting. Oh God, I thought, all I'd had to do was explain how the canteen worked and I'd already made a mess of it. And now Bert was going to feel silly on her very first lunchtime and it was all my fault.

It was OK though, in the end. I led her to the till and aside from a little bit of grumbling from the dinner lady when she wanted to pay with a twenty-pound note, we managed to complete the process without any problems.

When we'd finished eating – and much to my surprise Bert managed to clear her whole tray – I decided it was probably OK to carry out a few gentle enquiries about how it could possibly be that this was the first school she'd ever been to.

She was perfectly happy to talk about it actually, and by the end of that first lunchtime I'd found out that she'd been home-schooled for the first fifteen years of her life, most of that time spent travelling around the world. Her parents had recently decided to settle back in England and that Bert should go to a proper school for her GCSEs. It was no wonder that I'd thought she looked grown up – she was. Nearly sixteen in fact, when I'd not even been fourteen all that long. Whistle Down was the nearest school to the house they'd just bought, so here she was. She didn't seem to be at all annoyed about the decision. She didn't say anything to suggest she'd rather have carried on with the life she was used to. In fact, she seemed quite on board with the whole thing.

'I think it was time,' she said. 'Time to move on from all that business.'

I wasn't sure what 'business' she was referring to and if this could be in any way connected to the 'difficult time' Mr Hurst had mentioned, but it seemed rude to probe too much at this stage. I had plenty of time to get to the bottom of that one, I thought. I'd done well for a first day.

When we'd finished eating, I showed Bert how we had to clear our trays away and pile them onto the trolley in the corner. Then she bought a hot chocolate from the machine and I drank a cartoon of apple juice from my bag and we sat back in the corner to kill the last five minutes of the lunch break.

As Bert sipped her drink, she looked about at the people milling around us, that bewildered, overwhelmed look still on her face. Occasionally something that seemed to surprise her would happen – a boy would run in and vault over a table, someone would swear loudly, a Year Eleven would pick up a Year Seven by the back of his collar. Bert would flinch and blink, and then laugh, shaking her head.

Suddenly, she turned to me. 'You're going to have to look after me, Frances,' she said, looking at me hard. 'Or I don't know how I will ever fit in here. Promise me you will?'

I nodded and sucked on my straw. 'Uh, OK. I promise.'

6

What I didn't point out that first lunchtime was that the idea of me helping someone else to fit in was totally ridiculous. I'd never fitted in anywhere in my whole life. I can still remember one of my first days of school. I'd stood in the playground in my too-big navy tunic, scuffed second-hand shoes and fraying cardigan, all bought by Nan from the British Heart Foundation shop on the high street, and looked around at all the other little kids, some playing football, some with skipping ropes. I spotted two girls sitting in the corner on the steps to the nursery hall and I went over to get a closer look at what they were up to. I saw that they'd got a white chalk from somewhere and they were leaning forward, drawing pictures of flowers on the concrete floor. I thought that looked like something I could get on board with.

'Hello,' I said to them.

They both glanced up but didn't reply. They looked at each other, then put their heads back down and carried on with their project.

I pushed on, undeterred. 'Please may I play with you please?' I asked, in my sweetest, most appealing voice.

The girls peered up at me again. The bigger, darker one of the two pushed her mouth into a thin, determined line. She shook her head. 'No,' she said simply, and went back to her drawing.

I hadn't left at once though. I'd stood there watching them, not sure what to do with myself. After a minute, the smaller, ginger girl looked up at me.

'Sorry.' She'd shrugged. 'But you're not our friend.'

That incident pretty much set the tone for the years that followed. People didn't give me a hard time. I wasn't persecuted. I just wasn't anyone's friend. So, as you can see, the idea of Bert looking to me for support as she tried to work out the complex social rules and customs of the school environment was hilarious really, but it was actually a little bit exciting too. I found myself getting quite into the role.

The thing was, no matter how much of an outcast I might've been, socially speaking, I did still know a fair bit about the school and the people in it. I'd been with most of the kids in our year since St Paul's, after all. I'd been there through it all – the bad haircuts, the missing front teeth, the fallings-out, the makings-up. I'd seen it all from the outside, always as a kind of disinterested spectator, but I had been there nonetheless.

In our first few days together, Bert drilled me for details – about who was friends with whom and who were sworn enemies, about how the school worked and what she should be doing . . . about everything really. And I was happy to help. It wasn't often people came to me for advice – it wasn't often that people spoke to me at all to be honest – and Bert was a very rewarding audience. She'd look at me intently, listening hard and nodding seriously as I imparted my wisdom. On one or two occasions I actually saw her taking notes. It was really quite a responsibility, I realised. Any help I gave Bert in these early days would probably affect her whole school experience and it suddenly became very important to me that I didn't let her down.

Those first few days with Bert were a bit like finding yourself as a tour guide for an alien being. She was constantly bewildered and completely unfamiliar with normal school behaviour but, at the same time, full of the enthusiasm of a Labrador puppy. It was quite tiring a lot of the time, but quite fun too.

Bert liked to talk and she wasn't going to hang around and wait for people to come to her. She'd think nothing of marching right up to someone in the corridor – sixth-formers, teachers, it didn't matter who – and telling them she thought their scarf was 'exquisite', or sitting herself down next to someone in the canteen and giving them a detailed account of the summer she'd spent on a cattle ranch in Utah.

I got quite used to wading in and extracting her from those kinds of situations. 'She's new,' I'd explain, giving her ambush victims an apologetic smile. It was a difficult lesson to teach a person – why you couldn't just sit down and talk to whoever you wanted. Bert would just look hurt when I tried. In the end I gave up, and focused on coming up with distractions instead.

One day in that first week, I lost sight of Bert as we made our way from registration to our French lesson in Yellow Block. We were walking through Red Block – the art department – when I noticed she wasn't with me.

I scanned the area around me, expecting to find her trying to engage some unsuspecting Year Eight in a conversation about Beethoven. We were running a bit late, so the crowds

31

were thinning as people took their places in their classrooms. I started to panic a bit. She was so unpredictable back then I didn't know what kind of mischief she might be getting up to. I had visions of her swanning into the staffroom, making herself a cappuccino and putting her feet up with a magazine and a biscuit.

Suddenly I heard her clear voice. 'Do you have a favourite sculptor? Personally, I just adore Hepworth!'

I turned round and saw her sitting in one of the art rooms. She was at the back, on a table of four. She'd rolled her shirtsleeves up to her elbows and she was getting stuck in with some clay, rolling it into a long sausage and arranging it in a spiral. The group of Year Elevens she was sharing the table with were all busy looking down at their own clay, struggling to hold in their laughter.

'Alberta!' I hissed from the doorway.

Bert looked up. Her face broke into a smile. 'Oh, hi, Frances!' she called loudly.

'Shh!' I said, holding my finger to my lips. 'Come here!' I mouthed, beckoning her over with my arm.

She slid out of her seat and trotted over.

'What are you doing?' I asked.

'Oh,' she said, gesturing back to where her clay sausage was sitting on the table. 'I'm not sure exactly yet. I thought I'd just do something organic. You know, just let the piece take its own shape.'

'No,' I said, trying to stay patient. 'I mean, what are you doing in this classroom? We have French. This is a Year Eleven class. You can't be here.'

I peered in to see who the teacher was – I couldn't work out how she'd got away with sitting down even. But I saw my answer – it was a supply teacher. Their normal one must've been off sick.

'Oh, really?' Bert said, seeming a bit put out. 'I didn't really enjoy French the other day to be honest with you, Frances. It was all rather dull, wasn't it? All those verbs. You know when I lived in Paris we didn't bother with that sort of thing at all. We'd just, you know, flap our arms about and whatnot and do the right faces and that was much better than worrying about whether a word had an s or a t on the end. So I was thinking, I'll probably just stop doing that one now. I much prefer art anyway.'

I sighed. 'You can't just stop,' I said.

'Oh . . . No?' she said, perturbed.

'No. Not just like that anyway. You have to tell Mr Hurst and swap to another language and . . . oh God, would you just come *on*? We're so late!'

Bert looked mournfully over at her clay, but she didn't argue any more. She collected her bag and blazer, waved goodbye to her new Year Eleven friends and let me lead her to where we needed to be.

7

I felt sorry for Bert as the days went on and her first week turned into her second. She'd started off so full of cheer and enthusiasm, but it seemed to be slowly seeping out of her.

On her first day, when Megan Brebner had called 'Nice blazer!' to her, Bert had smiled and said, 'Thanks! It's jolly smart isn't it? Makes me feel like some wonderful old general.' By the end of her second week, when a Year Nine boy said the same thing to her in the corridor, she'd frowned and looked down, this time aware that she was being made fun of.

As Bert realised that she was getting things wrong – I suppose as she became aware of just how clueless she was – she seemed to need me more than ever. She appeared to get more anxious, less confident about striking out on her own. And it sounds awful I know, but I found I was almost enjoying myself. Of course I didn't want Bert to feel silly or shy or uncomfortable and I really was trying my absolute hardest to show her the ropes, it was just that, in a way, it was quite nice to be so needed.

The thing is, when you get so used to being ignored it starts to feel like you barely exist at all. It's almost like you're one of those film characters who's actually a ghost but hasn't realised it yet. And so when someone comes along and takes notice of you – waits for you after classes, wants to partner up in PE, actually wants to hear what you have to say – you start to feel a bit alive again. It's impossible not to find that just a little bit thrilling. It was just the sheer novelty of it all, I suppose.

It wasn't just that though, it wasn't all about my own stupid ego and about me being the centre of someone's attention. I was starting to realise that I really liked Bert. I can't say that if I'd been asked to describe my perfect friend that I would've come up with Bert – or even anything like her – but now she was here, I loved the way that she was nothing like anyone else at Whistle Down. She was nothing like anyone I'd ever met. She wasn't like a teenager at all really, I decided. Sometimes she'd be as bouncy and overexcited as a five year old, then other times she'd come out with some strange sentence like, 'I say, it's frightfully nippy isn't it?' and I'd feel like I was sitting next to an OAP or someone from another era altogether. Even though her quirks had been a bit difficult to manage at first, as the days went on, I grew to really enjoy them.

I just never knew what she was going to come out with next. She had a seemingly endless supply of bonkers travel anecdotes that she'd start up with, quite without warning. 'Do you know,' she said one geography lesson when we were meant to be reading a chapter on the Cape Peninsula, 'we once gave a lift to a jewel thief in South Africa. We didn't know that at the time of course. He was ever such a polite chap. It was only after we'd dropped him off in Pretoria that we found out he'd had a million pounds' worth of diamonds stuffed into his knickers.'

'Blimey,' I'd said, not quite sure how to respond to that kind of story. 'Must've been very uncomfortable.'

'Yes!' Bert cried, clapping her hands together in delight. 'Indeed it must! Oh, Frances, you're so funny.'

Bert wasn't one of those people who only talked about themselves though. She was interested in me too, asking me question after question about my life. She didn't seem to differentiate between polite chit-chat – 'And do they still work, your grandparents?' – and the kind of probing, personal questions that most people tend to avoid – 'Do you feel they resent you? As if your mother's suicide was your fault, in some way?'

At first it took me by surprise, but when I got used to it I found that I didn't actually mind answering her questions, even the personal ones. She seemed to find me so fascinating – the fact I'd never really known my mother, that I had no idea who my father might be – that I sometimes found myself over-egging the whole tragic past bit almost without realising. It was just so flattering to have all that attention.

One Friday – I suppose it must've been Bert's second or third week – it was last period and Bert and I were sitting at the back of the science lab waiting for the teacher to turn up. I was doodling a picture of a walrus on the back of my folder and Bert was lying on the desk, her head resting on her arm. She ran her fingers over the spine of my folder, tracing the letters of my name.

'Frances,' she read slowly. 'Frances Bird. It's a posh name, isn't it?'

'No,' I said, scrunching my nose up. 'Hardly. Anyway, you

can talk, Alberta Fitzroy-Black the Third, Duchess of England, Princess of all the World.'

I gave Bert a cheeky grin and she laughed and gently punched me on the thigh. 'Hey, you! Don't tease!'

I just smiled and carried on shading Mr Walrus's tusk.

'OK, not posh. Just smart. Grown up. Terribly . . . formal. Frances. Fraaaaarnces,' she said, stretching the syllables out. 'Let's make it shorter. More cosy. What do we think? What's good? Frankie? Yes, Frankie!'

The truth was, I had briefly tried rebranding myself as Frankie before. It was towards the end of Year Seven, when it'd suddenly occurred to me that all the other girls had friendly, chatty nicknames – Ella Dewsbury was calling herself Ellie, or even Elz sometimes, Laura Cox was Lolly and Megan Brebner seemed to have become Peggy, for some reason. I know it seems silly now but I'd suddenly thought that that could be it, my key to being accepted. I'd become Frankie – cool, fun, chilled-out Frankie.

I started writing the name on my exercise books and in the corner of my homework. But then one day, Mrs James was handing back a food tech assignment and she paused, squinting at the page. '*Frankie*, it looks like here. Who's that then? We don't have a Frankie, do we?'

'Me, miss,' I piped up, my hand in the air.

'Oh,' Mrs James said, looking confused. 'Frances. Of course.'

'Frankie Frankenstein!' Tony Hope called out, and the class cracked up.

'Frankenstein!' someone echoed. 'Stay away from Frankie Frankie Frankie-steeeeeeeeeiiiiin!'

More laughing and that was that. For the rest of Year Seven. I was Frankenstein. As soon as we got back to school in Year Eight, I reverted back to Frances and, luckily, no one seemed to have remembered my old nickname.

I didn't bother explaining all this to Bert though. I just shook my head quickly and said, 'Nah. Not Frankie. That's lame.'

'No?' she said. 'We don't like Frankie? OK then . . . what else . . .' She carried on running her index finger over the letters. 'Fran . . . Franny . . . Ces . . .' Suddenly she sat up. 'Bird!' she said, smiling. 'Birdy, I mean!'

'Birdy?' I said uncertainly.

'Yes!' Bert said. 'I love it, don't you? It's simple but cute, I think. Terribly British too. And it's a bit like Bertie! Like my name! Birdy, Birdy, Birdy. My great pal, Birdy. What do you think? Do you like the sound of that?'

I think this was the first point when I let myself think that Bert might actually become a real, long-term feature in my life, that maybe this wasn't just about her finding her feet and using me as a tour guide. And that meant that maybe it had happened at last. The big change I'd been waiting for: I'd found an actual friend.

'Yeah,' I said with a shy smile. 'I like it.'

8

As the term crept on and sunny September became damp October, I realised that it was just as I'd hoped: Bert and I had indeed become proper friends. For the first time in my life, I didn't dread going to school. The lessons were still pretty dull, the other students annoying and mean, but nothing seemed so bad when I had Bert to kick around with.

I think I laughed more in those first couple of months than in the rest of my life put together. That's the thing about laughing – you really need someone else around to be able to do it properly. Before Bert, when people near me had sat cackling in the corner, I'd always found myself stiffening. I know it probably didn't do me any favours, but I suppose it was a defence mechanism. I'd roll my eyes, almost automatically. Losers, I'd think. Immature. Pathetic. I suppose I was just trying to tell myself and everyone around me that I didn't even *want* to be part of the joke. But now Bert had arrived, I too was a laugher.

The silliest things would set us off: a classroom door squeaking in an odd way, a teacher sneezing mid-sentence. In one registration, a window cleaner appeared outside, grinning in at us as he soaped up the glass. For some reason, the sight of him gave us such a potent attack of the giggles that we'd completely fallen apart and Mr Hurst had had to ask us to step outside to calm down. Of course, that had set us off all over again and once we were out in the corridor, we'd clung to each other, gasping for breath, tears running down our cheeks.

Bert lived across the other side of town, on one of the wide roads that backed onto the golf course. Every morning we'd meet each other at the top of the hill and walk down together, across the main road and over the playing fields to school. Bert – who always seemed to have a fair amount of cash on her – would often want to stop at the paper shop on the corner to buy croissants or a sausage roll from the glass cabinet at the front. In fact, as her enthusiasm that first day in the canteen had suggested, Bert liked to eat a *lot*. Especially junk food. I have no idea how she managed to stay looking so healthy and fresh with all the grease and gunk she chucked inside her.

After school, we'd often wander up the field and through the grassy quayside area next to the river to the high street. We'd amble along for ages, looking in the shop windows. Sometimes we'd go inside and try things on, or go into Debenhams and play around with the make-up samples, dolling ourselves up like drag queens. Before Bert, I probably would've turned my nose up at such juvenile behaviour but I suppose that was because I would've always just been watching, looking over from the outside. Now I had Bert, now I could join in, it all seemed like brilliant fun. Really, everything with Bert was brilliant fun.

Those first few weeks, even though Bert and I seemed to be getting on really well, I still had that worry in the back of my mind that as soon as she got to know some of the others, she'd ditch me. I did want her to fit in of course, that was my whole job after all, it's just that I did so want her to still be my friend too. Every so often I'd get a wave of anxiety and decide that it was only a matter of time until she started spending her lunchtimes reading gossip magazines in the canteen with Megan Brebner and Laura Cox, or maybe organising science club outings with Polly Ratchet.

But then gradually I started to relax. The thing was, she actually wasn't having any trouble fitting in any more. She was still a little bit eccentric but people had got used to it. Some of them seemed to like it, even. She wasn't making a fool of herself. It seemed she had found her feet at last. But despite that, despite the fact she didn't necessarily *need* me any more, she didn't show any signs of going off with anyone else. I mean, she was polite to everyone, but that was as far as it went. It was me she'd sit with in lessons, me she'd wait for so we could walk home from school together. I seemed to be enough for her. She'd chosen me. She wanted to be my friend. It was quite a wonderful feeling, really.

Sometimes, when I look back now, I try to remember how much of that wonderful feeling was to do with Bert herself at that point and how much of it was just the sheer relief of finally feeling part of something after a lifetime of being on the outside of everything, of feeling that there wasn't a single person in the world who really knew me. It was sort of like being picked for the team after fifteen years of sitting on the bench and I suppose that was quite a powerful thing. Certainly powerful enough to stop me taking a step back and really taking a good look at Bert, carrying out a proper assessment of her character. She *was* lovely of course, totally charming, but I do wonder if I could've looked a little more closely at the person I was getting involved with.

Right from Jac Dubois's index finger sign on Bert's first day, I had a feeling that she'd be popular with the boys, and as time went on, there definitely seemed to be some truth in that. At first, there was the usual macho strutting about – wolf whistles, cheesy chat-up lines called across the canteen, but that always seemed as if it was more for the benefit of the other boys than any real interest. You know what they're like – just excited to have a new bit of meat to look at. After that all died down though, there were still one or two genuine admirers sniffing around.

There was Darren Hathaway for example, a grubby boy in our maths class, who liked to hover around a bit, and also a Year Eight boy who'd seemed to have developed a bit of a fixation and started leaving envelopes of rose petals tucked into Bert's locker. It was in the back of my mind that at some point Bert might succumb to the flattery and start going out with one boy or other. I didn't think Darren or the Year Eight were really in with a chance but if they were interested then I knew there'd be others. I knew that sooner or later another boy would pop up and it might just be someone who Bert liked the look of. I dreaded this happening to be honest.

I just knew what it would mean for me. For us. I'd be demoted to the third wheel, the spare part. The ugly best friend hanging around while the boy whispered, 'Can't we be *alone* for a bit?' into Bert's ear, at the same time tilting his head meaningfully in my direction. Bert would giggle and say, 'Oh, all right then,' before turning to me and asking me politely but firmly to make myself scarce. I know it makes me sound a bit neurotic, thinking like that, but when you've finally found something you've been waiting fourteen years for, I suppose you get a bit panicky at the thought of it being messed up.

Luckily though, for the time being, things were OK. Mostly Bert seemed happy to keep her distance from the boys. She was never rude; she never gave them cutting put-downs or withering looks. She just didn't seem that interested. It was also useful that if anyone more attractive than Darren seemed to be getting interested, the other girls in our year were pretty quick to act as bodyguards. Anyone who was even half decent-looking was usually declared spoken for, and if he was seen too near Bert, Megan or one of the others would step in. Once, for example, Matt Pereira had been hanging around us in the canteen. Matt was your classic tall-dark-handsome type. Big brown eyes and good at sports and all that. He was flirting with Bert I suppose, but more in a bored, lazy way than with any real determination. But Ella Dewsbury had caught sight of him and decided he was up to no good.

She called over. 'I see you, Matthew John Pereira, trying it on over there. Put your tongue back in and step away or I'll tell Laura what you've been up to.'

Matt had shot Bert one last cheeky grin and slunk away, obviously figuring she wasn't worth getting in trouble over.

By the time I'd known Bert for six weeks or so, I felt confident enough to ask a few questions around the 'difficult time' Mr Hurst had mentioned when he'd told me about her. So far, nothing she'd said about her life before school had given me much of a clue. I tried to think of a way to draw it out of her subtly, but there didn't seem to be one. I decided to just ask her outright. After all, Bert was nothing if not upfront herself.

We were in art one afternoon – one of my favourite lessons since Bert had joined because we were usually allowed to get on with our own work, which meant plenty of time for us to sit well away from everyone else and talk. I waited until there was a lull in conversation, then I dived right in.

'Bert,' I said carefully. 'Mr Hurst said . . . I mean, when he first told me you were coming, he mentioned that you . . . that things had been . . . *tricky* for you.'

I stopped, practically holding my breath. There. It was out there.

Bert didn't reply for a moment or two. She just carried on blending her charcoal with her fingers. I thought she was going to pretend she hadn't heard the question, or worse, snap at me for being so nosy. But then she looked up and gave me a mischievous grin. She looked sideways quickly, as if she was checking no one was listening.

'If I tell you, you can't tell anyone,' she said. 'Not a soul. People would think badly of me, I'm sure of it.'

'OK,' I said. 'I won't tell.'

'Promise?'

'Cross my heart,' I said, doing my most earnest, trustworthy expression. 'You can trust me.'

'I know. Of course I can. Good old Birdy.' She reached across the table and squeezed my hand. Then she grinned. 'I did criminal damage!' she said triumphantly.

I couldn't help but giggle. Bert sounded funny just saying the words 'criminal damage'. I couldn't for the life of me imagine her doing any.

'What do you mean? What did you do?'

'Threw a brick through a car window. *Richard's* car.' She pulled a bit of a face, like she found the name distasteful in some way.

I frowned. 'Who's Richard?'

'Oh, just this friend of my parents. He was a marine biologist.'

I waited for her to go on, to explain what he'd done to deserve such treatment, and whether it was somehow related to his marine biology antics, but she didn't show any signs of expanding on her anecdote.

'So . . . did you do it on purpose? Why?'

'Oh yes. It was quite deliberate,' she said, putting her charcoal down and looking at me. 'I was just so cross! Richard was being really unbearable. I'd just had enough. So I wrote him a little message, to tell him so. I was going to just leave it out for him to see, but that morning . . . well, let's just say he'd been particularly vile. So I tied it around a brick, and – smash! – popped it through the window of his car.'

I just looked at her for a minute, trying to take this image in. 'What do you mean, vile? What did he do?'

'Oh . . . you know.' She gave a little vague wave of her hand but didn't say anything else. Then she shrugged sulkily and added, 'What can I say? I'm a very passionate person.'

I laughed and shook my head. 'What did it say, then? The message?'

Bert looked back up, suddenly proud again. 'It said, "You are as loathsome as a toad."'

'What? Why?'

'It's from a play. *Titus Andronicus*. I was reading it at the time. I thought it was clever. Offensive, but classy.'

I nodded and we were quiet for a moment then, concentrating on our drawings.

'So what . . . then you had to come to school?' I asked. 'As a punishment?'

Bert shrugged. 'Not really a punishment as such. More for . . . socialisation. My parents talked a lot about boundaries and appropriate behaviour.' She scrunched her nose up. 'Don't tell anyone though.'

'Sure, OK. Whatever you want.' I wasn't really sure what I'd tell them anyway.

Bert smiled and shook the charcoal dust from her picture. 'Thanks, Birdy. Anyway, that's all in the past now. No more dramas for me, that's for sure. These days I am equanimity personified.'

I smiled back, feeling pleased that Bert had felt she could confide in me, even if I wasn't one hundred per cent clear on what she'd actually confided.

I have wondered about that day since, you know. I wonder if this was the first clue I had about what Bert was really like. She'd called it 'passionate', but with the benefit of hindsight, I wonder if another word might've been more accurate. Impetuous, perhaps. Volatile.

Definitely more than a little unpredictable anyway.

9

On October the eighteenth Bert asked me if I wanted to go to her house after school. I remember the date because it felt like such a milestone. Maybe I would've made a note of more of the dates if I'd known that one day this would all form part of a story.

'You can stay for dinner, if you like,' she said. 'Mum's so chuffed that I've made a friend so quickly. She can't wait to meet you.'

'OK,' I said, giving a nonchalant shrug to hide my delight. 'Sounds good.'

'Will you need to check with your grandparents?'

'Nah,' I said. 'They'll be fine. I'll just let them know I won't be in for dinner.'

The truth was, Nan would be likely to make such a fuss about the idea of me going to someone else's house for dinner that I knew I wouldn't even tell her. It was one of Nan's peculiarities – that we should never eat other people's food. In her eyes, it was somehow shameful. As if it was suggesting that we need to be fed by other people, like it made us look like a charity case. Still, I could easily tell Nan I was doing homework in the school library – as we didn't have the internet or even a computer in the house, I often had to do that, so she wouldn't think anything of it. I knew I'd have to eat a second dinner when I got home – Nan always kept mine for me when I was late, on the side with a plate over the top – but that was OK. I didn't want to worry her or stress her out but I did so badly want to go.

I'd actually walked past Bert's house loads of times before, when I was out for my Saturday afternoon walks. Weekends really drag when you haven't got any friends and you're only allowed to read real books when no one's watching. Sometimes I'd head to the library to escape the house but I'd often find it full of giggling five year olds and their drippy parents clapping and singing nursery rhymes. If I hung around at home, Nan would give me jobs to do – cleaning out cupboards, scrubbing the floors, starching Granddad's shirts – so I'd usually pass the time by taking myself out for long walks. I could be gone for hours, trudging around the streets. Sometimes I'd go into Flo's Cafe at the end of the high street and sit at one of the tables with the plastic red and white checked tablecloths. They'd give me a mug of hot water for free usually. They were never that busy in there so they didn't mind me taking up a table without paying for anything. If Flo was there she'd even slip me a biscuit sometimes. I guess I'm the kind of person people tend to feel sorry for.

Bert's road – Chestnut Avenue – was one of my favourites to walk down. All the houses were huge, and every one of them was different. Bert's one was light blue and white. It had big bay windows and the front door was right in the middle. I always think that's the sign of a really posh house – when it's perfectly symmetrical at the front.

We had to ring the doorbell because Bert had forgotten her key. When the door was flung open, a middle-aged woman stood in the doorway. She was older than I'd expected, I suppose around fifty. She had short, spiky hair, dark at the roots where her blonde dye was growing out. She was wearing an oversized man's shirt. Both her face and her shirt were splattered with green and purple paint. She smiled widely at us.

'Oh hi, darlings!' she said. 'You're home already! Gosh, hasn't the day whizzed by? You must be Frances,' she said to me. 'How lovely to meet you! I'm Genevieve.'

She leant forward and kissed me on the cheek. I froze, not quite sure how to respond. My nan had probably only kissed me twice in my entire life so I wasn't used to these kinds of spontaneous displays of affection.

'Yes, this is Frances,' Bert said, stepping into the hall and kicking off her shoes. 'I call her Birdy. But that's our thing really so you should probably just call her Frances. Is that OK with you?' she added, turning back to check with me.

I said it was fine and Genevieve laughed. 'Right-oh,' she said. 'Can you help yourselves to a snack or whatever you want? I'm just finishing up in here.'

Genevieve disappeared into a room off the hall that smelt like varnish and glue.

'Mum's studio,' Bert explained. 'She spends most of her life in there. She's an artist. Genevieve Fitzroy – have you heard of her? She does these ginormous paintings – all bright colours and splashes of paint everywhere. She sells them for thousands.'

I shook my head. It didn't exactly sound like the kind of artwork we'd be likely to have in my grandparents' house.

Bert's kitchen was warm and smelt like coffee. I sat at a huge wooden table and watched as Bert poured us big glasses of lemonade and made us jam on toast. I couldn't imagine Nan ever letting me raid the cupboards like that. Especially not before dinner. As we sat at the kitchen table, the back door opened and a tall, thin man with curly orange hair and muddy green wellies came in.

He seemed surprised to see us. 'Ah, hello there! Is it that time already? I thought it was still morning!' He stopped in the middle of the kitchen and looked at me, his head on one side. 'And who have we here?'

'Frances,' Bert told him through a mouthful of toast.

'Of course, of course! The wonderful Frances!'

He went to the sink and washed his hands, soaping himself right up to the elbows like a surgeon getting ready to go into theatre, then he turned back to me.

'I'm the father,' he explained. 'Also known as Charlie. Sorry about the attire.' He pointed down to his dirty knees and boots. 'Been planting hyacinth bulbs for hours. Got carried away.'

He seemed younger than his wife, I thought. But then maybe that was just because he had one of those fresh, jolly faces that redheads often seem to come with. He filled a glass with water and downed it in one, then headed towards the hall.

'Just getting in the shower,' he said.

From the hallway, we heard Genevieve shout, 'Charlie! Get those boots off the carpet!' and Charlie mumbling his apologies as he pulled them off.

Bert rolled her eyes and shook her head. 'Dad's a gardener,' she said. 'Although he mostly only does our garden. He's too scatty to run a business really. He does have a van though.'

I nodded and chewed my toast.

'It doesn't matter anyway,' Bert went on. 'Mum's dad was super-rich. An actual millionaire. He was horrible apparently and he's dead now, but he left Mum pots of money.'

'Oh right,' I said. 'Sounds good.'

I was slightly taken aback by this frank disclosure. I'd always been taught that it was rude to talk about money. Especially to show off about it. But the way Bert had said it, it was so matter-of-fact it didn't feel like showing off at all.

'Hey,' Bert said, grinning when we'd finished our snack. 'Do you want to see my den?'

10

Bert's house was huge. There were four floors. Bert led me up to the third floor, and then up a further set of stairs, narrow and winding, that led to the attic.

Her den took up the whole of the attic space and it was completely amazing. In my eyes, it was as close as you could get to paradise within the confines of a family home. Three of the walls were sloping, making the room feel all cosy and snug. In one corner there were three beanbags nestled in between two fully stacked book shelves. On the one vertical wall of the room, there was a big flat-screen TV with a whole pile of technological boxes and gadgets on a shelf below it. The whole room was decorated with framed prints of old-fashioned sketches of ballet dancers and trapeze artists. Most had French captions written along the bottom of them in swirly lettering.

In the middle of the room there was a kind of chair that looked like a giant wooden ball on legs. It had a stand that curled right around the back of it and the main chair – the ball – was suspended from a chain.

Bert went over to it and ran her hand over the smooth, dark wood. 'This,' she said proudly, 'is the Egg. Dad made it. Fab, isn't it? It's like a work of art, I think. But so comfy too. Like heaven. Look.' She hopped up and climbed inside. 'Come on!'

I hesitated. 'Will we fit? Will it hold us both?'

'Yeah, easy!' Bert said. 'This thing could hold a baby elephant.'

I took my shoes off and clambered in, letting myself sink down into the soft cream cushions. It really was comfortable.

'It's like a little hamster's nest, isn't it?' Bert said, lying back and resting her head against the cushions. 'It always makes me want to go to sleep.'

The Egg opened up taller on the inside, with the lip of the wood narrowing over the entrance, giving it a closed-in, cosy feel.

'It is lovely,' I said, shutting my own eyes and leaning back.

We lay in the Egg for an hour or so I suppose, half-watching cartoons but mostly just chatting. Then Bert announced she was 'ravenous' so we went downstairs to investigate when dinner was going to be ready.

Charlie was in the kitchen wearing a clean pair of jeans and a pink shirt that matched his cheeks but clashed with his hair. He was unloading the dishwasher, piling coloured bowls into a cupboard.

'When's dinner, Dad?' Bert said as I followed her in. 'We're *starved.*'

Charlie put his hands on his hips and looked around the kitchen, frowning. 'Uh . . . I hadn't really thought about it . . .' he said. 'What do you fancy?'

'Something *massive*,' Bert said.

Genevieve appeared at the door. 'Have we got anything in?' she said. 'I meant to go to the market today but I got side-tracked . . .'

Charlie opened a cupboard and shuffled tins about. 'Beans?' he called out. 'Mushroom soup? Or . . . more beans?'

'Takeaway it is then,' Genevieve said with a laugh.

Charlie poked his head out from behind the cupboard door and grinned at me. 'Good heavens, Frances,' he said. 'What must you think of us? Invited for dinner and no dinner in sight!'

I shrugged and smiled shyly. 'It's OK,' I said.

I couldn't imagine what it must be like to live in a house where you didn't know what was going to be for dinner, right up until the last minute. Where people hung about in clothes covered in mud and paint. Where people laughed and joked and teased each other. I thought it was all totally brilliant.

I thought of Nan and Granddad at home, sitting down to Tuesday's meal – fried liver and onions – and I felt a sinking feeling in my chest. I don't know if it was the dread of going back there that night, or guilt at the thought of them alone. As Granddad got worse, Nan would veer between attempting to keep things normal, trying desperately to think of questions to ask that wouldn't confuse him, and giving up, losing her temper and snapping at him, which only made him blink in confusion. I hated both. I pushed the image away.

I'd never had a takeaway before and I loved it all, the whole process. I loved choosing exactly what I wanted from the paper menu (not that I had any idea what any of the foreign-sounding names meant – I went for Kung Po and Foo Yung in the end, because I liked the way the words sounded). I loved listening

54

to Charlie order it all, reading out the string of numbers like it was a code. I loved it when the doorbell rang and Charlie carried in a plastic bag full of foil trays and spread them out across the table. I suppose the bit I liked most of all was the way it was all so relaxed – dishes passing between us, great piles of noodles slopped onto plates, everyone talking with their mouths full and laughing.

On the wall next to the table, above a dresser that was stacked with the kind of brightly coloured plates that make you think of an African tribe, there was a photo of a much younger Charlie. A baby with a squashed-up face was perched on his knee, scowling at the camera.

I nodded towards the photo. 'Is that you?' I asked Bert.

She pulled a face. 'Unfortunately.'

'Hideous, wasn't she?' Charlie said, with a grin. 'As soon as I saw her I said to the midwife, "Take her away. Send her back to where she came from. She's an eyesore."'

'Charlie!' Genevieve cried, and punched him playfully on the arm. 'Don't say that about my baby!'

Bert did an exaggerated comedy pout, her bottom lip sticking out. But then she laughed and her parents smiled back at her. Charlie pulled her in close and kissed her on the top of the head and I knew there was no way that anyone in this family could ever really know what it was like to be unwanted.

After dinner, Bert and Charlie scraped the dishes and loaded the dishwasher, Bert shrieking as Charlie pretended to try to juggle three plates. Genevieve and I stayed at the table. She leant back in her chair, swilling her red wine around in her glass. I sat on my hands and looked around the kitchen, not quite sure what to do with myself without Bert there.

Genevieve looked over towards Bert. 'I'm so pleased, you know,' she said. 'At how well it's all going for her. With the school, I mean.'

I nodded but didn't say anything.

Genevieve breathed out and shook her head, then she looked up towards the ceiling. 'I wasn't at all sure how it would work out, you know. Such a leap of faith.'

It was more like she was talking to herself than to me, so I just tried to listen politely.

'I mean, is it really OK to send a kid who's never really had to conform, who's never really had to be *part* of anything, into that kind of . . . institution? And to just expect them to take to it – to the rules and social hierarchy? God, I don't know if I could do it. But then, on the other hand, look how things were going here. Maybe it was a mistake, teaching her at home all these years . . . maybe if she was more streetwise then that Richard business wouldn't have got so out of hand. But then, well, I always think that someone's weak points are usually a by-product of all their best qualities and I wouldn't change Bertie's exuberance for anything really . . .'

I wasn't sure if I'd call throwing a brick through someone's car window 'exuberance' but I didn't like to say anything. Genevieve trailed off. She shook her head quickly and then she leant forward again, looking at me now.

'Anyway!' she said, smiling. 'Anyway. It all seems to be going marvellously, doesn't it? And, young lady, I have a pretty good idea that you have something to do with that. You've been such a good friend, looking after her like this. I'd so hoped she would meet someone like you. A clever girl. Someone grounded. We're very lucky she found you.' Genevieve reached forward and squeezed my hand. 'Thank you,' she said, looking me right in the eyes.

I shrugged, feeling rather pleased with myself, although perhaps just a little uncomfortable. I really wasn't used to this kind of talk from an adult, this kind of openness. 'It's OK,' I said. 'I'm lucky too. Bert is *really* nice.'

Genevieve laughed and looked over at Bert again. 'Yes,' she said. 'Yes she is.'

When dinner was over, we went back up to the den and climbed back into the Egg. We had the TV on in the background – some American programme Nan would never have let me watch, about beautiful tanned people driving around LA in open-top cars – but mostly we just talked. I can't remember what about now, I don't think it was anything particularly serious or important. I just remember that the time seemed to tumble by. I knew it was getting late and Nan would be working herself up into a stew but I so badly didn't want to go home. When it got to about half past eight though, I couldn't take the guilt any longer so I told Bert I needed to get going.

'Ohhh,' she moaned. 'OK . . . if you really have to.'

I said that unfortunately I did, and we hauled ourselves out of the Egg. As we did so, Bert's hair got tangled in her necklace, holding her head at an awkward angle and making us laugh. I stood behind her and undid the clasp to free her. I dropped the gold chain into her hand.

'Hey,' she said suddenly, holding the necklace up by its gold chain, dangling the charm in front of my eyes. 'Look!'

'What?'

'Look at what it is – I've never really thought about it before.'

I peered closely at the tiny bird shape with its outstretched wings. It was black, apart from a tiny speck of gold where its beak was. 'A bird?'

'A *black*bird!' Bert said, her eyes shining. 'It's funny, isn't it? I'm Bert Fitzroy-*Black*. You're Frances *Bird*. *Birdy*. So this is like, what we are together. A blackbird!'

I nodded slowly. 'Sort of like . . . our symbol? Our emblem.'

Bert shrugged and smiled. 'Yeah, I guess so.' She held the necklace out to me, the delicate metal bird swinging from side to side. 'Here. You should have it.'

I shook my head. 'No, I couldn't take it. It's yours.'

'Of course you must!' Bert said, holding me by the shoulders and spinning me round. 'I want you to. I insist.' She passed the end of the chain between her hands in front of me and fastened it at the back of my neck.

'Well, if you're sure . . . Thanks,' I said, turning round to face her. I held the tiny bird between my thumb and finger. 'I'll look after it. Until you want it back, I mean.'

Bert laughed. 'I don't want it back, silly. It's yours forever!'

11

Looking back, I think those autumn months were probably the happiest I've ever been in my life.

What with our matching timetables, our dawdling walks across the field and our after-school trips to town, Bert and I were barely apart. Bert seemed to have a never-ending supply of cash and was quite generous about buying me cans of Coke and bags of pic 'n' mix. I never accepted any more than that – I suppose Nan's reluctance to take gifts from others had rubbed off on me – but that didn't stop Bert offering. Sometimes when we were in shops I'd comment that I liked a particular top or had always wanted to read a certain book and she'd immediately offer to buy it for me.

There was only once when I was really tempted – when we were trying on clothes in one of the designer shops I'd never even looked at before I'd met Bert. It was a jumper made of the softest cashmere in the loveliest shade of blue I'd ever seen. It oozed quality and luxury. And expense. Bert insisted that I try it on and I didn't see any harm in that, at least.

'Oh, Birdy,' she said, reaching forward and stroking the soft fabric of the sleeve. 'It's simply *gorgeous* on you. You've got to have it. Here, give it to me. It'll be my treat.'

I hesitated for just a moment, letting myself imagine holding a carrier bag, the jumper neatly folded inside, then taking it up to my room and placing it lovingly on the top shelf of my wardrobe. But that's as far as it would ever be able to go really. There was no way I could wear it around the house – how would I explain to Nan where it'd come from? I shook my head firmly.

'No,' I said. 'Thank you, honestly. But no. I don't need it. I've got plenty of jumpers. I'm just being silly.'

Almost as if to torture me, I saw the same jumper a few weeks later in the fashion pages of one of Nan's magazines. I gazed at it, wondering if I'd made a mistake. Maybe I should've just let Bert buy the thing – she seemed to have plenty of money, after all. But the moment was gone; I certainly couldn't ask her for it now. I folded the corner of the magazine to mark its place, though I wasn't sure why.

There was one big thing I did accept from Bert though and that was a mobile phone.

Bert had been incredulous when she'd asked to take my number a few weeks after we'd met and I'd admitted that I didn't have one. Of course, the truth was that Nan would never have let me get one, even if she had been able to afford it – 'What makes you think you're so special that you need to be contactable at all hours of the day? Who do you think you are, Barack bloody Obama?'. I thought I'd played the whole thing quite well though, making it look like deliberate aloofness on my part – some kind of demonstration of my independence and individuality.

'But what if someone wants to speak to you?' Bert had said, frowning as she tried to get her head around the idea.

I shrugged. 'Then they can come over and talk to me. I don't want people pestering me all day and night.'

I'd almost laughed as I'd said that, at how ludicrous it was. I couldn't think of a single person who'd be interested in contacting me at all, let alone all day and night. Bert obviously hadn't been satisfied with my position on communications though, because when we met to walk to school together the next day, she handed me a small carrier bag.

'I know what you're going to say,' she said quickly. 'I know you don't want people phoning you and whatnot but then just don't give them your number. But *I* want to be able to contact you. That's OK, isn't it? I mean, it makes sense really. What if I'm late to walk to school or something? I'll need to get the message to you somehow.'

I reached into the bag and pulled the phone out. It wasn't one of the really swish models that people have these days – it was just a little boxy thing really with round plastic buttons – but even so, I could feel my heartbeat quicken. Blimey, I thought, an actual mobile phone of my own. And a hotline to Bert too. How brilliant, to be able to talk at any time. In fact, I was so overcome with glee that I almost forgot to do the polite thing and refuse to take the gift.

'Sorry, I know it's a bit of a tatty old thing,' Bert said. 'It's my old one. But it's in full working order. We can text and ring and everything.'

'Oh no,' I said. 'It's great. It's just, I can't take it from you.'

I pushed the bag back towards her but she held her hands up, refusing to accept it. 'Please, Birdy. Take it, honestly. As I say, it's just my old one. It's got heaps of credit on it so it would be a shame for it to go to waste. And I just can't bear the idea of not being able to get hold of you if I needed to.'

'Well, if you're sure . . .' I said, my stomach somersaulting with the excitement of it all.

At some point around this time I realised that even when Bert and I weren't together, she'd still be on my mind. It wasn't always a concentrated, conscious kind of thinking, but it was fairly constant. She was just always there somewhere – I'd wonder what she was doing, I'd replay conversations we'd had that'd made me laugh. Or, more importantly, where I'd made her laugh. I'd store up things I'd seen or thoughts I'd had, ready to tell her the next time we were together. I worried about her too, hoped she was OK and not getting into any trouble. I had to keep reminding myself that she'd managed for fifteen years before she met me.

I know it'll sound very strange if you haven't been in the situation yourself, but I suddenly felt that I knew what it must be like to have a religion. That sort of reassuring sense of always having someone on your side. A focus. A sense of meaning at last. 'What would Jesus do?' asked big black letters on one of Nan's old chipped mugs. *What would Bert do?* I found myself wondering, anytime I had to make a decision. And it couldn't have come at a better time, because at home, things were worse than ever.

Granddad's vagueness, his tendency for random comments or repeated questions, seemed to step up to a new level. He wouldn't just ask a question and repeat it half an hour or so later, he'd now started asking the same question over and over again, incessantly. 'When are we going home?' he'd say, fidgeting irritably in his chair.

'You are home, Granddad,' I'd say, trying to use a light tone, one that suggested this kind of question was perfectly normal and that we all forget where we are from time to time.

He'd leave it for a minute or two, but then he'd ask again. 'When are we going home? I told them, I want to go home.' He'd also started calling me Bridget – my dead mum's name. This had happened once or twice before, but had always seemed more like a slip of the tongue than anything more troubling. Now though, he'd call me Bridget more often than Frances and it felt like he truly believed I was his dead daughter. This made things really uncomfortable, not just because it showed that Granddad was definitely losing his grip on reality but because for as long as I could remember, it had been one of Nan's rules that we do not talk about Bridget.

These days I wouldn't dare mention her, but I remember even when I was small, if I asked questions – what did Bridget look like, where did Bridget live – Nan would shut me down. She'd pretend she hadn't heard, change the subject. Granddad though . . . sometimes he'd mention her from time to time – always when Nan wasn't there. He didn't generally go into any detail or take long rambling trips down memory lane, but sometimes, occasionally, he'd drop in a detail here and there: 'Bridget couldn't stand blackcurrants either,' he'd tell me after I'd turned down a glass of Ribena. 'Bridget had a lovely singing voice, you know,' he'd mutter, almost to himself, as we passed a lady busker in town. I decided that if I wanted answers, Granddad would be more likely to provide them than Nan, so one afternoon, when I was about nine, I brought up the subject.

I waited till Nan was at the shops and Granddad and I were in the garden sorting out his tools. We'd emptied all three of his toolboxes onto an old sheet spread out on the lawn and we were carefully cleaning each one with an old sock before placing it back in its proper place. I can't remember if it was deliberate but it was probably good timing – Granddad was sitting on the ground with his legs stretched out in front of him and his creaky old knees would've made it too difficult for him to just up and leave to avoid the question.

'Why don't we talk about Bridget?' I'd blurted it out quickly, before I had time to chicken out.

Granddad looked at me for a second. Then he touched my cheek with his grubby hand before going back to cleaning his hammer. I thought that was it – that he wasn't going to answer me at all. But then he started to talk:

'We never thought we'd have a baby, your nan and me. We wanted to, of course we did. Nan especially. But we waited and waited, year after year, and it just didn't look like it was going to happen. Until your mum came along, right when we were least expecting it. We were getting on a bit by then and we'd long given up hope, so we were delighted, Frances. We were beside ourselves! Your nan set about with all the preparations straight away – cribs, prams, teddies, you name it. We weren't well off but Nan was adamant – our baby would have everything. Everything. And then she was born, the baby. Bridget. Beautiful little thing, she was. Dark hair, brown eyes like chocolate buttons. Our little princess.

'She was naughty though, wilful. She was always that way. But that was fine, she made us chuckle. Nan lost her rag with her from time to time when she wouldn't eat her tea or put her shoes on to go to school, but they'd always make it up. They both had tempers so sometimes they'd . . .' Granddad pushed his fists together at the knuckles, like two bulls fighting each other. 'But they'd always sort it out.

'But then, Bridget got older. Thirteen or fourteen I think she was when she started staying out. Not all night, not then, but later than she said she would. And we tried to talk to her but she wasn't having any of it – we were too old to understand, she'd say. Past it. And that really got to your nan 'cause that was her big hang-up, you know – that we were old. Out of touch. Doing it wrong. Your nan so badly wanted to get it right, Frances, to be a good mum. But Bridget just . . . Bridget was wilful.'

Not for the first time in my life, I found myself feeling angry with Bridget. Who did this girl think she was, turning up, creating havoc, making everyone feel bad?

'Then it got harder,' Granddad went on. 'Bridget got older. Out more and more. In with a bad crowd, boys, drink . . . all of it. And you can't make someone, Frances. You can't make someone do what you want even if you know it's best for them. And Nan tried, believe me. Even locked her in her bedroom once! But she just went out the window. She'd stay out for longer and longer – two nights, four nights, a whole week. She'd come back a mess. Drink. Then drugs too. Every time we'd worry. We'd call the police but they didn't care, not really. She was known to them by this point. Just another tearaway teenager. No good.'

Granddad breathed out hard. He frowned and scrubbed at the blade of his palette knife.

'Then, when she was sixteen, she didn't come back at all. Two weeks went by, three weeks. A month. Three months. We looked, of course we did. The police said they were helping but I couldn't tell you to this day what exactly they were doing. She was a runaway. It was our fault she'd gone. They didn't say as much but you knew they thought it. We'd walk the streets for hours, asking everyone. We had leaflets – Nan got them all done up proper in the print shop. We took the bus all around. Even did a week in London – Bridget always talked about London – but where do you start with a place like that?

'We hadn't seen her for exactly one year when Nan flipped. I'd been expecting it really, in a way. I just came home once and found her sitting on the floor. Smashed glass everywhere. All the pictures, all the baby photos, first day of school, blowing out the candles on her ninth birthday, roller-skating on her eleventh . . . all broken. And Nan, just sitting there, cuts on her hands. Crying. Crying her heart out.'

Granddad's voice cracked then. I looked at him, alarmed, but he dragged his sleeve across his eyes and seemed to pull himself together.

'So I picked her up. I tidied away the photos, in albums, in drawers, tucked away for when she wanted them again. Then I washed her hands in the sink and tied them up with bandages and when I was doing it Nan says, "She's gone, hasn't she? She's gone." And she had, Frances. Bridget had gone from us. And that was it. No more searching, no more tears, no more photos.'

I'd never seen Nan cry. I couldn't even imagine it. I didn't want to. 'Poor Nan,' I said quietly.

'You've never known your nan how she was, Frances love. You never saw the best of her. What she is now . . . she's not the same. She's just a shell. When we found out Bridget had died, there were no tears, even then. Not from Nan anyway. She'd already accepted it. I hoped that when we got you home, it would . . . I don't know, snap her out of it. Give her a second chance or something. But it was too late. She'd already shut down.'

I looked at my hands then and swallowed hard. I was just so angry. That *stupid* cow Bridget. She thought she was so special but she was horrible. She'd ruined everything. She'd broken Nan. She'd broken them both.

Granddad must've seen me looking strange and assumed I was upset because he put down his dirty rag and held my hand. We stayed like that for a minute but it started to make me feel funny, so I wriggled free and placed my screwdriver in the drawer at the top of the red toolbox.

'Have we got time to have ice cream before Nan's home?' I'd said, forcing myself to be bright and cheery. I didn't want Granddad to say anything else. I didn't want to hear any more about Bridget, not ever. She'd taken up enough of everyone's energy as it was.

'I expect so, love.'

At first, we'd ignored it when Granddad got my name wrong.

'Hello, Bridget love, how was school?'

'Get Bridget to help you with the sweeping.'

Once though, I caught a look at Nan when he did it and

I saw the expression in her eyes – a brief flash of something that looked a lot like alarm. Panic, almost.

Then, one evening, we were sitting in the living room after dinner watching some awful quiz programme, and Granddad turned to me and said, 'Turn it up, would you, Bridget? Can't hear a word over here.'

All of a sudden Nan leant forward and turned the TV off. 'That's enough,' she snapped. 'That's enough of that rubbish. Come on, time for bed.'

'Is it?' Granddad asked. 'Already?'

'Yes,' Nan said firmly. 'It's late.'

It was barely nine o'clock, but Granddad nodded obediently and shuffled out of the living room. Nan didn't move for a minute. She just sat in the chair, staring at the blank TV. I wasn't sure what to do. I didn't want to move.

Neither of us said anything for a minute or two, then Nan spoke.

'She tried to kill you too, you know,' she said, her eyes still fixed on the empty TV screen. 'Never told you that. She dissolved some of those pills into your milk. Tried to get you to drink it. You wouldn't though, of course. Even a baby knows that's not right. Never told you that, did we?'

Her voice was strange. It was completely emotionless. It was scary. Much more scary than any of the angry, shouty outbursts that erupted when I broke one of her many house rules. I felt very much like I was in trouble, like Nan was saying this was all my fault somehow. But I didn't have a clue what I was supposed to do about it.

'No,' I replied quietly. 'You never told me that.'

12

My friendship with Bert started to affect my marks at school. It wasn't always dramatic, but it was enough for me to notice. Maybe I should've taken that as a sign to take a step back from her for a while, but the thing was, the impact wasn't all bad so I thought, on balance, it didn't matter too much.

In maths and science, my grades took a bit of a nose dive. Bert didn't have any time for those subjects. I'd always got on quite well with them. I liked the certainty, the right answers. Not to mention the fact that they were subjects you could mostly get on with on your own without the need for all that horrible group work that teachers are so keen on but that can be a real headache if you've got to scrabble around for someone to work with before you can get going. But Bert declared them 'boring and nit-picky' so we spent most of those lessons at the back of the class, talking quietly when we could get away with it, passing notes when we couldn't.

In art, though, I suddenly found my grades perking up. Cs, Bs . . . even the odd A. Art was Bert's favourite subject and her enthusiasm was infectious. Mostly because she was every bit as excited about my efforts as her own work.

'Oh, Birdy!' she said once as I put the finishing touches on a charcoal drawing of a stallion. 'That's just beautiful. I love the look in his eyes . . . he's so wistful and wise. Can I have him, once he's marked and everything, of course?'

I just shrugged and smiled a shy smile, the way I always did when Bert piled praise on me like this.

English was another subject where I found things improving. Although I'd always liked to read, I'd always felt a bit confused by English as a school subject. I liked spelling and grammar – stuff with rules – but all that woolly, creative business was a mystery to me. I suppose it just always seemed like such a strange way to spend study time.

Miss Lily, our English teacher, was a vague, drifty kind of woman and she'd usually set us vague, drifty kinds of tasks to complete. For example, once we had to 'describe the inside of a horse chestnut'. Another time, she told us to 'write a diary from the point of view of a snowflake'. I mean, I felt that I probably *could* do these things if that's what she really wanted, but I just wasn't quite sure what the point of it all was. I always felt a bit like I was missing something, or that those kinds of tasks were some sort of psychological test and they were going to use what we wrote to make a judgement about our character. I always approached those assignments a bit cautiously, being careful not to write anything too unusual or creative in case it gave anyone the idea I was not quite right.

It was the same with English literature. 'What is the significance of the fire in *Lord of the Flies*?' Lily would write across the middle of the board and I'd feel a sinking feeling as I realised we were going to have to spend the next hour – if not the next term – discussing something which as far as I could see was neither here nor there. Does it really matter? I'd think, looking around at the other people in my class to see if they were wondering the same thing. It's a work of fiction, isn't it? I doubt even William Golding himself was particularly interested in the significance of the fire. He probably just stuck it in there to give the boys something to sit around. And actually, these kinds of questions annoyed me too. I mean, what a way to ruin a good book! Picking stories to pieces like that. Spelling it all out. It was like having someone explain the punchline of a joke to you – it just didn't really work after that. Once, when I was looking for some past exam papers online, I found a copy with the examiners' marking notes attached. 'Examiners are encouraged to reward any valid interpretations,' it said. I knew it, I thought to myself. Just like I always thought: Any old rubbish will do. I felt a bit better then, less like they were trying to catch me out. But still, it seemed a very bizarre thing to be studying at school.

With Bert though, I tried to approach English with a new enthusiasm. After all, I thought, she seems to love it, so there must be something I'm missing. Like me, Bert was a reader – I guess most people who've grown up without many friends are – but unlike me, she loved nothing more than to spend hours talking over the motivations and personality traits of the characters. And to my surprise I found that, with Bert, I quite liked it too. It was fun with her. She had interesting ideas. She wasn't like drippy Miss Lily, head on one side, eyes getting all misty at the drop of a hat. When Bert talked, she was so passionate; it sometimes did feel like we were talking about real people. She was sparky. She made me laugh.

* * *

By this time, we were well into Bert's first term and the boys who'd been initially sniffing around her seemed to be losing interest. I think on the whole they just found Bert a bit too odd.

Once a scrappy little boy called Tom Coleman sidled up to her. 'Hey,' he said, 'you know what? I think there might be something wrong with my eyes. I can't take them off you.'

Bert spun round and looked Tom straight in the face – the poor kid probably thought he was in with a chance for a minute – but she just stood there, staring at him intently.

'What?' he said, backing away. 'What are you doing?'

'Checking your vision.' She held up a finger. 'Can you see this? Can you follow it with your eyes?'

Tom had batted her hand away and slunk away, muttering, 'Nutter,' under his breath.

I don't know for sure if those kinds of reactions were genuine – if she really was so out of practice when it came to teenage flirting stuff that she just didn't know what was expected – or if it was a bit more contrived than that, and playing the innocent was her way of letting people down without upsetting them. I wasn't really bothered either way, just as long as she kept turning them down. Even though I was pretty sure that Bert and I were quite solid friendship-wise by this point, I still didn't really fancy the idea of being ousted by some annoying boyfriend type.

The one boy who'd really stuck around despite Bert's slightly odd knock-backs was Jac Dubois – of index-finger salute fame. He was one of those who enjoys playing the role of the joker, whatever the situation. The whole act got a bit annoying at times, but he was harmless enough. He was the son of a French couple who owned the Parisian bistro in town and he was bilingual – a fact which lifted him a bit above the class clown status he'd assigned himself, I always thought. I used to like to hover around nearby when one of his parents picked him up from school and listen to them babble away in French together. How lovely, I always thought, to have another language that you could just slip into like that.

Jac would loiter around us in registration, trying to engage Bert in banter, alternating between outrageously sexist teasing and shameless flattery. I couldn't tell for sure what Bert felt about it but the whole thing made me nervous. He wasn't technically spoken for, but he was quite popular with the girls in general. I was worried someone might step forward to stake their claim if it looked like Bert was getting too involved, which might lead to tension all round. Luckily though, Bert managed to knock any romantic ideas on the head herself, one day in early November.

'I think he likes me,' she said that afternoon after school. We were in her den, sitting in the Egg and drinking big mugs of hot chocolate. 'Jac, I mean. Do you think he likes me?'

'French Jac?' I asked lightly, although I already knew who she meant.

Bert nodded and blew on her chocolate to cool it down. Then she giggled. 'I think he's handsome.'

I scrunched my nose to one side. 'Really? Do you? But he's got that . . . tail thing in his hair.'

Jac *almost* had a neat short back and sides, but right at the back, at the nape of his neck, he had a little straggly rat's tail hanging down. It was a bit odd, really.

'I like it,' Bert said. 'It's exotic. Do you think he likes me? I think he might like me.'

I shrugged. 'Maybe,' I said, not quite meeting her eye.

'Or do you think he doesn't? I don't know about this . . . about boys our age. Am I misreading the signs?'

I didn't say anything. I concentrated on trying to suck up a marshmallow from the top of my hot chocolate.

'Oh, I am, aren't I? I'm taking him too seriously. All those things he says . . . those comments . . . they're just part of his comedy routine, aren't they?' Bert said, shaking her head. 'Of course they are. What a wally I am.'

Conversations with Bert were often like this. I wouldn't necessarily need to say anything at all. She'd just gallop along on her own, jumping from one thought to another, making connections and drawing her own conclusions. I could just step in if and when I wanted to. I decided to step in now.

'I think it's just his way,' I said. 'He likes girls. Girls like him. I think it's because he's French.'

'I see,' Bert said, nodding thoughtfully. 'A veritable Lothario. Understood.'

We were quiet again as we sipped our drinks and listened to the rain on the skylight above us.

'Goodness, imagine if I'd said something,' Bert said after a while. 'He would've laughed in my face. Quite rightly too.' She shook her head and sipped her drink. 'And anyway, what am I thinking? What am I *thinking*? The last thing I need is to be getting into that kind of trouble. What's wrong with me? Why can't I just . . .? Honestly, what on earth would I do without you, Birdy? You must never leave me to my own devices. Think of the pickle I'd be in.'

I laughed. I wasn't totally sure what she was talking about, couldn't quite keep up with her leapfrogging thoughts, but I figured it didn't matter too much. Whatever idea about Jac she'd been briefly entertaining seemed to have been snuffed out. She'd managed to talk herself out of it. I was relieved. I could do without Bert getting us dragged into the middle of some hormonal cat-fight about boys.

And to be honest, I could do without anyone disrupting our peaceful little twosome.

13

So you'll probably remember earlier in the story when I told you about the two girls in primary school rejecting me when I tried to join in their chalk-drawing playground project. One of those girls – the bigger, darker one – was Pippa Brookman and, as bad luck would have it, she and I seemed to end up being thrown together almost every year – in the same classes at St Paul's and the same tutor groups at Whistle Down. I worked out pretty quickly that I'd had a lucky escape that day in the playground: Pippa was horrible.

She was annoying even to look at – she had a big moony face and the kind of smile that was about eighty per cent gums with little stubby shark teeth just peeping through. She was one of those people who fancy themselves as incredibly important, putting herself forward for anything and everything, from peer bullying counsellor to PE captain to recycling monitor. She had this loud, hooting voice that she'd use to broadcast whatever ever-so-important crusade she was on at the time. She could be mean too, in a really sneaky way. Even though she liked to make a big deal about all her fundraising and charity work, she never seemed that bothered about actually being a nice person.

This one time, in Year Eight, I'd come to school with a new haircut. It was just something I thought I'd try out to make me look a bit older – a bit shorter and a few layery bits. It didn't really work out as I planned though, partly because as soon as my hair gets shorter than my shoulders it puffs up like a mushroom but also because I'd tried to cut it myself and things had got a bit tricky around the back. I was feeling a bit self-conscious as I walked into school that morning, but I'd been trying to reason with myself: *No one cares about your hair, Frances. No one looks at you at all. They wouldn't notice if you walked in without a head*. But then, when I stepped into our tutor room and slipped into my seat, Pippa did this loud '*Woooo*' noise and everyone looked over to me.

'Look at *you*,' she called, making sure her voice was loud enough for the whole room to hear. 'New look, is it? Well, well, well. *Very* brave.'

I just ignored her and pretended to look for something in my bag.

She came over to me and made a big thing about circling around me, trying to get a look at me from all angles, everyone else still watching too.

'Ooh,' she said, doing a wincey face and shaking her head. 'It's so hard, isn't it? When you've got so much *body* in your hair. Does have a tendency to make you look like you've stuck your fingers in a plug socket if you go too short.' She shook her head again in mock sympathy. 'Still,' she said. 'Well done, you, for trying something new. You've got to try things, haven't you, before you can know they don't work.'

I glared at her but she just turned away from me and headed

back to the other side of the classroom, pulling an exaggerated horrified face as she went.

Luckily, by Year Ten, although we were still in the same tutor group, our timetables were different enough that I only really had to see her in registration. Even then we ignored each other. I knew we'd always remember the chalk day in the playground. I hoped she was ashamed. She probably wasn't.

In our school, assemblies were held every Thursday and, at the end, there was a five-minute slot for students to deliver messages to the school – stuff like updates on the football team's performance, requests for sponsorship for charity walks, that kind of thing. One Thursday in late November, Pippa Brookman stepped forward together with Ana Mendez, a dark, mousey girl from my French class. I rolled my eyes and looked out of the window.

Pippa pulled down the projector screen at the front of the hall.

'Sorry, could we . . . could we do the lights?' she called, looking around for someone to follow her command.

A sixth-former stood up at the back of the room and flicked the switch. Pippa gave Ana a nod and Ana darted forward to switch on a laptop on the table in the middle of the hall. An image flicked onto the screen of an old woman. She had one of those faces that's so crinkled and toothless it looks like it's going to crumple right in on itself. A couple of Year Sevens giggled at the sight of her, but Pippa shot them a fierce look to shut them up.

Pippa paused, waiting for everyone to have a good look at the woman, then she said, 'I'd like to introduce you to Edna.'

Another pause. She'd obviously been practising her dramatic delivery. 'Edna is ninety-four years old. She's lived through two world wars.' I did some fast maths and looked around me to see if anyone else had picked up on the obvious mistake here. It didn't look like they had. I looked at Bert, but she was staring intently at the image of Edna.

'She was married to George for sixty-two years, until his death ten years ago,' Pippa went on. 'She had one son, Jimmy, but he was killed in a motorbike accident in the seventies.'

At the side of the hall, our head, Mr Jeffrey, pointedly tapped his watch but Pippa wasn't put off. She was on a roll, and I was sort of fascinated by where she was going.

'So Edna is all alone. She has no family except for the family she's made for herself amongst the staff and residents of the Meadowrise Residential Care Home, up near the racecourse.'

She paused again, giving everyone a moment to take in this solemn news.

'Now,' she said, in a brighter tone. Hopefully she was getting to the point. 'As part of my Silver Duke of Edinburgh Award, I've been fortunate enough to work with some of the lovely elderly residents at Meadowrise and I've seen first-hand just how much the home means to them. So you can imagine my dismay when I learnt that the home was to be closed down due to cuts in council funding.'

Another pause. I suppose people were supposed to gasp or something but most people just looked at their feet, probably wondering when someone was going to shut her up.

'I'm sure you'll all agree that this can't be allowed to happen.'

Pippa gave Ana a small nod and Ana quickly replaced the picture of Edna with a slide showing text that said:

Save Meadowrise!
Action Group meeting, Saturday 1 p.m.
We will not be moved!

'Tomorrow, I'll be leading a protest outside the gates of Meadowrise. We need to show the council that we, the people, care about the elderly, that we won't be ignored. If you think vulnerable people like Edna have a right to live peacefully in the place they call home then join Ana and I. Meet us outside Meadowrise at ten to one. Bring banners, bring placards, bring enthusiasm!'

I think this last bit was meant to be rousing, but she was met with an echoey silence and the odd yawn.

Luckily, Mr Jeffrey stepped in before she had a chance to go on.

'Thank you, Philippa,' he said. 'Most . . . inspirational. I'm afraid we've run out of time this week, so any other student notices will have to wait till next week. Off to classes please, everyone.'

'*Me*,' I said to Bert as soon as we were out in the corridor. 'Why does she always say "I"? She means *me*.'

'Hmm?' Bert said, frowning.

'She said, "Join Ana and I." It's not *I* in that context, it's *me*. It should've been "Join Ana and me." She always says I. *Always*. It's like she thinks it makes her sound more intelligent. Sometimes I just want to tell her, I just want to say, "It's not always I! Sometimes it's me!"'

'Oh right, yes,' Bert said.

Bert and I had already discussed our shared intolerance of bad grammar so I'd thought this little rant would make her laugh but she barely seemed to be listening at all. She was frowning into the distance. 'Don't you think it's awful, though? About Edna?'

I shrugged. 'S'pose.'

'Oh, Birdy, I think it's dreadful! Don't you? After what happened to her son, and her husband, and now . . . being uprooted like this. She won't have a clue what's happening to her, poor love.'

'Won't she?' I said, looking at Bert out of the corner of my eye. 'I don't think Pippa mentioned that she was senile.'

'Well, whatever,' Bert said. 'I still think it's awful. We should go, Birdy. To the protest. We should make a stand!'

I couldn't think of anything I'd less like to do at the weekend than stand with Pippa Brookman outside an old people's home in the freezing cold, waving banners while Pippa would probably want to lead us through a selection of embarrassing chants. The truth was, I wasn't totally sure I was all that bothered about the old people. Is that terrible? I don't know. It's so hard, isn't it, when for all the excuses you might make about why you can't do something, the simple truth is you just don't *want* to do it. I had a feeling Bert would just see that as me being a bit mean. She didn't know Pippa well enough to see it from my point of view. She didn't know what she was really like. So that meant excuses were in order if I was going to get out of the protest without looking like a grouch.

'I can't, unfortunately,' I said, doing my best to put on a such-a-shame face. 'I've got to help my nan with some stuff. She wants to sort out the loft and she can't get up there now. Doesn't like going up the ladder.'

This was partly true, although it probably wouldn't take much more than an hour and Nan hadn't specified it had to be done on Saturday afternoon. Still, I thought it was the perfect excuse. Got me out of the ridiculous protest without making me look unkind. Luckily, this was exactly how Bert saw it.

'Oh, of course,' she said, turning to look at me. 'You've got quite enough on your hands, dealing with your own grandparents. Sorry, Birdy, I didn't think.'

'It's OK,' I said with a modest shrug. 'It's just . . . you know, they can't do everything they want any more. I need to be there for them sometimes.'

I was worried I was laying it on a bit thick, but it seemed to work quite well on Bert.

'Of course,' she said, putting her hand on my arm. 'Of course. I understand. You are good, you know. The way you look after them.'

I gave her a small, put-upon smile and assumed that would be the last I'd hear of the Meadowrise old folks protest. So you can imagine my surprise when, as Bert and I crossed the field on our way home that evening, Pippa cycled past waving and calling out, 'See you tomorrow, Alberta. Don't be late.'

'See you!' Bert replied, smiling and waving back.

I spun round to look at her. 'What?' I said. 'You mean, you're going to the protest?'

'Oh yes,' Bert said, wide-eyed. 'Of course. How could I not? I haven't been able to stop thinking about Edna all day.'

'Oh,' I said, trying to keep the indignation out of my voice. 'Right.'

I desperately wanted to talk Bert out of it. I thought about suggesting the two of us do something together instead but I'd already shot myself in the foot by telling her that I was busy with Nan and Granddad so that wasn't an option. What I really wanted to do was launch into a massive rant about what a cow Pippa Brookman was and how Bert really shouldn't be encouraging her by taking part in any of her stupid little projects. But I held my tongue. I knew if I looked like I was being bitter about things it would make her get all haughty, and would probably only make her think badly of me rather than Pippa.

I just sulked all the way home, saying a bit of a cool goodbye to her at the top of the hill where we went our separate ways.

14

The next day, I was distracted for a while when I was helping Nan heave Granddad's power tools up into the loft. She said it was just 'for the winter' but I think we both knew they wouldn't be coming out again anytime soon. When we were finished I spent the rest of the day with one eye on the clock.

I kept my phone by my side, picking it up to check it every few minutes and throwing it down in frustration when I saw that I had no new messages. I wasn't sure what I was hoping to see exactly. I suppose it was a message from Bert, saying that she'd realised just in time that Pippa Brookman was an idiot and asking me if I wanted to meet up today instead. That message never came of course, and I imagined Pippa and Bert arm in arm, clinging to the railings of Meadowrise and chanting, 'What do we want? To keep the old people! Where do we want them? Here!' This, I was sure, was the beginning of the end for me and Bert. She'd attach herself to Pippa now. They'd be the special friends now, not us. They'd spend their weekends saving the planet and rescuing people in need and I'd be discarded, the selfish, unkind one. On my own, just where I belonged.

But then, just after five, when Nan had gone to top up the

electric meter and Granddad was dozing in his armchair, I got a message:

What a day. Not exactly what I thought. Meet at the park?

I replied at once.

OK. *See you in ten minutes.*

I quickly checked on Granddad then let myself out of the house.

I found Bert sitting on the swing, gently swaying from side to side, poking at the dirt with the toe of her boot.

'How was it then?' I said, taking a seat on the swing next to her. 'Manage to save the world? Save Edna at least?'

I hadn't meant to sound so sarcastic and I regretted it straight away, but it didn't seem to matter. Bert was preoccupied.

She sighed. 'It was all rather disappointing.'

'Not many people turn up?' I asked, trying to be gentle about it. I didn't want to crow over her too much. That wouldn't have been very dignified.

'There were a few. Not a crowd as such, but maybe twenty or so. And the press were there too.'

'Really?' I said, imagining BBC news reporters and photographers jostling to get a good shot.

'Well, yes. A man from the *Echo* anyway.'

'Oh,' I said. 'I see.'

The *Echo* was the local newspaper. Its idea of 'news' was a minute-by-minute account of a family of ducks crossing the road. I wasn't sure I really considered it 'the press'.

'Well yes, and that's it really. I'd say Pippa was more interested in talking to the journalist guy and having her photo taken than anything else.'

I had to stop myself from grinning. That sounded like Pippa all right.

'And to start with, I thought, you know, fair enough. She's just trying to get the word out. That's the whole point really, isn't it? Raising awareness and all that. So they were doing that for a while, and everyone else was just sort of milling around. It felt like things hadn't really started yet, so I thought, I'll go inside and talk to the old people. I wanted to meet Edna, really. So I snuck in behind a man delivering potatoes and went into the lounge where they were all sitting around, watching the telly and playing cards and whatnot.

'There was a woman in a big cardy, sitting by the window, looking out at Pippa and the others. She was sort of chuckling and shaking her head. Then she looked up at me and said, "You know, when I was a teenager, Saturday afternoons were all about going down the pier and getting drunk. Lie there all day, we would. Hanky-panky too, sometimes, if you were lucky. We knew how to have fun. Not like this lot. What are they playing at, eh?"

'And I said, "Well I think they're just trying to stop the home closing –" but then I suddenly panicked because I thought maybe the old people hadn't even been told and I'd just put my foot in it. But it was OK because she said, "What for? Let them close the old dump. I'm sick of it. They're moving us to Glenferns, right by the beach it is. I can't wait. Wish they'd get on with it actually."

'And I said, "Really? But Pippa said . . . said everyone was really upset . . ." And we both looked out to where Pippa was posing for the camera. And by this time, one of the care-home nurse ladies had come over, and she laughed and said, "Did she now? And what would she know about it? She's only been here once."

'And I said, "Really?" again, because in that assembly Pippa was making out like she basically worked there, wasn't she? But the nurse woman just nodded and we all looked out at Pippa and Ana and the others, and then the old lady said – get this – she said, "Bunch of tossers, the lot of them."'

I couldn't stop myself laughing at this point. It was all too perfect. Even Bert cracked a small smile.

'It's awful, isn't it? But oh, Birdy, that's not the worst of it. Once that one old lady had wheeled herself away, I turned to the nurse and said, "Do you think I could speak to Edna?" I mean, I was thinking just because that one woman was happy about moving, it didn't mean they all were, did it? But the nurse said, "Edna who?" And so I described her, and said about the husband, George, and Jimmy, the son in the motorbike crash. And the nurse said, "Nope. Doesn't sound like anyone here. I've been here five years and we've never had an Edna."

'I was pretty confused by this point, so I went outside to ask Pippa. When I managed to get her away from the journalist and ask her where Edna was and *who* she was and all that, Pippa just gave me a rather pitying look and said, "Alberta, Edna was a persona. A representation. There's no *actual* Edna, obviously," and then she just turned away from me again. Can you believe that?'

I could believe it, actually.

'So what did you do then?' I asked.

'Well, I left,' Bert said, looking down sadly. 'What was the point? It was all a sham.'

Bert looked so dejected that I took her hand and squeezed it, but the truth was, I couldn't have been more delighted.

15

It was a couple of weeks before the Christmas holidays when Bert and I got drunk for the first time. I wasn't used to getting drunk really, not least because I was never invited to the parties or 'gatherings' down the field which seemed to be when all the people in my year did it, but also because I'd had a bad experience the first time it'd happened and so I hadn't touched alcohol since then.

That first time had come about quite unexpectedly, one warm evening at the beginning of Year Nine. I'd been heading home from school late but in no particular rush to get there and I'd decided to go the long way round, through the cemetery and then the park. As I took the path that ran along the railing that enclosed the kiddie bit with the swings and see-saw and all that, I heard a shout.

'Frankenstein!'

I looked up, surprised, because I hadn't heard that nickname for nearly a year by this point.

It was some boys from my year – Matt Pereira and Gary Chester – along with another boy and two girls who I didn't recognise as being from our school at all.

I put my head down and carried on walking.

'Oi, Frances!' Matt called. 'Come over here and say hello.'

I paused for a minute but then carried on walking.

'Oi!' he shouted again.

'Leave her alone, Matt,' one of the girls said. 'Don't be a bell-end.'

'What?' Matt said, pretending to look wounded. 'It's all right, I know her. She's my mate. Oi, Frances,' he called again. 'Come here and tell them you're my mate.'

I still don't know why I did it really, but I have a sneaking suspicion that it was because he called me his mate. I knew he was messing around, but even so, there was something about hearing him say that, just hearing those words. Seductive, I suppose. I'd known Matt a long time I thought, he'd never been nice to me as such, but then he'd never really been *not* nice either. It was the same with all of the popular ones at school really – they had their victims, the people they'd hassle, but I wasn't one of them. Not with any regularity. I suppose I just wasn't on anyone's radar. Maybe he was my mate, I told myself. In a way. I found myself sauntering over there.

They were all lounging around the roundabout. Gary was lying on it, pushing himself gently back and forward with his foot. The others were sitting on the ground nearby. Matt was leaning back on his elbows, his legs hanging apart. One of the girls was lying against him, slotted between his legs. Using him like a sort of human armchair.

'What?' I said, stopping in front of them.

'Christ, it actually talks,' Gary said, his head lolling a bit. That's when I realised – they were drunk. There was a half-empty bottle of vodka on the floor next to one of the girls and Matt was surrounded by empty cider cans.

Matt clambered to his feet with some difficulty. He stood next to me, swaying slightly. Then he draped his arm over my shoulders and slurred, 'Everyone, this is my mate, Frances.' Behind us, Gary sniggered.

'Hi, Frances,' one of the girls said, looking up at me. She had a weird look in her eyes, like she found me sort of mesmerising. Drunk too, I supposed. 'You wanna drink?' She held the bottle out to me.

I shook my head and turned away, ready to head home now.

'Oh, don't go!' the girl whined. 'Stay. Have a drink!'

I hesitated for a moment, and then I don't for the life of me know why, but I took the bottle from her and took a swig. It was rancid. Like what I'd imagine nail-polish remover to taste like, but I swallowed it down and wiped my mouth with the back of my hand.

At first I thought I was going to vomit, but then it settled into my stomach and it didn't feel too bad. Sort of burny, but in a good way. And then the girl cheered and Matt joined in. And so I smiled. There I was standing in the middle of the park holding a bottle of vodka with people cheering me and suddenly the whole scene struck me as so funny that I started laughing.

'God, she's pissed already,' Gary said.

The girl laughed a tinkly little laugh then she said, 'Have some more. Go on.'

I didn't move, so she said it again. 'Go on, Frances. Treat yourself.'

And then they all started chanting my name: 'Frances, Frances, Frances.'

So I took another swig, and another and another. I got used to the taste and I started to like the feeling. So I had some more. And then, in no time at all, I'd finished the whole bottle. I flopped down on the grass next to Matt. There's no rush to get home, I thought. I'll just sit here. Watch the sun go down. Have a chat.

I remember one of the girls peering down at me like I was something in a Petri dish. 'She's a funny little thing, isn't she?' she said to Matt.

It was strange really – I didn't even find it insulting. She just seemed so fascinated by me. I don't remember minding or feeling silly or anything. It all just seemed so funny, at the time. Flattering, almost.

'Yeah,' Matt said, laughing. 'A real nutjob.'

I don't remember anything else. I suppose I'd thought they'd carry on talking to me but I don't think they did. I don't remember saying anything at all. I think I just sat there, just being. The sun was warm on my face and my head felt like it was inside a cloud.

It was dark when the policeman woke me up, and freezing cold.

'Come on,' he said to me in a weary voice. 'Let's get you home.'

I'd frozen at the sight of him, not sure if it was a dream or a kidnap attempt or what. He'd bent down and hauled me to my feet and steered me out of the park and into the road where his car was parked. He wrapped me in a blanket, and laid me on the back seat. Then he drove me home.

When we got to the house he took me to the door. I realised

that at some point I must've started crying because I could taste the salty tears dripping into my mouth. I don't remember feeling very sad or anything though. I suppose it was all such a shock, finding myself outside in the dark with a huge chunk of time erased from my memory.

In the car, I'd been terrified that Nan was going to go crazy at me, maybe hit me even. I mean, it wasn't like she'd hit me before, and actually, her sudden fits of temper were usually reserved for silly, petty things – leaving soap-bubble smears on the glasses when I was meant to be drying up, leaving the light on in my bedroom all day by mistake – but here I was, being driven home by a policeman, a drunken disgrace. I was all too aware that this must've been exactly what Bridget was like. Surely, I thought, surely I'm going to get it this time.

But in the end, she didn't do anything very much. She thanked the policeman and when he'd gone she stood in the hall, just looking at me, not saying anything at all. I kept waiting for it to come, for her to explode. But she didn't. She didn't even look angry really. Just confused. Sad and confused. In the end she said, 'Your dinner's on the side,' and went back upstairs. I'd assumed Granddad was in bed but then he'd appeared at the top of the stairs. He'd just stood there for ages, looking down at me, and I stood at the bottom looking up. I wanted to say sorry or to explain myself but the words didn't come. Eventually he shook his head, and said, 'You've let her down, Frances. You've let your nan down.'

Anyway, this time getting drunk was totally different. It was indoors, it was with Bert and we did it in style – on real champagne.

When Bert told me her parents were going away for a Saturday night and asked me if I wanted to sleep over at her house, I thought it sounded like an amazing idea. 'A bit of a girls' night,' she'd called it. A whole evening, just me and Bert. No having to worry about getting home. No being interrupted by lessons or by boys trying to chat her up. Just the two of us, hanging around, chatting and relaxing. But I also knew there would be no way Nan would let me stay out all night. In all the years I'd lived with Nan and Granddad, the only night I'd spent away from them was when I had my tonsils out when I was seven. Still, I was determined that I would get to go. It sounded too much fun to just turn down. I came up with a plan.

I knew that the only chance I had of Nan letting me stay out for a whole night was if the occasion was a) supervised and b) educational, so that's precisely what I told her it was. I'd read an article once about how the Natural History Museum stages sleepovers for schools where whole classes are allowed to bring their sleeping bags and bed down at the feet of a brontosaurus. I knew there'd be no way our school would ever get to take part in that kind of thing – not unless they wanted to find someone trying to ride the triceratops, can of lager in one hand, cigarette in the other – but Nan didn't need to know that. So, one lunchtime, I snuck up to the library and typed out a letter, complete with authentic-looking permission slip, and printed it off. I presented it to Nan that evening.

She frowned at it, moving it back and forth in front of her face until she found the distance from her eyes where she could focus well enough to read.

'Sleeping?' she said at last. 'In a museum? I've never heard anything like it.' She put the paper down on the kitchen table. 'No, I don't think so. And on a weekend! What a load of rubbish schools get up to these days. No, not for us, I don't think.'

I felt myself panic. I'd just assumed she'd be fine with it, once she had an official school letter to back it up.

'But, Nan,' I said, following her out to the garden where she was starting to hang the washing on the line, 'I have to go. It's part of my course. My GCSE. I have to go for my project. I'll lose marks otherwise.'

I could see the cogs going in Nan's brain as she moved up and down the washing line, pegging up pants and socks at lightning speed. 'We can't pay,' she said. 'I can't afford fancy trips like your mates. I've told you before.'

'No, you don't have to pay,' I said quickly, daring to hope that victory might be in sight. 'It's free.'

Just then, there was a crash from the lounge. We both looked towards the window and saw that as Granddad had tried to take a book off the top shelf, a pile of photo albums had fallen down on him. He was standing in the debris, looking at his feet. 'For God's *sake*,' Nan said, darting towards the back door. 'I can't leave him for two minutes.'

'So I can go, then?' I called after her.

'Yes, yes. Fine.'

When the Saturday came round, I was worried that Nan might change her mind. I wasn't sure whether to mention it early on to check or to just wait until the time came for me to leave. On the one hand I didn't want to remind her and give her all day to stew about it in case she worked herself up into a frenzy and changed her mind about letting me go. On the other, I didn't want to spring it on her in case she had forgotten and the surprise of it had the same effect. In the end though, I didn't have to remind her. Nan came to find me in my room.

'I've made you a sandwich,' she said, placing a square, foil package on my desk.

'Oh,' I said. 'Thanks. But . . . I'm not going till after dinner.'

'You might get peckish, I thought. In the night.'

I smiled up at her. 'Thanks.'

Then she ran her finger along my bookshelf. 'It's filthy in here. Make sure you clean it before you go.'

Seven-thirty couldn't come soon enough. At exactly seven-thirty-one, I stood on the Fitzroy-Blacks' doorstep and knocked three times with the big metal knocker.

Bert flung the door open almost at once. For a minute, I wondered if she'd been standing there, waiting for me. I sort of hoped she'd been looking forward to our evening together as much as I had. But I suppose that was wishful thinking. She got to do whatever she wanted every Saturday night. It wasn't a novelty for her like it was for me.

Bert was wearing some loose pink trousers and a matching vest. Over the top she had a cotton robe-type jacket. Her hair was in a messy bun, with strands falling around her ears. She looked amazing. I thought of the fraying grey pyjamas in my bag. I decided I'd have to sleep in my clothes.

'You're here!' She pulled the door open wide for me to step in.

She lifted my bag off my shoulder and chucked it at the bottom of the stairs, then she took my hand and pulled me down the hall to the kitchen.

'I thought we could have a little Christmas party!' she said.

'What do you mean?' I asked. I was suddenly afraid I was going to find that she'd invited half of Year Ten to join us for a wild house party, and that they'd be there already, hiding in the kitchen. But it was OK. It was just two bottles in the middle of the kitchen table, dark green with gold tops.

'Champagne?' I asked, gazing at them.

'Yep!' Bert said, bounding over to the table. 'The real deal. Fancy a glass?'

'But . . .' I said, 'your parents . . . they'll . . .' For some reason I couldn't take my eyes off the shiny foil wrapped around the necks.

'Oh it's fine,' Bert said. 'One of Mum's customers brought them round when Mum and Dad had already gone. We'll just drink one bottle and leave them the other. That way, if the customer says, "Did you enjoy the champagne?" Mum and Dad will still be able to say, "Yes, thank you, it was terribly kind." The customer isn't going to say, "Did you enjoy the TWO bottles of champagne?" is he? So we don't need to worry – they'll never know. Anyway, I've had wine with dinner heaps of times before so they're fine with that sort of thing.'

I didn't say anything but I don't think Bert was waiting for my approval. She was already peeling the foil off one of the bottles. I jumped when the cork popped out and Bert giggled as she sloshed the foaming liquid into two elegant champagne flutes.

'To the den?' she asked.

I nodded. 'To the den.'

Fifteen minutes later and we were squashed up together in the Egg – fast becoming my favourite place in the world. I'd already downed most of my glass. I'd got used to the sharp taste by now and I was enjoying the warm feeling in my belly and cheeks.

'Have you ever had champagne before?' Bert asked me.

I shook my head. That was the good thing about Bert. I didn't worry that she'd laugh at me or turn her nose up at my inexperience. She never seemed to find anything odd.

'Have you?' I asked.

Bert nodded and took another sip. 'A couple of times,' she said with a modest shrug. 'With my parents sometimes. Just a glass at New Year and whatnot.' She giggled suddenly. 'And . . .' she said, shooting me a mischievous little grin, 'and with Richard.'

I had to think for a minute to remember where I'd heard the name before. 'Wasn't he the one whose car you smashed up? Your parents' friend?'

Bert nodded and giggled into her glass again.

'I thought he was a plonker,' I said. I drained the last of my drink and Bert topped me up. The foam flowed over the top and we squealed as it splashed onto our legs.

Bert didn't say anything. She just looked into her glass and then smiled at me over the top. She giggled again and she shook her head. I wondered if she was drunk.

'What?' I asked, confused. 'What's funny?'

'I can't tell you,' she said, miming an exaggerated zipping action across her lips.

Now I really was curious. 'What? What can't you tell me? Tell me what you can't tell me!' I poked her playfully with my toe.

'Maybe after one more drink,' she said.

I nodded and we made quick work of our second glass. As soon as she'd finished, I was on her again. 'Go on then,' I said. 'Tell me.'

Bert topped up our glasses again, then she leant back into the cushions.

'If I tell you, you can't tell anyone. No one from school.'

'Of course not,' I said indignantly. 'As if I'd tell them anything.' I kept staring at her, afraid she might lose interest and change the subject if I took my attention off her for a second.

She didn't say anything for a moment, looking down into her glass and swilling her drink around. I wanted to prompt her, to ask again, but something told me to hold back and give her a minute.

'He was my boyfriend,' she blurted out eventually. She didn't look mischievous any more. She seemed nervous. She looked at me carefully, her eyes serious.

I frowned. 'Who? What?'

'Richard.'

16

I pushed my hair away from my face. 'Huh? Really? I thought he was horrible? And how *old* was he?'

'Forty –'

'Forty!'

'Five. Forty-five. I know it sounds old but . . .' She let the sentence trail off. It did sound old. It *was* old. 'He hadn't been friends with Mum and Dad for that long. Really it was his wife that they were friends with. Jane . . .' Bert looked down, her hair falling over her eyes.

'His *wife*? He was married? You . . . you can't have a married man as your boyfriend!'

Bert picked at a loose thread on a cushion. 'That's what Mum and Dad said,' she said quietly.

I just stared at her. Everything was spinning and fuzzy round the edges.

'But he was.' She chewed on her bottom lip. 'He was my boyfriend. Just for a little bit. But then he broke up with me. And then I . . . broke his windscreen.'

I tried to take it in, to think it through. But thinking felt like wading through glue.

I grinned suddenly. 'You're joking, aren't you? Bert! Stop messing about!'

But Bert just scrunched her mouth up and moved it from side to side like she was swilling mouthwash around. She shook her head and my smile fell.

'I don't . . . I don't understand . . .' I whispered.

So Bert explained.

She told me that Jane was her mum's friend from some artists' guild and whenever they did exhibitions together Richard and Jane would have dinner at their house. As Richard was a marine biologist he'd offered to tutor Bert in science and Bert's parents had jumped at the chance of the help because Bert was 'such an absolute dumbo' when it came to the sciences. She told me that when the two of them started spending time alone together, they'd hit it off straight away. He had crazy hair and beautiful teeth and such an enthusiastic way of talking that she felt anything was possible when they were together.

'He told me Jane was a nightmare to live with – always in a bad mood about her work and taking it out on him. He said they should never have got married in the first place. He said he liked talking to me, that he felt I understood him better than Jane ever had. He was ever so kind to me, you know. He never made me feel like I was younger than him or anything like that.

'And then one day, we were talking and he just leant in and kissed me. I mean, I think he was as surprised as I was, but straight away it just felt so *right*, you know? We did try to leave it there, to stay away from each other, but it was just so hard. And then after a while we just thought, well, why *not*? Why can't we be together? Jane had already ruined their marriage anyway by being such an unbearable grouch, and the age thing . . . well, in countries all around the world girls are married long before they're fifteen. It's only silly old England where everyone makes such a fuss about sixteen being a magic number. As if people suddenly turn into adults overnight! And to be perfectly honest about it I've probably seen and done a lot more than most people three times my age. That's what Richard always used to say anyway . . .'

I didn't speak at all during Bert's confession. I just stared down at the cushions of the Egg, steadily drinking my champagne one big gulp after another. I could feel the tips of my ears burning.

'We still had to do our lessons. We had to keep it professional. But we'd meet up at the weekends. He'd come round when Mum and Dad were out.' She smiled shyly. 'We'd sit up here for hours,' she said. 'Talking and . . . everything.'

I looked down at the Egg. Suddenly I didn't want to be in it any more, all squashed up against the cushions. I didn't move though, I just stayed there. And Bert told me how after a couple of months Richard had started to get cold feet.

'We'd been planning to tell Mum and Dad – I didn't like sneaking around in secret, I wanted to tell them – to tell *everyone* – how in love we were. I thought Richard felt the same but he kept stalling. He just got scared, I think,' she said. 'Started talking about how he'd get sent to prison, that the whole thing was a mistake and we had to end it . . . But I wouldn't have it. I wouldn't take no for an answer.' Bert looked down, embarrassed for a moment. 'So then he started to get nasty. He said I had to forget it all, said he was going to move away anyway and not even be my tutor any more. He called me silly once. "Silly kid." I think that's when I got really cross. When I threw the brick through his car window. And then of course Mum and Dad wanted to know what the hell had got into me and I . . . I'd had enough. I was exhausted. All the emotion. All the lying. I'm not used to keeping secrets, especially not from Mum and Dad. I just crumbled. Told them everything.

'I tried to make them understand, to explain how it was real, *pure* love, not just some silly fling, but they were furious. They wanted to report Richard, go to the police, but in the end he managed to persuade them not to. Kept asking them to remember how hard it would all be on Jane if it came out . . .'

'Maybe he should've thought of that first,' I said. I was surprised by how bitter my voice sounded.

Bert didn't reply. She just sunk back into the cushions and brought her knees up to her chest, curling herself in a little ball.

I don't know if it was the champagne or the surprise of it all or what, but I was just so angry. I couldn't stop thinking about them both – Bert and slimy, disgusting Richard – curled up in the Egg. In our Egg. Their hands and legs entwined, talking and laughing and . . . 'everything'. It made me feel sick.

We stayed like that for ages. Me just sitting upright, staring at the wall, steadily making my way through my drink. Bert curled up, cowering in the corner.

'Birdy?' she said eventually, in a voice almost too quiet to hear. 'Please don't be cross.'

'I'm not,' I said in a voice that came out too loud. I tried to make myself smile, to soften the atmosphere, but it just didn't come. I think I was just shocked to discover that she'd had this big secret. This huge thing had happened in her past and she hadn't wanted to share it with me before now.

'I know it was . . . silly,' she said, still quiet. 'But it was . . . I mean, haven't you ever felt like that? Like as long as you can be with that person, just sitting close to them, then everything will be OK? Like nothing else mattered?'

I made a hard 'hmph' sound, as if to say, 'Don't talk rubbish,' and we were quiet again.

After yet more sitting and staring and not talking, Bert shifted and I felt her warm, soft hand on mine. She prised my clenched fist open and curled her fingers around mine. We sat there for ages, just holding hands. I felt my anger seep away. I just couldn't be bothered with it. I wanted to forget it. I didn't want to let revolting Richard spoil our evening. I wanted to go back to how we were before.

'Shall we open the other bottle?' she said, sitting up and smiling.

'We can't . . . your parents . . .'

Bert climbed out of the Egg. 'It'll be fine,' she said with a wave of her hand and she galloped down the stairs to get it.

I can't remember much after that. I know we put the music channels on loud on the big TV and that we danced around the den. It could've been for minutes, it could've been for hours. I just remember that at one point, I'd stopped to get my breath back. I'd watched Bert trying to bounce on a beanbag and getting her legs tangled up. She'd fallen over and we'd both laughed and laughed and at that moment I remember thinking that being drunk was the best feeling in the world and that I couldn't believe people weren't drunk all the time.

And then a feeling of triumph crept over me. Look at us, Richard, I'd thought. Look at Bert, here with me, having the time of her life. You're gone. I'm here now. This is my time.

We fell asleep in the Egg itself, which shows how drunk we must've been because it's really not the right shape for one to sleep in, let alone two. The next morning, the light streamed through the skylight and straight into my brain like a laser. My mouth felt like I'd drunk a pint of sand. I tried to heave myself out of the chair, feeling like my head was going to explode. The movement made Bert stir. I guess she had a similar set of symptoms because she let out a long groan.

'Oh God,' she said. 'Need water.'

We shuffled to the edge of the Egg and perched on the side, looking at the detritus around us. Cushions were strewn across the floor and crisps were ground into the carpet. Our eyes stopped on the two empty champagne bottles. One was lying on its side, a tiny trickle of liquid escaping from its neck.

'We should get rid of those before Mum and Dad get home,' Bert said.

I nodded and reached down to pick one up. It stunk like chemicals and vinegar and made me want to puke.

The smell of coffee and toast wafted up as soon as we opened the door to the den.

Bert turned to me, her eyes wide. 'No!' she said. 'They must've come home early! We'll have to sneak straight out the back, dump the bottles there.'

I nodded, my eyes barely open. I just wanted to climb into bed and pull the duvet over my head.

We were halfway down the stairs when Charlie appeared in the hall. He was wearing a dressing gown and his face was covered in bright ginger stubble. He curled his hands around his mug and looked up at us. Bert and I froze. I turned to her, my heart beating.

'Well,' Charlie said. 'Good morning.'

We didn't reply. I just stared at him. My brain wasn't working well enough to process this development, and anyway, Charlie's expression was impossible to read.

He nodded towards the bottles in our hands. 'Put those with the recycling, then come and join us in the kitchen please.'

Bert nodded and we got rid of the bottles in silence. I didn't know what was going to happen to us. I didn't know how much I cared at that point. I felt like someone else had taken possession of my body. I was just watching, from the outside.

Charlie and Genevieve were sitting at the kitchen table. There was a pot of coffee and a plate of croissants in front of them, Charlie in his navy towelling robe, Genevieve in a long white nighty. I half-wondered what Nan would make of that. In our house, we weren't allowed to wear pyjamas downstairs at all – 'If you're up, you're up. You're not lazing around here like it's a dosshouse.' She'd probably have had a heart attack at the thought of people sitting down to a full meal in their nightwear.

Bert and I stood in the doorway, looking down. 'I thought you were . . . were out all night?' Bert said in a small voice.

'Came home late last night,' Genevieve said, looking at us over the top of her coffee cup. 'Thought we'd rather sleep in our own bed. I did look in on you two but you were out for the count.' There was the slightest raise of her eyebrows.

'I'm sorry,' Bert mumbled.

Suddenly Genevieve let out a loud, posh laugh. 'I bet you are, now!' she said.

Charlie's expression cracked too, and a smile spread over his face. I just stared at them, looking from one to the other.

'Sit down, for heaven's sake,' he said. 'Have some food, soak up the alcohol.'

I looked at Bert and we skulked over to the table. The sound of the chair scraping back cut right through me. We chewed our croissants in silence.

'I do wish you could've chosen something from the wine rack, rather than pinching the champagne, you know,' Genevieve said after a while. 'That stuff was probably sixty quid a bottle.'

Bert didn't say anything.

Charlie laughed. 'Expensive tastes, eh? That's my girl.'

Genevieve drove me home. For one awful moment I thought she might come in and tell Nan everything that'd happened, but she didn't. She just gave me a wry smile and said, 'I'd get back in bed, if I were you,' and I nodded and thanked her and dragged my sorry self inside.

As you can imagine, Nan really isn't the kind of person to let people get into bed in the daytime just because they fancy it. The only exception is genuine and serious illness. Luckily, I felt confident that I couldn't have felt more awful if I'd had a life-threatening debilitating condition so I had no trouble convincing her that I'd 'picked up a bug' from the museum. I lay under the covers, shivering even though I had a thick jumper on over my pyjamas. I felt terrible. Not just physically, but in my head too. It was like there was a black cloud hovering above me, but I couldn't quite put my finger on what it was.

I could only remember snapshots of the night before. Every time I thought about Bert and Richard I felt that hot wave of anger again. It was all so confusing. Was I angry with her? Was she angry with me? Why did it all matter so much anyway? I suppose part of me was just so hurt that this huge gap had emerged between us suddenly – she'd had this proper, adult lover and I'd never even had a real friend before her, much less a boyfriend. It made me feel like a little kid, left behind. Embarrassed. In the end I decided that my anger was probably meant for Richard. I was angry at how he'd taken advantage of Bert. He'd treated my best friend badly and so it was only natural that I'd be furious with him about it. Yes, that was it.

I felt a bit better once I'd decided that and eventually I fell asleep. By the time I woke up, it was dark outside.

17

The next week or so at school was all about the lead-up to Christmas. Tinsel sprung up in the classrooms, draped along windowsills and framing the board, kids and those teachers who liked to think of themselves as 'fun' started wearing Santa hats, mobile phone ringtones were set to tinny renditions of Christmas songs. Bert joined in the festivities with gusto, declaring Christmas her 'absolute most favourite' time of year, but despite her cheerful exterior, despite the foam reindeer antlers and the flashing Christmas tree brooch, I still felt there was a little bit of an atmosphere between the two of us.

Neither of us had mentioned our drunken night since that weekend, and neither of us had mentioned Richard. Her confession was definitely on my mind though, and I had a feeling Bert was thinking about it too. There was something about the way she was around me – sort of tentative and on edge – that told me she was nervous. I thought perhaps she was worried that I'd get cross with her again. Or maybe she was just scared that I might give her little secret away and everyone at school would realise what she was like.

I didn't like it, that uncomfortable feeling. We were still the best of friends on the outside but it felt like there was an invisible wall between us and I couldn't work out how to get round it. But then, quite by chance, something happened that seemed to break the wall down. Something that flung us back together again.

We'd just finished maths and we'd headed over to our lockers to dump our textbooks and collect our painting shirts before going up to art. Bert was moaning about trigonometry and how it was all totally pointless and I was nodding along and agreeing even though to be perfectly honest I'd never had any problems with it. She was so up in arms about the whole thing that she didn't even see it at first. She just grabbed her lock and started fiddling with the combination. It was only because I was staring at it that she looked up at all.

It was written across her locker, right from the top to the bottom, the words scratched into the paint in angry, spiky letters:

STUCK UP BITCH!!!

The exclamation marks were an odd choice, I thought. Made the message look a little bit too enthusiastic, made the person who wrote it seem more excitable than menacing.

'Oh!' Bert said, reeling back. She turned to me. 'What's this? What's happened? Who would do this?' Her brow furrowed. 'And *why* would they?'

I looked at the words, my eyes narrowed slightly, trying to work through the possibilities.

'Don't know,' I shrugged eventually. 'Could be anyone.' Then I realised how that sounded. 'Well, I don't mean *anyone* as in lots of people might think . . . I just mean . . . Oh, I don't know, Bert.' I shook my head. 'People are idiots. It probably doesn't mean anything. It might not have been for you at all. Might just be a random thing.'

If I'm being completely honest I wasn't totally convinced of this myself. If it'd said something else – just the 'bitch' perhaps – then maybe it might have been a random attack, but if there ever was anyone to criticise Bert – and as I've said before, there weren't many who did – 'stuck-up' would often be the phrase that was used. It wasn't totally fair, I didn't think, but I could see where it'd come from. It was that slightly plummy way of talking she had, the little bit of haughtiness about her. I suddenly felt very protective of her. Poor old Bert, so cheerful and innocent. Why pick on her? It was like kicking a puppy.

I could see Bert still fretting about it as we shared a tray of sausage rolls and potato smiley faces in the canteen at lunchtime. I wasn't sure what to do to put her mind at ease.

'Bert,' I said gently. 'You're just going to have to forget it. Everyone gets that kind of crap at some point. It's not a big deal. Let it go.'

She looked down sadly at her plate, picking at a bit of pastry.

'I just . . . I just try really hard to be nice to people. Why would they be so . . . so mean? I just don't know what I've done to deserve this kind of treatment.'

I sighed. I felt sorry for her but I also worried that she was making too much of it. I mean, I'd seen some quite vicious stuff at school – harassment campaigns going on for years, violent attacks, the works – so I knew that a bit of casual graffiti was pretty small fry. And I knew that the truth was, she needed to learn to be a bit more resilient if she was going to really fit in at a place like Whistle Down. I realised that a good friend would tell her that. I had to be careful about how I phrased it though. Tough love didn't really work on people like Bert and I really didn't want to upset her any more when she was already feeling fragile. I realised I was going to have to go for a softly-softly approach.

'Bert,' I said, putting down my fork and giving her my undivided attention. 'You're a lovely, kind, generous person. I know that. Anyone who knows you at all knows that.'

She opened her mouth to say something but I carried on before she could get a word in.

'But you need to realise, most of the people here aren't like you. They don't go out of their way to be kind, to see the best in people. They get their kicks from seeing other people suffer. Like I said, they might even have picked a locker at random. They're just bored, most of the people in this place. Bored idiots. You're just going to have to accept that some people . . . some people just aren't that nice.'

Bert puffed her cheeks out and blew air out slowly. 'OK,' she said. 'OK, I know you're right. I need to toughen up. Not be so sensitive. It's just such a . . . such a disappointing realisation to come to terms with, isn't it? I suppose I just wanted to believe that . . . everyone liked me . . .'

Even Bert could see that this sounded a tiny bit conceited and she gave me a bashful little smile. I laughed, but not in an unkind way.

'No one's liked by everyone, silly,' I told her. 'But *I* like you. A lot. And you'll always have me on your side.'

'I know,' she said, nodding. 'And I'm so pleased about that.'

She slid out of her seat and gave me a hug.

And as it turned out, having that little crisis to overcome together – me having the chance to deliver some honest but well-meaning advice – seemed to clear the air between us a bit. That afternoon, for the first time since the champagne night, Bert brought up her Richard confession.

'You know I am sorry,' she said as we sat together in our usual seat at the back of the science lab. 'I know you're still cross with me.'

'I'm not!' I lied.

'It's OK,' she said. 'I'm cross with me too. I know I was an idiot . . . but it was ages ago. I'm different now, honestly.'

'It's fine,' I said. 'People make mistakes. I just wish you hadn't lied to me.'

'I didn't lie,' she protested. 'I told you about the brick, I just . . .'

'Left out some fairly crucial details?' I raised my eyebrows, just a little.

Bert looked down. 'I know,' she said. 'I'm sorry.'

'It's OK. It's fine.' Although I did want Bert to know I was disappointed in her, I didn't want a repeat of the awkwardness there'd been between us when she first told me. It was time to move on, I thought. Put it behind us. 'I understand. I do. But just . . . don't keep secrets from me again, OK? We're supposed to be friends.'

She nodded hard. 'We are,' she said. 'Best friends.' She sighed.

'Oh, Birdy, I just want to fit in here at school. I want to do well at my exams and that's *all*. No getting into trouble, no boys, no drama. No *nothing*.'

I nodded and gave her an encouraging smile, but she still looked a bit stressed.

'I have an idea,' I said suddenly. I took her hand and pulled it towards me, setting it just in front of me on the bench. I took my black Biro and on the back, just by her thumb joint, I drew a tiny symbol. A silhouette of a bird in flight.

'It's a blackbird,' I explained. I pushed the pen into her hand. 'Here, you do one on me.'

Bert shrugged and nodded and did the same on my hand.

'Now we're tattooed!' I told her with a grin.

She looked at the neat drawing on my hand and the slightly more lopsided one on hers. 'Until we wash our hands . . .'

'That's my idea,' I said. 'We keep redrawing it on. Every night. Every morning. Then it will be like it's permanent. Blackbirds forever!'

Bert smiled. 'OK,' she said. 'Sure. Blackbirds forever!'

I ran my fingers over the little drawing, being careful not to smudge the ink, and I smiled to myself.

I couldn't help feeling a little bit grateful to the mysterious exclaiming graffiti artist.

18

I was invited to spend Christmas Day with Bert and her parents. Although I was obviously delighted by the invitation to start with, my joy quickly began to fade away as I realised that I'd have to turn it down. There was no way that Nan – who didn't like me accepting so much as a chocolate digestive from a 'stranger' – would allow me to spend the whole of Christmas Day in someone else's house, eating their turkey and sprouts, pouring their cream on my Christmas pudding. That didn't stop me thinking about the idea though – fantasising about being in Bert's big house, sitting around the dining table in the kitchen, pulling crackers and groaning as Charlie read out the terrible jokes. Bert's parents would ask me questions in their kindly and interested way. Bert would insist that I had first pick of all the food on offer. I'd feel like one of the family, only better. I'd be like a VIP.

I enjoyed these daydreams so much that the idea of them never coming true seemed to become really quite painful. I didn't want to upset Nan by suggesting I didn't want to spend Christmas with them, but then Nan had never made any secret of the fact she thought the whole festive period was a total waste of time and money. Anyway, two days before Christmas I thought, What the hell, there's no harm in asking. I've got to at least try.

'On Christmas Day?' Nan said, frowning as she scraped the bottom of a saucepan clean with a knife. 'They don't want a stranger in their house on Christmas Day.'

I couldn't be bothered to point out I was hardly a stranger, having been to the house at least fifteen times over the past three months. Besides, Nan didn't know about most of those visits. She just thought that the pressures of GCSE coursework meant I'd had to start staying late at school several times a week.

'They do, Nan. They asked me. It's fine.'

'I'm doing a perfectly good dinner here,' she said. 'Butcher's saving me a bit of lamb's neck. We don't need their charity.'

I didn't reply. There was no point. There was no reasoning with her. She wasn't open to negotiation. I missed Granddad then, the real Granddad, how he used to be. Sometimes when Nan was being rigid like this he'd step in and fight my corner. It didn't normally get him anywhere but it was nice to have him on my side. Then, if Nan was being particularly severe, he'd come and see me in my room, to check if I was all right I suppose, to explain. 'She does love you, Frances love,' he'd tell me. 'I'm sure of it. I know she's strict about rules and what have you, but she's just scared . . . scared of what happens when she's not in control. You understand, don't you?' I suppose I did understand, but it didn't make me like it any more.

I took a tea towel from the drawer and started drying the plates on the drainer, telling myself I'd been stupid to let my imagination run away with me like that. But then, fifteen

116

minutes later, as I was spraying the worktop with cleaner, Nan sighed and said, 'OK, fine. If you're going to sulk about it, you can go over after dinner. In the afternoon. Just for a couple of hours. I don't want you eating their food.'

I froze mid-wipe, wondering if I'd heard her right. But before I could check, she'd marched out of the kitchen and I could hear her grumbling and cursing as she tried to squeeze the Hoover back into its tiny space under the stairs. I smiled to myself, and sprayed the kitchen cleaner extra hard onto the kitchen table – five jubilant, celebratory pumps. Then I quickly wiped the foam away before Nan came back and caught me being so frivolous.

I'd already been working on Bert's Christmas present for a few weeks. It was a detailed pencil sketch of a blackbird, standing on a branch with a worm in its mouth that I'd copied from the old *Encyclopaedia Britannica* Nan and Granddad kept on the shelf in the hall. On Christmas Eve, I added the finishing touches to the beak and eyes and carefully positioned the sketch in the frame I'd bought from the 99p shop a few Saturdays ago. The 99p had technically been Bert's – she hadn't asked for her change back when she'd sent me to the canteen to buy doughnuts one breaktime – but I didn't think that mattered too much. The sketch was the important bit.

Then, in a swell of panic, it suddenly occurred to me that perhaps I should be taking Genevieve and Charlie a present too. Was that the right etiquette? I wasn't sure. I was hardly a seasoned Christmas Day guest. I decided that, as I was in doubt, it was better to take something than to not, but that left me with the problem of *what* I could possibly take.

I had precisely thirty-two pence in my purse and even if I managed to think of anything reasonable that could be bought for that price, it was Christmas Eve evening and all the shops were bound to be shut by now. I expected that the paper shop on the way to school might be open – I don't think I'd ever seen that one close – but what would I get from there for thirty-two pence? I couldn't exactly present the Fitzroy-Blacks with a packet of chewing gum or half a box of value Jaffa Cakes.

I sat down on my bed and chewed on my nail, looking around my bedroom for inspiration. Maybe I could just give them something of mine and pretend I'd bought it. Would they want a Bible? A jigsaw? I half-wondered if I could wait until Nan had presented me with the standard-issue pair of socks that I got every Christmas morning, then re-wrap them and take them round. But even if I could get away with that for Genevieve, it wouldn't do for both of them. What would I do – tell them to wear one each?

I mentally pictured their house, hoping that something would jump out at me, some kind of clue as to what they'd like. Suddenly I remembered something. On perhaps my second visit I'd been staring up at a big painting in the kitchen. It was just big blocks of colours really – a smudgy pink rectangle with a rough yellow rectangle on top and a black line across the middle. I'd assumed that Bert had done it, when she was much younger probably. It looked like something a four or five year old might produce the first time they were let loose with a set of powder paints and big sheet of paper. But luckily I didn't say anything out loud because Bert had come and stood alongside me.

118

'It's Mark Rothko,' she said. 'It's splendid, isn't it? Mum and Dad love him. It's just a print, of course. The original's in the Guggenheim I think.'

'Yes,' I agreed, not wanting to appear uncultured. 'It's magnificent.'

In the library the following day I'd found a book on Mark Rothko and flicked through, trying to familiarise myself with his most famous works in case he ever came up in conversation at Bert's house. I was a bit surprised to see that all his paintings were like the one in Bert's kitchen – just squares of random colours. They weren't even neat squares and the colours didn't even match half the time. Strange, I thought, closing the book up. Talk about the emperor's new clothes.

But now I was suddenly grateful to Mark Rothko and his primitive style. I thought back to that book, trying to picture one of his pieces. I remembered there was one that I'd found particularly odd – one big square of orange together with a big square of navy. That was it. That was his whole 'work of art'. I tore a page out of my school sketch book and got out my chalk pastels. I wasn't sure exactly what media Mr Rothko used to bring his genius to life but I thought chalks would be best for getting those smudgy edges.

I drew a big block of orange and below it a big square of navy. Then I rubbed the sides with my finger to give them the trademark Rothko blurred look. When that was done, I shook the loose chalk dust from the page and in the bottom right corner I wrote *Mark Rothko* in tiny, squiggly letters with a Biro.

With the piece complete, I rummaged around in the drawer next to my bed until I found what I was looking for – a picture of Mum slouching in an armchair, her hair tumbling over her eyes. The only picture I had of her, in fact. The photo was sitting in a clear plastic frame, so I undid the clip at the back, tipped Mum out and slotted my drawing in its place. I held it out in front of me to survey my handiwork.

Yes, I thought. That'll do nicely.

19

I still had to get through Christmas morning and dinner at home before I could escape to my fantasy Christmas at Bert's. It was just as painful as it was every year. Perhaps more so. There's nothing like having somewhere better to be to make it starkly obvious how awful Christmas in your own home is.

There was one brief moment of excitement that morning though, when instead of the usual sock-shaped parcel, the package Nan handed me was bigger, softer.

'I saw you looking,' she said gruffly, 'in me magazine. Folded the blasted corner over as well, didn't you. Weren't exactly sly about it.'

My heartbeat quickened slightly. Could this be it – the first year that Nan had actually got me something I wanted?

I lifted up the flap of red paper at the end and unpeeled the Sellotape – Nan didn't approve of any kind of unrestrained ripping and tearing; why waste good paper that could very well be used again? – and peeked in. Blue wool! I upended the parcel and tipped the jumper out, beaming. I unfolded it on my lap.

I felt my smile fade. It wasn't the same jumper. Not at all. It was made of something cheap, something rough. Acrylic probably. The collar was all loose too. It was just all wrong. I kept my cheeks in position, but I knew the smile had gone from my eyes.

'S'not the exact same one obviously,' Nan huffed. 'Not paying those rip-off prices. But it's almost identical and a quarter of the price.'

'It's great, Nan,' I said. 'It's perfect.'

I really hoped Nan couldn't tell I was disappointed. If I hadn't expected it to be the other jumper it would've been a good present. And the thought of Nan tearing the photo out of the magazine, trudging down to the high street and carefully scouring the shops for something similar just about broke my heart.

'Good,' she said crossly. 'So it should be.' Then she got up and went to check on the potatoes.

I handed out my presents to Nan and Granddad. Without any money of my own bar my dinner money – which Nan gave me anyway and which was barely enough to buy a bag of chips a day with – I was a bit limited, so Nan and Granddad had to make do with homemade efforts too. Luckily, as I had all year to prepare for Christmas, I'd been working on their presents for a few months.

First, I handed Granddad the scarf I'd been making at lunchtimes in the textiles room, with the spare balls of wool I'd found in the drawer. He smiled and nodded, and laid the scarf on his lap, stroking it like it was a cat. Then I gave Nan the project I'd been working on in woodwork for the whole of the autumn term. It was a kind of letter rack, with little hearts carved on the front. She unwrapped it and held it up in front of her.

'What is it?' she said. 'For toast?'

I shook my head. 'No,' I said. 'It's for letters. To keep them safe.'

Nan frowned. 'Right,' she said, 'I see.' She turned the rack over in her hands. Then she put it down on the arm of the chair. 'Shame we don't get much post then really, isn't it?'

'Yeah,' I said, running my finger over the dovetail joints that had taken me so long to get right. 'I s'pose.'

When I was allowed to leave, I felt like skipping my way to Bert's but I was held up by a very old lady walking in front of me, hunched over almost double and dragging a shopping trolley behind her. She was walking painfully slowly but I was reluctant to overtake. I hate it when I'm out with Nan and Granddad and people overtake us. Even if they don't mean anything by it I feel like they're making a point. Nan always purses her lips and puts her head down and tries to walk faster. I didn't want to be that person. I didn't want to make the shopping-trolley lady feel old and weak. Not on Christmas Day.

When I finally got to Chestnut Avenue, Charlie let me in and I found that, as usual, the Fitzroy-Black house was full of music and laughing and energy.

There was a roaring log fire in the lounge and Genevieve was sitting in an armchair next to their spectacular tree, her legs curled under her and a big glass of red wine in her hands.

'Frances!' she said as I stepped in, rubbing my hands to get warm. 'You're here!'

She stood up and came over to me. She kissed me on both cheeks and then held me by the top of my arms, looking into my face like she was searching for something. 'Merry Christmas, darling. How are you? Have you had a good day, so far? Take your things off, get warm. Get comfy.'

'Yeah, good thanks,' I said, laying my coat over the arm of a chair.

I heard Bert before I saw her, bounding down the stairs and calling, 'Merry Christmas, Birdeeeeeeee!'

She bundled into the living room, tripping over slightly on account of the enormous slippers she had on her feet. They looked more like teddy bears than any kind of footwear – huge grey fur things with ears.

'Do you like my elephants?' she beamed. 'Smashing, aren't they? Only I keep falling over the trunks!' She laughed and threw herself down in an armchair, her legs draped over the arm. But then straight away she was on her feet again. 'Oooh, presents!' she shouted. 'Let's do presents!'

Charlie came in to join us. 'Do stop shouting, Bertie!' he said with a smile. 'Honestly,' he said, turning to me now. 'She's been like this at Christmas since she was two. You'd have thought she would've grown out of it by now, wouldn't you?'

'Never!' Bert called from where she was now on all fours under the tree, rummaging around in a huge mountain of wrapped gifts. 'Christmas is too magical. How can you *not* be excited!'

Charlie rolled his eyes but he was smiling as he flopped down onto the sofa.

'Here!' Bert called eventually. She held up a parcel triumphantly. 'This one's yours, Birdy.'

She brought it over to me and dropped it into my lap. It was wrapped beautifully – in matte gold paper, tied with rustic-looking string. It seemed a shame to spoil it.

'It's from all of us,' Bert said. 'But I chose it.'

'Thank you,' I said, picking at the knot of the string. 'Thank you so much.'

'Oh just rip it!' Bert said. 'Don't take all day about it!'

She reached forward to take the parcel from me but Genevieve held her back. 'Bertie!' she said, laughing. 'Give the girl a minute. Let her do it her way!'

'Sorry,' Bert said, leaning back in her chair and sitting on her hands. 'I just can't wait to see her face!'

I finally got the string undone and peeled the paper back. I knew what it was straight away, as soon as I saw the blue wool. I didn't say so though, I just played along, making 'Ooh, what's this then?' kinds of noises as I unfolded it and held it up in front of me. This was it. This was *the* jumper. The real deal this time.

'The jumper,' I smiled. 'You got me the jumper!'

'Yep!' Bert said, bouncing back onto her feet again now. 'We got it for you! Do you like it still? You still like it, don't you?'

'I love it,' I said, standing up and holding it up against me. 'I absolutely adore it.'

'Put it on!' Bert demanded.

I did as I was told. It was perfect.

'Oh, it fits a treat, doesn't it?' Genevieve said. 'Good choice, Bertie, darling.'

'Thank you,' I said, smiling around at them. 'I really, really love it.'

Then I remembered my own gifts, lying in my bag.

'I got you things too,' I said, reaching in and passing one square package to Bert and the other to Genevieve. 'That one's for both of you,' I said. 'You and Charlie.'

125

'Oh, darling!' Genevieve said, sitting up and setting her wine glass down on the coffee table to give the unwrapping of my present her full attention. 'You didn't have to get us anything, you mad girl!'

I shrugged modestly, and looked down. 'It's OK.'

Bert opened hers first.

'A blackbird!' she said, holding the picture up in front of her. 'Did you do this?' she said to me.

I nodded.

'Look, Mum,' Bert said. 'Birdy's drawn me this – isn't it brill?'

Genevieve took the picture from her and squinted at it. 'Yes, it certainly is,' she said. 'Look at the detail on the feathers! You clever old thing,' she said, turning to me. I felt my cheeks get hot.

'Thanks, Birdy,' Bert said. 'I'm going to put it on the wall, in the den.'

'My turn now,' Genevieve said and we all turned to watch as she tipped her own picture out. She frowned at it for a minute, as if she was trying to make sense of it. Charlie and Bert looked on expectantly.

'What it is, Mum?' Bert said.

'It's a Mark Rothko,' I explained.

'Oh,' Genevieve said slowly. 'Of course it is!' She looked up and smiled. 'Did you do this one too, darling?'

I hadn't been expecting that question. I'd just assumed they'd accept it as a real one. Not an original, obviously. But a print. Like the ones you get on postcards in the library gift shop.

'N-no,' I said. 'It's a real one . . . a copy, I mean.'

There was a tiny twitch at Genevieve's eyebrow, but then her smile was back. 'Of course,' she said. 'A reproduction.'

I realised straight away that I hadn't fooled them. I felt ridiculous. Why had I said that? Why didn't I just tell them I'd drawn it myself? They probably would have liked that even. I mean sure, it all looked the same to me, but these people knew about art and all that rubbish. They could probably spot a forgery a mile off. But what could I do? I couldn't change my story now. It'd look totally insane. I just had to sit there, grinning at them like a fool, and just wait for the whole excruciating episode to be over.

She passed it to Charlie and I saw a similar twitch at his eyebrows and a little amused look pass between the two of them.

But then he smiled too. 'Wonderful,' he said. 'Wonderful – we love Rothko. We'll put it up, of course.'

He placed it on the mantelpiece. Face down.

Once the presents were out of the way, Charlie got out the Scrabble set and we sat on the floor in front of the fire to play. Charlie gave me and Bert mugs of hot milk spiced with cinnamon to drink. The radio was on in the background, playing old-fashioned Christmas songs. The lights on the tree blinked happily and the glow from the fire flickered on our faces.

How fantastic, I thought, for this to be your Christmas Day, to have this every year to look forward to. No wonder Bert had been so chirpy in the run-up – *this* was something worth getting excited about. And how I wished it was *my* Christmas Day. My real one. That I could stay for the whole evening, not just a couple of hours. That I could stay forever.

Being rather a slow game – especially with Charlie, who liked to think very long and very hard before placing his letters – Scrabble left a lot of time for chatting. I just listened mostly, enjoying the banter between Bert and her parents, hearing about their Christmas so far and their plans for New Year.

Genevieve seemed very interested in how I spent my Christmases with Nan and Granddad so I described our routine, keeping it deliberately vague. I left out details like how I get the same present every year and how we eat in silence, struggling to chew our cheap cuts of meat and over-boiled vegetables.

'It must've been ever so hard for them,' Genevieve said. 'After what happened to your poor, dear mother. Suddenly finding themselves with a toddler on their hands, just when they were in the midst of all that grief . . . terrible. I can hardly imagine.' She shook her head and gazed into the flames of the fire.

I suppose I should've been used to it by now, but I was still slightly taken aback by Genevieve's candid way of speaking about things. I couldn't imagine Nan suddenly passing comment on someone else's family situation like this. Not to their face, anyway. And definitely not with any tone of sympathy. I didn't know what to say. I just nodded.

'Do you miss your mum?' Genevieve asked, looking me straight in the eyes, trying to read my face.

I thought this was a funny question. Why would I miss someone I couldn't even remember?

Genevieve spoke again before I had time to reply. 'Of course, I suppose you didn't know her that well, but do you . . . I don't know . . . feel the lack of something? Feel that . . . that maternal figure is missing in your life?'

I know I'd hammed up the whole *Little Orphan Annie* bit when Bert and I were alone, but it felt silly to do that now, with all of them there. To be honest, I wasn't all that comfortable with the line of questioning. In the end, I opted to just tell them the truth.

'Not really,' I said with a shrug. 'I'm just used to it.'

Genevieve nodded thoughtfully, running her finger around the top of her wine glass. 'And I'm sure your grandparents are terrific, aren't they. I expect they dote on you . . .'

I didn't get the feeling Genevieve was really talking to me at all at this point. She was gazing off into space, a faraway look in her eyes. I felt like she'd created her own mental image of my family – the weary, grieving grandparents cherishing what they had left of their daughter. I wasn't sure how interested she was in the truth of the situation.

'They do their best,' I said, which I knew was true. 'They try.'

It was time to go home all too soon. I said my goodbyes and trudged home through the streets. Even the icy wind and the light drizzle that had started to fall couldn't spur me into rushing and I let the journey take twice as long as normal. Just before I got to my road, I stopped and took the blue jumper off. I shoved it into the bottom of my bag. I really didn't want Nan to find out I'd been given an upgrade just a couple of hours after I'd opened her present.

But I needn't have bothered. When I got in, I found Nan dozing in her chair. She looked up as I went in but nodded straight back off again within seconds. I realised I could've been wearing a gorilla suit and she wouldn't have noticed.

The TV was on quietly, showing coverage of some carol concert in a huge old cathedral. I sat on the sofa beside Granddad and listened to him hum along, trying to sing the odd word but getting the timing all wrong.

Suddenly he reached across and held my hand. His skin felt rough and cold. 'Happy Christmas, Bridget love,' he said.

I smiled sadly and squeezed his hand. 'Happy Christmas, Granddad.'

20

I didn't see Bert much over the rest of the holidays as her parents took her away to her aunt's house somewhere in the countryside for New Year so I was pleased to be reunited with her when school began again in January. The days were cold and dreary as they always are in the middle of winter but January plodded by peacefully enough, Bert and I passing the time snacking and chatting at the back of lessons, huddling together for warmth as we trekked across the field on the way home. Then in registration one morning a few weeks later, we found Pippa Brookman parading around the classroom, handing out some sort of flyer.

'*An Outing to Oz!*' she was calling breezily. 'A unique twist on the classic tale! Join in! Take part! It's all for charity!'

I swiped one of the flyers that'd been left on a desk.

An Outing to Oz: A Musical
A modern retelling of the much-loved story,
written to raise awareness of the treatment
of the elderly in our society.
All profits to charity.
Put your name down for auditions!!

I made a snorting noise. 'Another one of Pippa's noble charity efforts. Great. What would the old folks do without her?'

I passed the flyer to Bert.

'I love *The Wizard of Oz*!' she said, looking down at it. 'Don't you? It's just magical, I think. Gosh, I'd love to have the chance to be in it.'

'It's not *The Wizard of Oz*, Alberta,' Pippa called across the classroom. 'It's *An Outing to Oz*. Similar, but with some important differences. Come along to the meeting if you want to know more!'

'I wouldn't touch any of Pippa's projects with a barge pole,' I sniffed. 'It'll just be another excuse for her to show off and polish her massive ego.'

Bert shrugged and sat down on the edge of a desk, her legs swinging underneath her. 'I don't know,' she said. 'This is different I think. Sounds like it's an official school idea this time, not just one of Pippa's plans.'

I raised my eyebrows but we couldn't say any more about it because Mr Hurst had come in to take the register and was calling for everyone to sit down.

As I made my way to my chair, Pippa snatched the leaflet I was holding out of my hand. 'No need for you to get too interested, Frances,' she hissed. 'We wouldn't want to put the punters off.'

I glared at her and looked around to see if Bert had heard what she'd said, but she was busy looking for something in her bag.

Bert disappeared after third period so I queued in the canteen and sat at a table in the corner on my own, picking at the crust of my pizza and wondering where she could've got to. She was gone for most of lunchtime but eventually, ten minutes from the bell, she turned up, rosy-cheeked and smiling.

'Where have you been?' I said, trying not to sound too grumpy.

'Oh, I'll tell you,' she beamed. 'Just let me get some grub first. I'm ravenous.'

Bert collected a plate of chips, four sausages and a chocolate brownie, and slid her tray down next to me.

'Oh, Birdy,' she said, piling chips into her mouth. 'I've been in the hall, with Pippa and the others.'

'What do you mean?' I said, frowning. Just hearing Pippa's name was enough to put me in a bad mood.

Bert slipped two sausages onto my plate and I chewed at them grumpily. I don't know why she always had to buy so much food if she didn't even want to eat it.

'It was a meeting, about the play!' she said, her eyes shining. 'About *An Outing to Oz*. It sounds like it's going to be really wonderful. It's such a clever concept, you know. They've taken the whole idea of *The Wizard of Oz*, but changed it to show how elderly people struggle if people don't help them. So rather than the lion, the tin man and the scarecrow, there are these three old people – one's ever so lonely, one's losing his memory, one's . . . oh, I can't remember . . . but the other one's the equivalent of the lion so I suppose she must be fearful about something or other. Anyway, they all hear about this mythical land – Oz, of course – where they can be young again, if they can just get there. So the whole play is all about their journey on the long road to Oz, and all the people who help them on the way. But *then*, when they get there, they discover it's all been a myth and there's no magic potion or whatever. There *is* no being young again.'

'Great,' I said, fiddling with my straw moodily. 'Sounds really depressing.'

'No, not at all!' Bert said, spraying chips everywhere. 'Because the thing is, as they've been making this long journey, so many people have looked out for them, helped them on their way and whatnot, that they realise they don't really mind being old at all, that it's not so bad if only the people *around them* would be a bit more helpful and understanding!'

I rolled my eyes. 'Oh wonderful,' I said dryly. 'I love a story that hammers home a moral.'

Bert either missed my sarcasm or deliberately ignored it. 'Oh, I do too,' she said, nodding. 'It's such a powerful one too, don't you think? And it should be such a good show, because the thing is, it's not just for the school. It's all being organised by this national charity – Age Awareness UK or something – and they want a certain number of schools across the country to take on the performance of the show and then sort of tour around the local area, showing it to other schools and in youth centres and social clubs, you know, to sort of . . . spread the message. So that means there's a bit of a budget for costumes and music and things, so it should be really quite professional.'

Bert paused to take a gulp of lemonade, then she said, 'So anyway, that's why I've put my name down.'

My head jerked up then. 'What do you mean, put your name down? To be in the play?'

Bert nodded, her mouth stuffed full again. She forced herself to chew and then swallowed hard so she could go on talking. 'Yes. Well, for the auditions. Of course, it's ever so popular, so there's no guarantee but . . . oh, I do hope I get a part!'

'You could've told me you were going to the meeting,' I said sulkily. 'I might've wanted to come along.'

'Oh really?' she said, stopping chewing for a second and looking up at me. 'Would you, Birdy? Sorry, I didn't realise. You didn't seem keen earlier? It's not too late though. You can still put your name down to audition.'

I did a hard laugh. 'No thanks,' I said. 'I don't want to get involved in anything Pippa's in charge of.' I knew I could've told Bert about Pippa's snide remark to me that morning, but I just couldn't bring myself to for some reason. I was embarrassed really, that people spoke to me like that. And I didn't want Bert to pity me. I decided I'd rather she thought I was bad-tempered than pathetic.

Bert shook her head and rolled her eyes. 'Oh honestly, Birdy, talk about cutting off your nose to spite your face. Pippa's not in charge, she was just organising the meeting. I think it's going to be brilliant.'

She polished off the last of her sausages and started on the brownie.

'It just sounds such fun, I think,' she said, her eyes bright. 'Learning lines, going to rehearsals together, the singing, the dancing . . .'

I had to admit, it *did* sound sort of fun, if we'd be doing all those things together. And rehearsals for a school play would be the perfect excuse for me not to have to go home straight

135

from school. It would definitely be more fun to stay and hang around with Bert after school. I wouldn't even have to lie to Nan. She couldn't complain about a school production, especially one that was all for charity.

I suddenly had an image – Bert and me, on stage together. We were looking out across a sea of smiling faces, all clapping and whistling. Imagine that, I thought, people cheering for little loner Frances.

I sighed. 'OK,' I said. 'I'll put my name down. I doubt I'll get through the auditions though.'

I took my tray back to the front of the canteen and headed off to the hall to find the audition list.

21

The auditions were two weeks later, on Valentine's Day. I'd been so preoccupied by the thought of them that I'd forgotten that first we'd have to get through the awful annual Valentine's card ritual.

Every year at school, for the first two weeks of February, there'd be a makeshift postbox stationed in reception – an old cardboard box covered in pink tissue paper and printouts of heart shapes. The idea was that people label their cards with the name and tutor group of the object of their affection and leave it for the 'postman' to deliver on the day, in order to ensure absolute anonymity.

The postman was actually Mr Parker, head of Year Eight, and every year he'd get all dolled up in a ridiculous cupid costume, complete with fluffy wings, golden bow and a white smock-like dress which I was pretty sure must be his wife's nighty. Mr Parker would come around in morning registration with his sack of cards and there'd be loads of silly shrieking and giggling as he delivered them.

At some point, I reckon one of the parents must've complained that the system wasn't fair on ugly, unpopular ducklings like me who never got a single card, because for the last couple of years there'd been some cards that were clearly faked, sympathy-vote ones. I'd get one myself sometimes. They were always thin, cheap-looking things, the type you get from the bargain bin in Smith's. There would always be some cheeky, chirpy message inside – the type of thing that looked like it'd been copied from a packet of Love Hearts – 'be mine', 'cutie pie', 'groovy chick'. You'd only need to take a look at the cards received by some of the other class sad sacks to spot that the handwriting was the same in all of them. They probably got Mrs Warboise, the school secretary, to write them in bulk the day before.

But, as I say, this year, the upcoming auditions had been such a distraction I'd barely given Valentine's Day a second thought. That was until the morning of the fourteenth itself, when I bumped into Jac Dubois standing next to my locker and the whole thing was catapulted to the forefront of my mind.

I thought he looked shifty the second I saw him – the way he was loitering in the shadows like that, looking around him, all furtive and on edge.

'All right?' I said to him as I opened my locker.

'Oh, hi, Frances,' he said, coming to stand at my shoulder.

'Hi, Jac.'

'How are you?' He looked up and down the corridor again, like he was expecting someone.

'Uh, fine, thanks,' I said.

'Cool,' he said, still looking around him. He was sort of shifting from one foot to the other and fiddling with the rat's tail at the back of his head.

'You?' I said, having to continue the conversation because, although he didn't show any signs of saying anything else, he didn't seem to be moving on either.

'Uh . . . yeah,' he said. Then with another quick look down the corridor he suddenly reached up the front of his jumper and whipped out a bright red envelope.

I remembered what day it was at once, and for one moment I thought Jac was actually going to present me with a Valentine's card. I was surprised of course, but pleased too. I mean, I wasn't really interested in Jac, but I was looking forward to telling Bert about my admirer. Especially as he'd once been *her* admirer. I hoped she might be jealous, just a little bit.

But he didn't hand me the card. Instead he said, 'Would you do me a favour?'

He lifted the flap of the envelope and pulled out a card. It had an unfussy design – a simple sketch of a red heart on thick, cream parchment.

'Would you look at this and tell me . . . tell me . . . what you think?'

He opened the card and held it under my nose. I took hold of it to keep it steady while I read.

Dear Alberta,
I'm not much good at clever poems or rhymes, so I'll just say:
I think you're lovely.
From

I had to read it over a couple of times before I made sense of it. It was for Bert. Jac had written a card for Bert. He was still hung up on her. It seems silly now but I really hadn't seen it coming. I'd assumed he'd moved on to someone else ages ago.

I just looked at him as he stood in front of me chewing on his thumb nervously, waiting for my verdict.

'What?' he said. 'Is it awful? I mean, you know Alberta pretty well . . . Is it OK, do you think?'

He always pronounced 'think' as 'sink'. I guess that's what happens when you learn to speak English from people with French accents.

I blinked and turned away from him, pretending to rummage in my locker. 'Uh, no . . . it's just . . .'

'Ah, bollocks. It's terrible isn't it?' He looked down at the card, a pained look on his face. 'Maybe I should just forget the whole thing.'

I didn't reply. I just closed my locker with a bang and clicked the lock into place.

Jac looked down at the card again, opening and closing it.

'Fuck it, I'm going to send it,' he said, sounding determined. 'I've been thinking about it for weeks. I'm just going to put it out there. I won't put my name on it though. I'll just put it in the postbox.'

Then he took a pen out of his pocket, rested the card against the wall to lean on and drew a careful question mark at the bottom. Then he slipped the card into the envelope and sealed it up. He did it all quickly, like he wanted to complete the whole action before he could change his mind.

He looked at his watch. 'I better get a move on . . .'

He tucked the card back up his jumper and headed off towards reception but not before Gary Chester caught sight of him.

'What you got there, frog boy?' he shouted from the other end of the corridor. 'A love letter for a laaaayddeeee?'

'Fuck off,' Jac said, but he was laughing. He didn't hang around for Gary to question him any further.

Gary came over to me. 'Was that a card for Alberta?' he asked, still smirking.

'Uh . . .'

'I knew it!' He laughed and shook his head. 'What a muppet.'

Gary sauntered away, chuckling to himself, and I walked to registration feeling a bit miserable. I suppose I wondered if this was it – this was where Bert and Jac got together and started walking hand in hand across the field every day, me trailing a few paces behind, excluded. Forgotten.

I sulked through the whole of registration. Not only did I get my usual embarrassing fake card – 'Forever yours, from ????' – but I had to put up with Bert's squealing and giggling while she opened *four* separate cards. Most of them were full of exactly the kind of cheesy, sexist rubbish you'd expect from your average fifteen-year-old boy, but Jac's seemed to have an effect on her.

'Oh,' she whispered to me. 'Look at this one.'

She pushed the card under my nose and I had to read Jac's neat handwritten message for the second time that morning.

'Mmmm,' I said. 'Great.'

I passed the card back to her and made a show of tearing up my own card and dropping it into the bin.

'It's so sweet, don't you think? I love the way it's so simple. Completely unpretentious. Oh I wish I knew who sent it . . .' She looked around the room as if hoping to spot a clue.

'Why?' I said, screwing my nose up. 'What would you do about it anyway?'

Bert shrugged and pushed the card into her bag. 'I'd just like to know, that's all,' she said quietly.

22

I was glad that we had the afternoon's auditions to focus on so I was spared listening to Bert puzzle about who her secret admirer might be all day. The auditions were held in the hall, in groups of four, organised alphabetically. That meant that Bert and I were auditioning together, which was good. It also meant that Pippa would be there too, which was less good.

'I'm hoping for Dorothea, of course,' she told us, referring to the granddaughter of two of the elderly people and leading lady of the show. 'I mean, you've got to aim for the top, haven't you?'

Still, I was pleased to see that she was at least having to audition like the rest of us. I'd half-suspected that with all her busy-bodying and organising she'd be assured a lead role without having to do anything.

When we got to the hall, I was annoyed to find Mr Allenby there.

Mr Allenby was the school music teacher and although he seemed to be quite popular with lots of the other students at Whistle Down, I thought he was an idiot. He was young, as teachers go – only in his third year of teaching – and that was a fact he liked to remind us of all the time: 'It was only yesterday I was sitting where you guys are,' he'd say, at every available opportunity.

'Guys.' He was always calling us that. It drove me crazy. 'Hey, guys, are we feeling the vibe today?' 'Guys guys guys, what's with the beef? Calm it down, yeah?'

He was sitting at the piano as we traipsed in for our audition, playing a kind of relaxed jazz tune, his eyes closed as if he was lost in the music.

He pretended not to see us at first, but then he looked up and made a big show of standing up and pretending to be embarrassed. 'Oh, hey there, guys!' he called cheerily. 'Just caught me having a tinkle on the old ivories.'

This was typical of him. No doubt he'd been keeping an eye out for us for the last ten minutes, just waiting for us to walk in so he could get into position and have us 'catch' him showing off how talented he was.

'You're so good!' Bert said. I glared at her for taking his bait like this, but I don't think she noticed.

Mr Allenby shrugged. 'Bit rusty now, I'm afraid. Been concentrating on the woodwind too much lately . . .'

'Oh, what do you play?' Bert asked.

'Just getting into oboe,' Allenby said, his hands in his pockets. 'You know it's really –'

'How long's this going to take, Mr Allenby?' I interrupted, trying not to sound too grumpy. 'Only we shouldn't really be out of lessons too long.'

Allenby nodded and hopped back behind the piano. 'Sure,' he said, shooting me a little glare. 'Won't take long. We'll start with a read-through. Do you want to take a script each?'

144

He pointed to a pile of papers on top of the piano and we took one each. The scene was about the three elderly protagonists trying to complete part of their journey to Oz by bus, only to find that the forgetful one had mislaid their money. Luckily though the day was saved when a punky teenage boy the old people had earlier crossed the road to avoid stepped forward to pay their fare. It was just like I thought it would be – the 'Be nice, folks!' moral message was about as subtle as a punch in the stomach.

The read-through was pretty straightforward really. The fourth member of our group was Michael Boon, a big fat boy from our art class. He'd always seemed a bit backwards to me – the type who might've been dropped on his head at some point. Poor old Michael struggled with a few of the longer words in the script, meaning that he read all of his lines quite slowly, normally taking a couple of attempts and a prompt from Mr Allenby before he got the pronunciation right.

When that was out of the way, we had to move onto the singing. Truth be told, I hadn't given much thought to this bit. I'd never been especially known for my singing voice, but then as I saw it, when you go down to the nuts and bolts, singing was nothing more than talking in tune. I thought I could give it a good shot, at least. The song we had to sing was a version of 'We're Off to See the Wizard' and the words were on our sheets. I felt myself getting a bit pink when it got to my solo bit, so I just stared down at my song sheet, trying to block the others out. My memory of the song was a bit hazy, so there were a couple of lines where I wasn't one hundred per cent sure of the pitch but I managed to find my way eventually.

When I finished, Mr Allenby thanked me for my 'interesting interpretation'. I glared at him and Pippa sniggered. I glared at her too.

When the audition was finished, Mr Allenby told us that the casting list would be on the hall board tomorrow. I thought I'd probably done OK. I mean, I wasn't deluded, I knew I was never going to be good enough for a lead part, but that didn't matter to me. I wasn't in it for the glory. As long as I got a part – any part, even a tiny one – then I could go to rehearsals and hang out with Bert and actually join in with something for once.

As promised, at lunchtime the next day, the list of parts was posted on the notice board outside the hall. People approached nonchalantly at first, pretending to have only a passing interest, but then as more people saw what was going on, the crowds began to jostle, everyone trying to get a look, hoping they'd been given the starring role of Dorothea, or failing that, one of the old folks.

'Alberta,' I heard someone say. Then a few seconds later, someone else, 'Alberta. Alberta got it.'

Bert looked at me. 'Was that my name? Do you think I got a part?'

I shrugged and craned my neck but I couldn't read the list from our position at the back of the crowd. When we eventually got near enough to the board to be able to see, I spotted Bert's name straight away. It was right at the top.

Dorothea – Alberta Fitzroy-Black

'Birdy!' Bert said, spinning around. 'I got Dorothea! I'm going to be Dorothea!'

'Yeah!' I said, making a real effort to sound pleased. 'Brilliant! Well done. The star!'

People were patting Alberta on the back and congratulating her, and she was nodding and thanking them.

'What did you get?' she called to me. I looked down the list, searching for my name.

I saw that Pippa had got the woman who was scared of everything – which was a bit of a joke I thought, as I'd never met anyone with a confidence like Pippa's – little Harry Derbyshire had got the part of the forgetful old man and Laura Cox the old woman looking for love. I scanned further and further down the list, watching the parts get smaller and smaller – 'Bus Driver', 'Teenage Punk', 'Angry Builder', 'Man with Umbrella'. But I wasn't there. My name wasn't on the list at all.

There was even a 'backstage crew' section. Mr Allenby was 'Musical Coordinator/Director' – trust Allenby to feel the need to put his own name on the list – Jac Dubois was on lighting and mousey Ana Mendez on sets. Just as I was about to step away from the board I caught sight of one name that made me do a double take – Michael Boon from our audition group. Special needs Michael Boon, who could barely read and who had once wet his pants in the middle of a cross-country run, had got a part. It was only 'Man at Bus Stop #3', but still, it was one better than me. I honestly think I must've been the only person to audition to not get any part at all. I stuck my chin out and shoved my way through the crowd.

Fine, I thought. I didn't want to be in your stupid play anyway.

I looked around for Bert and saw her standing in the middle of a little group made up of Pippa, Harry and a couple of other people who'd been given decent parts. The key cast members, congratulating each other. She saw me looking over.

'Birdy!' she called. 'What did you get?'

I didn't really want to call it out, publicly announcing my shame, but I didn't exactly have much choice. It was either that or turn around and ignore her and have everyone making stupid, 'Oooh moo*dy*,' noises. I skulked over and joined them. Luckily Pippa and Harry and the others were too caught up in their own conversation to pay me much attention.

'Nothing,' I shrugged. 'But it's OK. I wasn't really that into it anyway.'

'Oh,' Bert said, sounding disappointed. 'Well, you tried your best. That's the main thing.'

Her patronising tone annoyed me so I just nodded and picked at a bit of loose paint on the wall.

'We've got to go, Alberta,' Pippa called over. 'But see you at rehearsals tonight?'

'Yep, see you later,' Bert called back.

'Oh, is there a rehearsal tonight?' I asked, looking up. 'Maybe I could come and help out? I could test you on your lines and stuff?'

'Sorry, Frances,' Mr Allenby called, coming from nowhere. 'Cast members only in rehearsals. I can't have all the hangers-on drifting around or it'll be bedlam in there.'

'Sorry,' Bert said, looking a bit uncomfortable.

'Fine,' I said, looking down. 'It's fine. I hope you and Pippa and Mr Allenby all have a great time together.'

I knew how stupid I sounded straight away. Like a petulant child. I just felt so disappointed. I'd wanted it to be *me* and Bert, not Pippa and Bert, leading the show together. And I felt silly too. Stupid for even auditioning. I must've been really terrible if even Michael Boon was better than me. I blinked hard, forcing the tears back.

Suddenly, Bert laughed. 'Oh, Birdy, please don't look so glum! It's not the end of the world! I mean, drama's not really your thing anyway, is it? You know you didn't get all the notes in the audition. Singing's just not for you obviously, but there's no need to get cranky about it. And there's no need to take it out on Mr Allenby. Or on Pippa for that matter.'

I couldn't fight the tears away then. They pricked my eyes, hot and sharp. I turned away from her and strode off towards the canteen.

23

In the next couple of weeks, Bert and I didn't actually acknowledge how I'd stormed off that day, but I could tell she was being careful around me. She kept up a deliberate facade of cheerfulness, prattling on about this and that – homework, telly, what she was having for dinner. She never mentioned how things were going with rehearsals, even though I knew she was spending an awful lot of time on the play, both after school and at lunchtimes. She extended a few half-hearted invitations to go over to her place after school, but I generally turned them down, telling her, perhaps a bit snootily, that I had 'things to do'.

I don't really know why I still felt so cross with her. I tried to reason with myself – so she'd got a part in the school play. So I hadn't. So what? She hadn't asked for things to work out like that. She hadn't planned to spend every spare hour singing and dancing and messing around with Pippa. But I just couldn't shake the irritated feeling. I suppose the truth was, I felt just a little let down by her. She could've been a bit nicer about me not getting a part. She could've just left a *little* gap to comfort me before she started making arrangements for rehearsals and defending Pippa and precious Mr Allenby.

Lying in bed one night I stared up at the shadows on the ceiling and tried to remember what my life was like before I met Bert. I just couldn't really picture it now. What had I thought about all day? What did I focus on? Schoolwork, I suppose, and the prospect of eventually being able to escape to university and having another shot at making some friends. But that was years away still – how had it ever been enough? And anyway, who was I kidding? I was never going to fit in anywhere. University wasn't going to be any different.

For a moment, I actually toyed with the idea of ditching Bert altogether. Formally ending our friendship. It'd been fun while it lasted, but we'd grown apart now. It was time to move on. I looked at her number on my mobile, the mobile she'd given me, my finger hovering over the delete button. But I knew I could never do it, not really. The thought of life without Bert was just too, too bleak. If I wasn't friends with Bert, if I didn't have her, then what would I have? My depressing home life in that silent, miserable house with Nan and Granddad and my equally dismal school life, where I'd go back to watching everything from the outside, sitting alone in lessons, eating my lunch on a bench in the corridor. The thought of it was too lonely to bear. I may have been all right before, before I knew anything better, but now I'd known what it was like to have a friend like Bert, I knew I could never go back. That, I decided, was probably why I was so miffed at her. I'd realised that she had control over me. She'd made me dependent on her. She hadn't done it on purpose, I did realise that. But still, she *had* done it.

* * *

My telling Bert that I was too busy to spend time with her turned out to be not entirely untrue, because later that month, Nan got ill and, for a while at least, Bert wasn't the only thing I had to worry about.

It started as a bad cold. I'd hear her coughing and sneezing in the kitchen, followed by impatient mutterings of, 'For Christ's sake,' as she reached for the tissues.

But then, one afternoon, I got home from school to a quiet house. On further investigation I found Granddad asleep in his chair, but there was no sign of Nan. I wracked my brain to see if I could remember her mentioning any errands she had to run but I came up with nothing. I thought about waking Granddad to ask him but I knew there'd be almost no way he'd remember even if she had told him, so I'd only end up worrying him.

I eventually found her in bed, which immediately told me that she must've felt really awful. I don't think I'd ever known Nan to go to bed in the daytime. She'd barely enter her bedroom at all between the hours of 8 a.m. and 9.30 p.m. It'd always been a point of pride, I think.

'Nan?' I called gently, pushing her bedroom door open. 'Are you OK?'

She was lying on her back, not sleeping, just looking at the ceiling. I could hear her breathing, laboured and rasping.

'Fine,' she said, not looking at me. 'Just this bloody cold, isn't it. Gone on me chest.'

'Should I call a doctor?' I asked, stepping into the room. As I got closer I could see Nan's skin, grey and clammy. It gave me the shivers. She looked so old. So tired. I wished I could've gone over to her, put my hand on her forehead. But she would never have stood for that.

'Don't you come in here,' Nan said, lifting her arm and trying to wave me away. 'Last thing I need is you getting ill. You've got school. And I need you to feed your grandfather. Do you think you can manage that?'

I nodded and retreated back to the doorway. 'OK,' I said. 'But . . . what about the doctor? Or some medicine? Shall I go to the chemist's?'

'No!' Nan barked. 'I don't need no doctor. Just a good night's sleep. Now get out of here and let me rest. Shut the door!'

I did as I was told. I went back downstairs and made a dinner of beans on toast for Granddad and myself. We ate on our laps because I couldn't face the thought of sitting at the table with him, trying to engage him in a conversation he wouldn't be able to keep track of. It was easier if we had the telly to focus on instead.

He turned around and grinned at me, a bit of bean juice dripping down his chin. 'This is fun, isn't it, love?' he said. 'On our laps. Like the old days, eh?'

I nodded and smiled back. As far as I could remember, we'd never eaten on our laps together, so I had no idea which 'old days' he was referring to. I supposed it was probably something he'd used to do with Mum and he was confusing me with her again. But then it was just as likely that the whole thing was a figment of his imagination.

Nan was still in bed when I got home from school the next day. She didn't seem any worse, but she didn't seem any better either – she was still awake, still doing the same rattly breathing. I was worried now. Nan was still saying she just needed 'rest' but it was so unlike Nan to take to her bed like this and she was getting older now . . . I really thought I ought to do something.

I didn't know if you could really get doctors to come out to houses or if that was just something they did in the olden days, but either way I figured the surgery would be shut by now. I knew if things were really bad I could just call an ambulance but that felt rather dramatic and I knew Nan would be furious about that kind of fuss. In the end, I settled for going to the pharmacy. I'd seen people talking to the ladies behind the counter a few times so I figured they knew their stuff. I slipped five pounds out of Granddad's wallet – I didn't want to confuse or worry him by asking him for it, and anyway, I figured that, morally speaking, this kind of stealing was pretty acceptable – and headed out the door.

I waited patiently in the queue in the pharmacy and when it was my turn I described Nan's symptoms to the lady in the white coat.

'How old is she? Your grandma?' she asked me.

'Nan,' I corrected her. I don't know why. It felt important at the time, that we get her name right. 'She's seventy . . . something.'

The woman nodded. 'And how long have her symptoms been going on for?'

'Not too long,' I said. 'A few days.'

'Well, flu can be quite dangerous to the elderly so really, you ought to get her to the doctor's.'

'Oh I don't think it's flu,' I said. 'Probably just a cold.'

Of course, I had no idea if it was flu or not. But I was afraid that if the pharmacist thought it was too serious she'd insist we got proper help and send me away empty-handed. And then I'd be right back where I started – no medicine and no chance of persuading Nan to see a doctor.

'Hmm, OK,' the woman said. I could tell she wasn't totally convinced. 'Well, I can give you this.' She handed me a small red box labelled 'Cold and Flu Relief'. 'But if she's no better by this time tomorrow, she should see a doctor.'

'OK.' I nodded. 'I'll tell her.'

At home, Nan barely resisted at all as I poured out the medicine. I'd been expecting an almighty fuss – complaints about me interfering, about how she was perfectly fine thank you very much. Again, I felt nervous at how out of character her behaviour was. I prayed that the medicine would work.

Luckily, it did. Or maybe it was just that Nan's own immune system kicked in and did the job. Either way, although Nan was still in bed when I left for school the next day, by the time I got home, she was up and about. She still looked tired and the bags under her eyes were bigger than ever, but she was dressed and that awful grey sheen had gone from her face.

Still, the whole episode had given me a fright. I realised that no matter what I said about Nan, without her, if it was just me and Granddad, I wasn't sure I'd be able to cope.

That's when I realised how much I needed Bert. Nan and Granddad weren't going to live forever and without them I had no one. No one except Bert. She was my refuge, my sanctuary. Without her, everything in my world was grey and cold and dark.

And so I decided: I had to get Bert back on side.

24

Unfortunately, getting Bert back on side was easier said than done.

The tricky thing was, I didn't want to come right out and apologise for storming off because, frankly, I didn't think it was *all* my fault – she'd been pretty out of order too, telling me off like that, and defending Pippa over me – but then I didn't want to start throwing blame around either because that could only lead to more awkwardness. What I really wanted was for things to go back to how they'd been before, just like that, and for the past few weeks to just be forgotten without the need for any kind of confrontation or heart-to-heart.

My strategy to bring this about was to be as friendly and cheerful as possible – I figured that really it'd been me who'd been a bit cool over the last few weeks, so it was up to me to warm up a bit if I wanted to fix things.

So, I did all the things I could think of to show I was back to normal – I greeted Bert with a big smile every time I saw her, I chatted away quickly, filling any silences that could be interpreted as awkward. My Biro blackbird had started to fade in the last few weeks as I'd only kept it up sporadically, so I made a point of colouring it in and then, in one history lesson, I took Bert's hand and reapplied hers as well. I even asked Bert about *An Outing to Oz* and how rehearsals were going, aiming to make it crystal clear that there were no hard feelings. But the problem was, I just wasn't sure any of it was working. Whatever I did, I still got the definite feeling that Bert was holding me at arm's length.

She often seemed distracted, like her mind was elsewhere. Sometimes when I tried to engage her in upbeat chatter – funny things I'd heard people say, new food I'd spotted in the canteen – she'd turn to me and say, 'Sorry, what was that?' and I'd have to repeat it all again, even then only getting a small smile in response. She seemed happy to let our conversations lapse into silences. She didn't seem to feel any particular urge to fill them.

I began to get despondent. During the weeks immediately after the casting, when I'd been deliberately a bit off with Bert, I'd felt confident that as soon as I decided to rekindle our friendship, Bert would be receptive. Grateful, even. I'd arrogantly thought that I'd had all the power. Now though, I started to doubt that that was true. I wasn't sure if Bert had actually been just as miffed as I was during our cold war, or if perhaps, by keeping up my moody act for so many days, I'd actually pushed her away for good. I was furious at myself. I felt sure I'd ruined things. There was no getting things back to how they'd been before, and it was all my own stupid fault.

But then, one lunchtime about a week into Operation Get Bert Back, I was waiting for her outside the canteen (we were at least still having lunch together – things hadn't got that bad yet) when I spotted her coming along the corridor, looking down at something in her hand. As she got close I noticed her brow was furrowed, her eyes anxious.

'Hey,' I said.

She didn't reply. She just thrust something into my hand. A piece of notepaper, folded in two. 'Look at this,' she said urgently. 'I just found it.'

I unfolded the paper. It was that squared kind you get given in maths to draw graphs and tables and things, obviously torn from a notepad. The message was written in the careful block capitals of someone trying to disguise their handwriting.

YOU NEED TO WATCH YOURSELF, POSH GIRL.

I looked up at Bert. 'What's this?'

She took the note back off me and looked down at it again. She rubbed the patch of forehead just above her nose. 'It was in my pencil case. I just found it now. What does it mean, "watch yourself"?'

'Like, be careful, I guess?'

Bert rolled her eyes. 'Yes, obviously be careful. But why? And more importantly, who's it from?'

She looked a bit of a sorry state, her face screwed up, all bewildered and anxious. She was pulling on a strand of her hair, twirling it around her finger.

I took the note off her and tore it into four pieces. I dropped it into the bin.

'Bert,' I said gently but firmly, 'this is a school. Not even a particularly nice school. This kind of crap is just what people do.'

Bert looked over to the bin where the fragments of the offending note were now sitting. She chewed on her lip.

'Thing is, Bert, if someone wanted to do anything to you – to rough you up, to teach you a lesson or whatever – they'd just do it. They wouldn't send you a letter to book an appointment.'

Bert looked at me, alarmed. 'Do you think that's what they're going to do? Rough me up?'

I sighed. 'No,' I said. 'That's exactly what they're *not* going to do.'

Bert pursed her lips. 'Really? But how can you be so sure?'

'I've been coming to school almost my whole life, Bert. I know how these things work. This'll be as bad as it gets. The type of people who leave notes . . . that's all they do. Leave notes. Draw graffiti on things. The type of people who want to punch you in the face . . . they just get on and do it.'

'Really?' I could see I was starting to get through to her. Her features began to relax. 'So what do you think I should do?'

'Do nothing,' I said, leading her to a table in the corner and sitting her next to me. 'If this kind of thing really bothers you, then just . . . keep your head down for a bit. Don't do anything that could wind any of the pathetic morons up.'

'Like what? What do I do that winds them up?'

'I don't know,' I said, looking in my bag for a Kit Kat. 'I don't know for sure. We'll just have to keep ourselves to ourselves, mind our own business. Soon someone else will be in the firing line instead.'

She nodded and swallowed. 'OK. Right. OK.'

'Let's get some lunch, shall we?' I said brightly, sensing it was time to move Bert onto a different subject. 'Curly chips today – your favourite!'

Bert managed a small smile and let me steer her to the queue. I could tell she wasn't going to forget the note that easily though. The worried expression stayed with her all through lunch and she was only ever half-listening to me. Then, as we were stacking our trays on the trolley, she said, 'It's just a horrible feeling, you know? That someone's got it in for me. I just feel a bit . . . shaken.'

'I know,' I soothed. 'I know. But, like I said, it'll be over soon. I won't let them get you!' I gave her a grin and squeezed her arm.

'Thanks, Birdy,' she said, giving me a tired smile. 'Do you want to come over later? I feel like a bit of company this evening . . .'

I smiled. 'Of course. We'll have a nice relaxing evening and tomorrow this will all seem like the silly, playground rubbish that it is.'

Later that evening, we sat squashed up together in the Egg. I was feeling full from an amazing Mexican dinner that Charlie had cooked us and very pleased to be back in the den again. I realised just how much I'd missed being there. Bert had been adamant that she didn't want to tell her parents about the note, not wanting to worry them when they'd been so pleased that school was working out for her, so we hadn't mentioned it since arriving at her house earlier that afternoon. Now we were alone again though, Bert seemed keen to analyse the whole episode again.

'I just can't work out *who*,' she said. 'I've been through the type of people who I think might go for this kind of thing. You know, those girls who you always think could be a little bit sly if the mood took them – Megan, Ella – but they're always relatively pleasant to me, I think. I just . . . I just thought I was, you know, not popular but definitely not *unpopular*. Is that terribly naive of me?'

I didn't think it was naive but I did wonder if it was just a bit egotistical. And possibly part of the problem. In fact, I'd had a thought brewing all afternoon – a theory that I wanted Bert to consider – and I decided that now was probably the time to share it.

'Maybe . . .' I began, 'maybe that's it. You are popular. Maybe a bit *too* popular . . . if you know what I mean.'

She looked at me. 'What? No, I don't know what you mean.'

I sighed. 'OK, so think of all those Valentine's cards you got for starters. You know how the boys like you – there's always been at least one or two circling you.'

Bert frowned. 'Well I didn't know who any of those cards were from . . . I expect they were probably those made-up ones from the school that you told me about.'

I shook my head. 'Unlikely,' I said. 'Very unlikely. But I don't think it really matters who they're from. The girls will have seen that you've got them and that will be enough. They'll be jealous. You're treading on their ground.'

I thought about Gary Chester catching me and Jac in the corridor and I wondered if he'd told anyone about Jac's card. I knew that just because Bert didn't know it was him who had sent it, other people might still know what he'd done, know that he was still after Bert.

Bert sighed. 'Maybe you're right, I don't know. I still wish I knew which one though – which girl I've offended. And which boy I'm meant to be staying away from. That would make everything a lot simpler.'

I decided not to name Jac himself here. Admittedly it would've been better if I could've advised her to stay away from him in particular as he was the obvious problem, but that would mean telling her about the Valentine's card. And then she'd want to know why I hadn't told her before if I knew who it was from and anyway, to be honest, I didn't want her to realise it was from him. She'd been quite taken with that card and I didn't want her to go up to Jac and say anything to him about it. That would only lead to all kinds of drama.

'It doesn't matter,' I said. 'It doesn't matter who it was. They're probably just letting off steam. They're just jealous and pissed off. Just forget it now. If they were going to do anything else about it, they'd come and tell you to your face. The best thing for you to do at this point is to steer clear of the lot of them. I know you're not doing anything on purpose but, just for now, try to avoid doing anything that could wind anyone up.'

Bert nodded sadly, then she leant back into me and I put my arm around her. We were quiet for a while.

Eventually she sighed. 'Thanks, Birdy,' she said. 'Thanks for coming over and . . . you know, helping me keep things in perspective and whatnot. It's funny really, even after all these months, I still feel like school, boys . . . everything is all such a mystery. I don't know if I'll ever make sense of it.'

25

After that, things with Bert seemed to get back on an even keel for a few weeks. It'd been similar after the locker graffiti incident really – it was like Bert was actually better after these little wobbles. It was a shock at first for her, to discover that not everyone around her was as lovely and honourable as she'd like, and that there were situations where she'd have to tread carefully, but once she'd accepted that, she bounced back to her old self, albeit with a bit more caution than before.

I suppose I might've been a bit insulted that she was only back to normal with me once a little fright had reminded her that she still didn't entirely fit in at school, but I decided not to dwell on that thought. I wasn't exactly in a position to start getting fussy about those kinds of details. And anyway, wasn't that what friends were for? Being there to support each other when other people had let them down?

As March crept on, the weather got warmer, little buds started to appear on trees and everything had a hopeful, new-beginnings feeling about it. Things were easier at home for a while. Granddad was always better when the days were longer and lighter. Sometimes he'd sit on his bench in the garden instead of staying holed up in the lounge all day. He'd still keep his blanket over his knees, but he'd lean back and look up, letting the sun fall on his face. He looked peaceful like that. He stopped seeming so agitated. He didn't call me Bridget or say anything else obviously muddled for over a week and that had a positive impact on Nan, too – she was less frantic, less snappy.

I tried to make myself relax and enjoy things, to tell myself that this was as good as it was likely to get in my life – Granddad calmer, Bert and I as tight as ever – but I had this nagging, foreboding feeling constantly in the back of my mind. I suppose I was just all too aware of how precarious everything was. Tomorrow, the clouds could gather and rain could come. Granddad could blurt out something random or call me Bridget and Nan would spin into a frenzy, cleaning, shouting, trying to control the little things to make up for the fact she couldn't control the big things. Bert could . . . I don't know. Bert could do anything. That was the thing with Bert – you never knew what was around the corner. I suppose it was what made her interesting, but it also made it very difficult for me to relax. And as things turned out, I was right to be worried.

One Friday afternoon, I suppose it must've been around mid-March, we were unpacking our books into our lockers and I asked Bert if she wanted to come up to the high street with me on the way home. It seemed a nice evening for a stroll and I thought we could even share a can of Coke in the park afterwards, maybe get a trashy magazine and have a laugh at some of those stories about people who accidentally marry their brothers or believe that their goldfish is a reincarnation of their grandmother or whatever.

But Bert shook her head. 'Sorry,' she said, flicking through a textbook like she was looking for something. 'Mum and Dad are getting the lounge decorated at the weekend so I've got to get home to help them shift the furniture about.'

'Oh,' I said. 'OK.'

I was disappointed, not so much because she'd declined my invitation, but because she hadn't even bothered to look at me when she'd done it.

There had been a time when if she'd had to let me down she would've looked truly pained, rubbed my upper arm and said, 'Sorry, Birdy. Next time, I promise. For absolute sure.' This time though, she hadn't really looked sorry at all.

'You ready?' I said, closing my locker and turning to head towards the door at the back of the science lab, the exit we always took before we cut across the field and made our way home together.

Bert hung back. 'Uh . . . I'm not walking today,' she said. 'Dad's picking me up on the way back from the paint shop. He wants us to get cracking straight away.'

'Oh, OK then.' I nodded and waited for Bert to offer me a lift – they'd be driving practically past the end of my road after all – but she just rummaged in her bag, and then headed off in the opposite direction, calling, 'See you later,' and giving me a distracted wave over her shoulder.

I just stood there in the middle of the corridor for a minute. The whole conversation had seemed odd and left me with an unsettled, uneasy feeling but I couldn't really put my finger on why. I tried to tell myself I was being silly – she was allowed to get a lift home for God's sake – but I still felt a bit flat. I suppose I'd expected that Bert would jump at my offer of a lazy afternoon strolling around town so I was disappointed to find myself on my own, at a loose end.

I toyed with the idea of going up to town anyway, but that seemed a bit pointless. It'd be no fun without Bert. Instead, I decided to stay behind at school and head to the library to make a start on some of the week's homework. I figured it made sense to get all my chores out of the way tonight when Bert was busy anyway, so I'd be free for any possible get-togethers over the weekend. I told myself I was being stupid to feel so put out by her rejection and tried not to think about it.

As it happened, I didn't hear from Bert at all that weekend and I didn't contact her. I assumed she was busy helping her parents and I didn't want to ask to see her again only for her to turn me down. I might have relented by the Sunday afternoon when I was really bored but I knew that she had an extra show rehearsal that evening so she was busy anyway.

In the end, I decided to go for one of my walks to get some fresh air and wait out the last of the weekend. I read my book in the park for a while but it started to get cold so I ambled over to Flo's Cafe for my usual mug of hot water to kill a bit more time before heading back for dinner. As I sat down at my usual table I noticed that there were two boys from my year in there – from the same crowd as Gary Chester and Matt Pereira and all those other popular types. One of them was a boy I'd known since St Paul's called Billy Carr. The other one I didn't know well, but I'd heard people calling him Hoover. I didn't know the reason for that for sure but he certainly seemed to be living up to his nickname now as he attacked a huge fry-up. I casually listened in to their conversation, just for something to do really. I worked out they were talking about some party that Jac Dubois had hosted on the Friday night, upstairs in his parents' bistro.

'Imagine that though, seriously,' Hoover was saying as he slurped up beans. 'Having, like, an actual bar of your own. Man, I'd be pissed twenty-four-seven. I'd have a party every day of the week. At least.'

Billy laughed. 'Totally, mate. Totally. I reckon old Jac will be in for a right earbashing from his old man when they find out though. Especially when they see what's happened to their fancy French brandy.'

'What, did it all go?' Hoover asked. 'Did we get through the whole lot?'

'Oh, mate, and that's not even the worst of it. When Jac started freaking out and throwing a hissy fit about it, Gary was all like, "Don't worry about it, mate, I'll take care of it. I'll replace it. I'll sort it right now." Ten minutes later he comes back and it's topped up and he just puts it back on the shelf, all like, you know, no dramas.' Billy laughed again, shaking his head.

'What?' Hoover asked. 'What was it, like some old cheap shit or whatever?'

'No, mate. Not quite. It was piss! The dirty bastard had pissed in it, then just slipped it back on the shelf, calm as you like.'

'Oh, man.' Hoover was laughing too now. 'That *is* dirty.'

Over in my corner I rolled my eyes and shuddered at the thought of the reaction of the customer who next ordered a French brandy at the bistro.

'Still,' Billy went on, 'well decent party, wasn't it? Not often we get a blowout like that.'

'Totally,' Hoover agreed. 'And do you know, everyone's saying he put the whole shindig on just to get that Alberta chick to come over to his?'

Billy frowned. 'That posh girl in 10KS?'

Suddenly I was all ears. I leant forward, anxious to make sure nothing was drowned out by the sound of clinking mugs and sizzling bacon.

Hoover nodded. 'Yeah. Been after her all year, he has. Think he set the whole thing up just to get her pissed.'

'And did it work?' Billy asked. 'I think I saw her . . . she did look quite wasted, actually.'

Hoover nodded and grinned. 'Absolutely, mate. She was smashed, I reckon. I heard her talking to Megan and Ella and all that, telling them about aborigine spiritual festivals or some shit.'

'So did Jac get a go on her then?' Billy asked.

I found myself pulling a face at the way they were talking about her – like she was a merry-go-round.

Hoover thought for a minute as he chewed on a sausage. 'Not sure, to be honest. I saw him having a good go, giving her all the lines and that, but she didn't seem to be having none of it, when I saw. Mind you though, they love all that fighting-them-off act don't they, women. Treat them mean, keep them keen and all that. And I didn't see her later on, so either she went home early or else . . .' He raised his eyebrows suggestively.

'Or else they were doing the business.' Billy grinned and

nodded. 'God, it's always the posh ones, innit. They're always properly filthy, those ones. Get *in*, Jac lad.'

They both laughed loudly and Flo had to ask them to keep it down.

I looked down into my hot water. I felt sick. Not only had Bert lied to me to get out of spending time with me but she'd gone to a party. A party I didn't even know anything about. And she'd got drunk and now Jac had ... who knows what Jac had done to her. I was angry of course and I felt stupid that I'd just accepted her lie, but I tried to bury that and focus on the constructive emotion here. I was worried. Bert's judgement wasn't great at the best of times. I dreaded to think what kind of trouble she might get into if she got drunk, especially with people like Jac Dubois hanging around. She was just so ... 'exuberant', as her mum would say. She just ran headlong into things and didn't think about them properly. And even if she'd gone into this with Jac with her eyes open that night, did she have any idea about what it was doing to her reputation? Reputation is everything at school. Bert wouldn't have learnt that yet. And I really didn't want Bert to have to find that out the hard way.

I sat for a moment, trying to think clearly, to work out what I could do, if anything. I badly wanted to go and find Bert and demand to know why she'd lied to me but I knew that would make me look bitter and petty and, anyway, that would be missing the point. I'd had enough of listening to Billy and Hoover's sniggering and I noticed my drink had a fly floating in it so I didn't want to finish it now anyway. I slipped out of my seat and headed home, still going over and over

169

the boys' conversation in my head. When I was nearly at my road, I stopped abruptly. I stood for a second, not moving, just squinting into the distance. In the end I told myself something I often try to remember when I'm feeling torn: there's no way to really know if you're making the right decision. You just have to go one way or the other and hope for the best.

I turned around and started walking quickly in the other direction. Doing something was better than nothing, I reasoned.

26

I stood on the doorstep, not moving for a moment. I suddenly felt a bit nervous. I'd been imagining the scene all the way here, rehearsing.

Charlie would open the door, I thought. Genevieve often didn't hear the knocker when she was in her studio. He'd look down at me, his ginger hair tousled as usual. He'd look surprised to see me, but still quite pleased.

'Frances!' he'd say with a smile. 'What a lovely surprise – long time, no see. Bert's not here, I'm afraid.'

'Actually, Charlie,' I'd say, in a low, clear voice. 'I'm not here to see Bert. I'm here to see you. You and Genevieve. May I come in?'

Charlie would look confused but he'd nod and show me in. We'd sit at the kitchen table, the three of us, Charlie's greeny-grey eyes fixed on me, Genevieve leaning forward, her hands clasped in front of her. I'd tell them everything. I mean, I'd make sure I phrased it all a bit more sensitively than Hoover had. No parents want to hear about some slimy teenager boy 'having a go' on their daughter. But they did need to know that it was like Richard all over again – the lying, the bad decisions.

Knowing Genevieve, she'd probably take my hand and get all emotional like she does and say, 'I'm so glad Bertie found a friend like you, Frances,' or something like that.

I rang the doorbell and waited. I could hear sounds on the other side of the door. Lots of sounds actually – thumps and scrapes and shouts of words I couldn't make out. But no one came so I rang again, holding the button down for a good few seconds. This time the door was flung open almost at once.

In front of me was a man I didn't recognise. He was youngish, I thought. Maybe twenty-something. He was unshaven and a bit on the fat side. He was wearing navy-blue overalls spattered with paint and he had a tool belt fastened around his bulging belly.

'All right?' he said, looking me up and down.

'Uh . . . hi,' I said. 'Are Charlie and Genevieve here?'

The man nodded once but didn't say anything. He let go of the door and it swung back, almost closing in my face.

'Charlie!' the man called, stomping back down the hall into the house. 'Some kid here for you.'

Charlie appeared a moment later. He too was wearing navy overalls, his cheeks were pink and there was sweat on his forehead.

He frowned. 'Oh, it's you, Frances,' he said. 'Is Bert OK?'

I was thrown by this question. How could he possibly already know that Bert was in trouble? Was it just some kind of parental sixth sense?

'She's at rehearsal tonight, isn't she?' he said. 'First run-through with the band or something, she said?'

'Oh, yes, I think so,' I said. I wanted to get these preliminaries out of the way so he'd get on with asking me in to talk properly.

'Yes, that's what I thought. Good. So . . .' he said, looking down at me, obviously waiting for me to announce the purpose of my visit. I decided to plough on with my script.

'Actually, Charlie,' I said, trying to make my voice sound serious but actually sounding a bit like I was trying to do a voice from a movie trailer. 'I'm here to see you. You and Genevieve. May I come in?'

Charlie hesitated for a moment. He rubbed the back of his head.

'Um . . . it's not a great time right now . . . we've got the decorators here and there's furniture and paint cans and God knows what else all over the house. Can you just give me whatever message it is now, and I'll make sure I let Gen know too?'

I blinked a couple of times. I hadn't imagined having this conversation on the doorstep. I thought about leaving it, telling Charlie I'd come back another time, but I realised there was a good chance he'd mention to Bert that I'd called round and then she'd want to know why. And that would mean my subtle, under-the-radar, word-in-your-ear approach would be all messed up.

'Uh . . . OK,' I said. 'Well, it is about Bert actually. I'm worried about her. About what she's been doing . . . and there's this boy. A bad influence, you know.'

Then I told him about what Billy and Hoover had said – about how Bert had gone to a secret party and how she'd been way too drunk and that Jac had been all over her.

Charlie scratched his stubble. He was frowning. 'Well, I knew she was a little worse for wear at the party, that's for sure.'

'You mean you knew she was there?' I was surprised. I'd assumed she'd snuck out, told them some lie about where she was going. I suppose I forgot that Charlie and Genevieve were nothing like Nan.

'Oh yes, we knew all right,' Charlie said. 'She was sick all over the back seat of my car. It'll take days to get the smell out. Still, she's been paying for it all weekend.'

'Oh, so you've already punished her?' I asked anxiously. I hoped I hadn't said anything that was going to get Bert told off any more than she already had been. I wasn't meaning to get Bert in trouble with her parents here; I just wanted to stop her getting into a situation with Jac. Apart from anything else, if Charlie started giving her a hard time about Jac, Bert would want to know how Charlie had found out about him and he'd be bound to tell her it was me who'd reported it.

'We didn't need to,' Charlie said, his eyebrows slightly raised. 'The hangover's been quite punishment enough.'

'Oh,' I said, feeling a bit silly. That's what he'd meant by 'paying for it'.

I hesitated for a moment. I wanted to ask Charlie what he was going to do about Jac. I guess I just wanted reassurance that someone else was going to look after things now, that I didn't have to worry. But I didn't want to keep going on about it. Charlie might think I was questioning his parenting skills or something. I decided not to labour the point. I'd said what I'd come to say.

'Right, anyway then, Frances. Thanks for letting us know your concerns. I'll talk to Bert when she gets in. Make sure everything's OK.'

'No,' I said quickly. 'No. You can't say anything to her. She's so terrified of worrying you. She doesn't want you to think that she's making a mess of things at school. She knows you think that she's silly sometimes, manages to get herself into trouble. You know, after what happened with . . .'

Charlie nodded. I didn't need to say Richard's name. We both knew what I meant.

'But it's not Bert's fault, really it isn't. She didn't bring it on herself. It's this boy – Jac – he's well known for it. He's got quite a reputation. And you know what Bert's like – so trusting, always wants to be nice to everyone – she . . . well, she sometimes gives the wrong impression.'

'Right,' he said, his brow so furrowed that his eyebrows almost met in the middle. 'I see.'

'It's him,' I said again. 'Jac. He's the one who needs the talking to.'

'Yes,' Charlie said, with another sigh. 'Quite.' He closed his eyes briefly and rubbed his face with his hand. Then he stood upright, his hand on the door, and said, 'Thank you, Frances,' in rather a brisk way.

Then he shut the door in my face.

27

The next day, when I met Bert on the corner to walk to school she looked tired and she greeted me without much enthusiasm.

'What's up?' I asked.

She sighed. 'Oh, just Dad being a pain this morning. Nagging me.'

'Oh, yeah? About what?' I asked breezily.

'Oh you know – making sure I'm focusing on school, doing my work, not getting distracted by . . . stuff.'

I didn't reply, but I was worried. I thought Charlie had understood when I said this was all Jac's fault. It was no good talking to Bert about it. I just had to hope that Charlie hadn't mentioned any specifics, and that he hadn't said anything about my visit. To be honest, I felt fairly confident that he hadn't brought me into it. Bert would've said something straight away if she'd known I'd been there.

I decided my best bet was just to move on and change the subject. 'So how was the party on Friday?' I said in the lightest voice I could muster. I didn't want to start going in heavy, asking her what she'd been playing at, but I did want her to know I'd caught her out on her lying. I didn't much like the idea of her treating me like an idiot.

Bert stopped dead. I turned to look at her.

'You *know*,' she groaned, closing her eyes for a second and breathing out. 'Oh God. I'm sorry, Birdy. I've always been such a terrible liar. I knew you didn't buy it when I said Dad was picking me up. It's just I knew you hadn't been invited and I didn't want you to feel bad. It wasn't that good anyway. I drank too much and got sick.'

I smiled and gave a small shrug. 'It's OK,' I said. 'Don't worry about it. But you don't need to keep stuff from me, you know.'

'It wasn't a total lie though,' she said as we began to walk again. 'We *are* doing the decorating at home.'

'I know,' I said without thinking, and then immediately cursed myself silently. I only knew they were doing the decorating because I'd been at her house the day before and had seen the overalls man myself. Luckily Bert didn't seem to notice though and the rest of the walk to school passed peacefully enough.

When I'd told Charlie about Jac, I'd sort of assumed that he'd warn him off her himself. Go round to his house or to his parents' bistro for 'a quiet word'. I mean, Charlie isn't exactly the scary type but he's tall enough and can be quite grumpy when it suits him. More to the point, he's a dad and everyone knows that boys are scared of girls' dads. I had a pretty good idea that Jac was exactly the type to run a mile from a girl if he encountered any kind of hassle, so I thought a little word from Charlie would have the whole business sorted. But what actually happened wasn't exactly what I'd imagined.

When we got in for morning registration that day, Mr Hurst was standing in the doorway and people were crowding around, trying to bundle in as usual.

'One line, please,' Mr Hurst called. 'Everyone in one line down the corridor.'

Bert and I were near the back so we couldn't quite see what was going on at the front, but pretty soon, indignant whispers were passed down to us: 'Seating plan? What the fuck – since when?'

Megan Brebner was in front of us in the line. 'What's this about, sir?' she shouted. 'Why we all got to sit in places now?'

'I want to restore some order to my classroom,' Mr Hurst called back. 'I've had enough of all this loafing around, eating packets of crisps and lounging on tables. This isn't a youth club. Or a zoo. From now on, you'll come in and sit down in your assigned seats and behave like civilised humans until I've finished the register. Over there, next to Neil please, Megan.'

'Oh, sir!' Megan whined. 'But Neil smells like piss!'

At this, Mr Hurst put his arm across the door, blocking Megan's path. 'You're not coming in at all if you say things like that.' Mr Hurst pointed to one of the wooden benches that lined the corridor. 'Sit down there please. I'll deal with you in a minute.' Megan slumped down on the seat, her arms folded across her chest.

I didn't think anything of it at first, didn't make the connection at all, but then, when everyone was in their places, I looked around and saw immediately what Mr Hurst had done. There was Jac, at the front of the classroom, on the desk by the bookshelf right in the corner. And then there was Bert, at the back of the classroom, next to the book trays. Almost as far away from Jac as it was possible to get. And now with Mr Hurst enacting his 'sit-down, shut-up' regime, I didn't think there'd be much chance for any early morning harassment before the register.

And there were further developments that morning.

After registration, Mr Hurst kept Jac behind. It was a fairly common occurrence really – Jac was always falling behind in one class or another, too busy playing the fool and chasing the girls to keep up properly. He'd never really been one of those kids clever enough to cruise by on minimum effort. I don't think he ever did anything bad enough to get any serious grief from teachers, but I gathered there were plenty of 'buck up your ideas, pull your socks up' type pep talks as he'd often boast about them to his mates afterwards.

A few minutes later, when Bert and I were at our lockers and I was trying to look cool and bored while Pippa was going over some Very Important Rehearsal Business with Bert, the classroom door was flung open and Jac stomped out.

'Wanker!' he said through gritted teeth, kicking the bottom of the lockers and making them rattle.

Pippa, Bert and I looked up. 'What?' Pippa asked.

'He's banned me, hasn't he? From Oz. Says my maths is too shite. Been messin' about too much, test results not good enough. All the usual bollocks. Why give it to me then, I said. Why let me do it in the first place? He reckons they were giving me a chance and I've "blown it". Tosser!' Jac shook his head and marched off down the corridor, his bag slung over his shoulder and his head down.

'Oh brilliant,' Pippa said, tutting and rolling her eyes. 'What are we supposed to do for a technician now?'

'An adequate replacement will be provided,' Mr Hurst called from the classroom. 'The show won't be compromised. No need to panic.'

Bert and Pippa launched into urgent talks about what this would mean for the production and who would be best to take over, but I wasn't listening. I was having a slow but wonderful realisation: it looked very much like my plan had worked. It hadn't all gone exactly as I'd thought but actually, if anything, this was better.

This is what I guessed had happened:

Charlie would've been angry, I suppose like any father would, at the thought of his little girl being molested by a creep with a dodgy haircut. But I realised my early assumption had been a bit silly – Charlie wasn't one of those Neanderthal types. A man like Charlie, with his gangly legs and rosy cheeks, wasn't going to storm over to Jac's place to start roughing him up and making threats. What I realised was far more likely, once I'd thought about it properly, was that Charlie would phone the school. He'd use the official channels. He'd be reasonable and pleasant, and ask for some discreet but firm action to be taken. He wouldn't shout for Jac's head on a spike – he wouldn't want him expelled and he wouldn't want his Bertie embarrassed by Jac finding out that the complaint had been made at all. Charlie would just ask for the situation to be quietly managed so that some distance was put between the two of them. Bert and Jac didn't share any lessons, but registration and rehearsals – the only real harassment opportunities – had been quietly shut

180

down. That was far more Charlie's style. Get our Bert out of harm's way but without making too much fuss.

I was relieved. The problem had been taken out of my hands. Good one, Charlie, I thought. Nicely done.

28

The end of March was warm and sunny. People even started to declare that it was 'boiling', the way they always do when the sun finally comes out after a long and damp winter. In fact, everyone was so relieved that dreary February was over that they got quite over-excited and started walking around the place in short sleeves, stripes of sun cream lining their noses.

Bert and I started sitting on the field at lunchtimes. She'd collect her mountain of junk food from the canteen and tip it into a polystyrene carton and we'd take it out there with us for a greasy picnic. From time to time, Pippa would sit with us too, which was incredibly annoying.

I was having a hard time working out exactly where Bert stood when it came to Pippa. On the one hand, I knew she'd been annoyed with her about the whole Meadowrise Care Home debacle – I could still picture her disappointed face as she told me about what had happened that day – but then I wasn't sure if their close collaboration on the show had worn Bert down. I wondered if Bert was starting to confuse familiarity with friendship. When Pippa came over to us, the two of them would start by discussing official Oz business, but it often seemed to lead on to other totally unnecessary chat.

Pippa would usually dominate things, talking about what she'd done, projects she was investigating, successes she'd had. Me, me, me, as always. Bert generally seemed to indulge her, nodding along and saying, 'Really? Gosh,' in all the right places. I'd originally assumed that this was just Bert's natural good manners in action but then, one lunchtime, Pippa had harped on for fifteen solid minutes about a letter she was writing to her MP on the importance of sustainable fishing practices in such a self-satisfied, puffed-up way that I'd had to fight to hold back an attack of the giggles. Honestly, the girl was like a comedy sketch – a parody of a self-important Girl Guide.

When she'd finally left, I'd laid back on the grass with my arms stretched out above my head and groaned. 'God!' I said. 'I thought that would never end!'

Bert didn't reply and so perhaps I should've left my comments there, but I really wanted to offload some observations. I think I just wanted someone to bitch with for once. The thing about Bert was that she always tried so hard to seem so constantly, relentlessly *nice*. And sometimes, just occasionally, I wished she'd let the act slip. I wished she would have a bit more . . . edge.

'Seriously though,' I said, propping myself up on my elbows, 'what really annoys me is the way she acts like she's such a saint. All that sighing and acting so obligated all the time, like she must tend to her parish. Pippa Brookman must save the world, because who else is going to do it?'

Bert just smiled in a faraway sort of way and lay down on the grass, closing her eyes. I felt a bit annoyed that she wasn't taking the bait, wasn't joining in.

'And you know what really gets me,' I ploughed on, 'is that she isn't even as angelic as she likes to make out.'

Bert batted a fly away from her face. 'Well, I know that Meadowrise thing wasn't exactly her finest hour, but I suppose she meant well . . . she just got carried away with the excitement of the occasion.'

'Well, yeah, but it's not just that. There are other things too,' I said and that's when I told Bert about what'd happened with Pippa and the chalks in the playground in that first year of school.

Bert opened her eyes and looked at me, a funny expression on her face. For a moment, I thought she was going to say something sympathetic and disapproving, but she didn't. She just shook her head and laughed, then closed her eyes again.

'Birdy, you're so peculiar,' she said. 'Still upset about something that happened when you were five years old. That's quite a grudge to hold!'

I didn't reply, I just lay back down on the grass and closed my eyes, sulking. It might've been a long time ago but I knew that people didn't change, not really.

29

Even the nice weather wasn't enough to help Granddad for long. His short run of lucidity spluttered to an end and his symptoms returned, more worrying than ever.

He started waking up at night, screaming and shouting out. The first time it'd happened I'd woken up with a jolt. At first, I'd thought it was someone outside, some drunk person staggering past my window, but when I realised it was coming from inside the house, I opened my bedroom door and peered out onto the landing. Nan was standing at the top of the stairs in her long blue nightdress, a steaming mug in her hand. My grandparents' bedroom door was open and I could hear the shouts coming from there. Mostly they didn't make any sense; they were just yelps really. The only words I could make out were 'No!' and 'Bridget!'

Nan's head jerked up when she heard me. 'What are you doing up?' she snapped. 'Get back to bed.'

'Granddad . . .' I said, looking towards their bedroom.

'Granddad's fine! Bed!'

I ducked back into my room and closed the door behind me.

A few days later, when I came down for breakfast, I turned around when I heard Granddad coming down the stairs only to see him wander into the kitchen wearing nothing but his underpants. I'd never even seen him without his shirt on before – in fact, it was an event if either he or Nan took their shoes off in the house – so I knew this was a bad, bad sign.

I didn't know where to look. In the end, I just got up and took my cereal to my bedroom without saying anything. I suppose Nan must've come down and sorted him out because by the time I left for school he was sitting in the lounge as normal, shirt, tie and shoes in place.

That day, I found myself bringing up Granddad's deteriorating mental state with Bert. I didn't normally let Bert know many of the details about what was going on at home. It was funny really, I was happy to soak up the sympathy when it came to talking about my dead alcoholic mum or my anonymous absent father – things that I actually couldn't care less about – but when it came to talking about Nan and Granddad and the increasing panic I felt about what was going to become of them both, I clammed up. I just didn't feel comfortable letting Bert in. I don't know why really. Maybe I was scared of admitting how sad and pathetic my tragic little life was. But actually, to Bert's credit, when I gave her a brief rundown of the things that had been happening over the last few days, she was really quite good about it.

'Oh goodness me,' she said, her face full of concern. 'How upsetting to see that happening to someone you love, their personality just . . . fading away like that.'

I nodded. 'Yeah,' I sighed. 'It's horrible really.'

'Of course,' she said, putting her arm around me. 'So horrible. You know you can always stay at mine. Anytime it gets too much.'

I smiled gratefully. 'Thanks,' I said. 'That's nice to know.'

But I knew I'd never be brave enough to ask if I could stay. I'd wait to be invited. Then Bert would get distracted, the invite would never come and I wouldn't want to mention my worries about Granddad again.

One lunchtime, when it was really a bit too cold to be sitting outside, we were lounging on the grass, lazily watching the Year Ten boys' football team, who were practising over at the far side of the field. One of the boys was Jac Dubois, darting about in his little shorts, dribbling the ball between orange cones, and at one point he saw us looking. He paused, his foot on the top of the ball. He winked and blew a kiss towards us.

I rolled my eyes and shook my head. 'Dickhead.'

I'd meant it to sound jokey. I'd meant to follow the comment with a little laugh and a gentle shake of the head. But it didn't really come out like that. In fact, it came out sounding quite bitter.

Bert sighed. 'For God's sake, Frances, give the boy a break, would you?'

I was shocked, both at Bert's tone and at the sound of my real name which I hadn't heard her use since the week she'd joined Whistle Down. And I was angry too. What *was* it about this boy? Could she seriously not see what he was like? He was a moron. He was so clearly only after one thing. Everything from the disgusting 'I'd give her one' sign he'd made with his finger the second he'd laid eyes on her, to his sly little plan to get her into bed. It was all horrible. Creepy. Why couldn't she see it? Was she really that clueless?

'You know what I think,' I said, looking at Bert through narrowed eyes. 'It was him who sent you that note. And the locker graffiti thing too, probably.'

I didn't know where the accusation had come from really. It was just a spur-of-the-moment thing, an eruption of irritation.

Bert frowned. 'What are you talking about?'

'I think it was him,' I said again, more firmly this time. 'It makes perfect sense. He's angry with you because you won't go out with him.'

Now I'd said the theory out loud, it seemed to be gaining momentum in my mind. It was entirely plausible really – I couldn't believe I hadn't thought of it before. We could forget that theory about it being some jealous girl. This was much better. It was the boy himself.

'That's so ridiculous,' Bert said. 'Jac thinks the notes are sick. He said he'd like to beat up whoever left them.'

This revelation took me totally by surprise. 'What?' I said. 'You mean, you told him about the notes?'

Bert shrugged. 'Yes, of course. In rehearsals once. He was there just after and . . . I was upset. He was rather sweet about it actually.'

'Ha!' I shouted before I could stop myself. 'I bet he was. I bet he was so *sweet*, I bet he was a real shoulder to cry on, wasn't he? I bet he offered you tissues, put his arm around you . . .'

I shook my head, astounded by her naivety. And then a new scenario began to form in my mind. This one was even more credible than the rejected lover version, I thought. She couldn't deny this one.

'It all makes perfect sense, doesn't it?' I laughed again, a hard laugh, my head thrown back. 'God, Bert, seriously, can't you see it? He left those notes to get to you, to . . . weaken you and get you to turn to him. He wanted to break you down so he could be there to pick up the pieces. Kind, *sweet* Jac.' I shook my head again. 'Utter, utter bastard. And you've played right into his hands by going running into his arms.'

Bert was staring at me. She wasn't frowning any more, she just looked bemused.

'Birdy,' she said quietly. 'Listen to yourself. A minute ago he was cross with me because I wouldn't be his girlfriend. Now it's all an elaborate psychological game designed to reel me in. You're not making any sense.'

I didn't reply. I just sat there, looking at the ground, breathing fast. I could see her point. I hadn't presented my hypotheses very clearly. I needed to rein myself in a bit, to calm down before I tried again.

'Is it . . . is it about your granddad?' she said. 'Is the stress getting to you?'

I looked up and made myself smile a weary smile. 'Yeah,' I said quietly. 'You're probably right. I'm just stressed.'

We were quiet again, the little storm seeming to have passed. We carried on looking over towards the football training. There was something almost hypnotic about watching them knock the ball between them, hearing the dull rhythmic thud as it bounced from one boot to another. I started to calm down. I'd been silly. Rash and impulsive. I'd try the whole thing again later. I'd make a more convincing case, one Bert would realise she couldn't deny.

'You know, you shouldn't worry,' Bert said after a while, her eyes still on the boys. 'Be . . . jealous, I mean. There'll be a boy for you soon, you know. When you're least expecting it.'

I couldn't even begin to think of a reply to this. I just turned away from her, staring out over the field, hot tears in my eyes.

30

The first few weeks in April were all about frantic preparations for the premiere of *An Outing to Oz*. The plan was that there'd be a performance to the school first, followed by a couple more shows just for parents and governors, and after that it would go on the tour and the kids of Whistle Down would educate the world in the proper treatment of the old and infirm.

The premiere performance was due to be held over fourth and fifth periods one Friday afternoon near the end of April. The fact the whole school had been excused from two full lessons was a good indication of how worked up everyone was about the whole thing. As you can imagine, Bert, Pippa and the rest of the cast were almost beside themselves with excitement by the time the Friday came around. That day, there were lots of toings and froings to the hall to check on things, lots of passing of notes and messages and a huge number of embarrassing high-fives and group hugs. It was all a bit irritating but I made myself smile encouragingly whenever Bert mentioned how nervous or excited she was and reminded myself that it was only a few weeks until the whole stupid operation was over.

I ate lunch on my own that day, Bert having to spend lunchtime backstage making last-minute adjustments to the set and costumes. After lunch, I joined the rest of the school as they filed into the hall, ready to watch the show. Outside, a quite spectacular April shower was in full flow, creating a ferocious background roar, and Mr Allenby was hovering by the window, looking out anxiously, no doubt hoping his expert 'musical coordination' would be able to compete with the sounds of nature. I took my seat and watched as the drops of water on the window snaked down from the top to the bottom.

Suddenly I realised there was some giggling going on at the back of the hall. I turned round and craned my neck to see what was happening. People were bent forward, leaning over something. Whatever it was seemed to be making its way along the row because the laughter was travelling with it. Everyone was looking over now, wondering what it was. I stayed in my seat and waited. I figured it would get to me eventually. It did.

It was an email. It'd been printed out. The paper was crinkled and the ink slightly smudged from where a hundred pairs of grubby hands had passed it around the school.

From: albertafitzroyblack@gmail.com
To: ross.allenby@whistledown.ac.uk

Dear Mr Allenby,
You won't be surprised to get this email because we both know there's been something between us for

weeks now. I just wanted to say I think your gorgeous and would you like to meet up outside of school and see wear things go?

I know you might be nervous about our relationship getting out but you don't have to worry. I've been with older men before including one who was married so you can trust me to be discrete.

Lots of love from
Alberta xxxxxx

I'd only just got the bottom when someone snatched it from me. It was Billy Carr, from the cafe.

'Told you, Hoov!' he yelled over the crowd to Hoover, waving the email above his head. 'The posh ones are absolute filth!'

Someone else took the email off him and it continued down the row, a Mexican wave of sniggering.

'You do realise Bert didn't write that,' I told the people around me.

'She did!' Gary Chester said. 'Had her name on it. Her email address.'

'No way,' I said. 'Didn't you see the spelling? Bert's not an idiot. Wrong type of "your". Wrong type of "wear". In fact, it wasn't even the right type of "discreet".'

Gary shrugged. 'Whatever. Guess her mind wasn't exactly on spelling when she wrote that.' He stuck his tongue out and waggled it around. It was gross.

Eventually Mr Jeffrey managed to wade through the crowds and confiscate the piece of paper. He read through it quickly, his face darkening. Then he folded it in two and tucked it inside his jacket.

He made his way to the front of the hall and called for quiet. For a minute I thought he was going to say something about the email, demand to know where it'd come from, but he didn't. He'd obviously decided we should go on with the afternoon as planned and he just gave a bit of a speech about the show, talking about how hard everyone had worked and how the production was going to really make a difference to the community and blah blah blah, and then it was time for curtain up.

The play opened with a scene where Dorothea's cantankerous, demanding grandparents and great aunt sit around whinging about how miserable they are and how they wish they were young again. The reference to the original *Wizard of Oz* was actually quite clever – Pippa played the fearful grandmother, complete with a lion-like mane of wild orange hair, who sits and worries about how she's too afraid to go out any more, what with all the feral youths running around the place, ready to push her over. The old aunt had a neat grey bob, spray-painted silver and shiny as tin. Her problem was with the fact that she couldn't find love, believing that if she was young and pretty again people would be more interested. The grandfather, with scarecrow hair and a ragged green jacket, was sick of his dodgy memory and just wanted to be as quick as he was when he was young. That part was a bit irritating actually – the forgetfulness was presented as a series of jokes involving things like pairs of glasses turning up in the fridge and misunderstandings when messages weren't passed on. If only these people knew what it was really like to live with someone who was losing their mind, I thought to myself. Wouldn't be laughing then, would they.

Bert did a good job of Dorothea, and it was nice to see her enjoying herself. All in all the show was fine really. Better than an afternoon of French and geography anyway.

When the cast had performed the final song and the curtain went down, there was a roar of applause and even a few whistles, but it wasn't long until people had moved on from the show and were talking about Bert and the email again.

'Did you see?' one girl behind me was saying. 'She kept looking over at Allenby the whole time. She's definitely into him.'

'Definitely,' her friend agreed. 'And I think he'd go for it, you know. After all, he did cast her as the lead. I think there's something dodgy going on there, for sure.'

Over at the front of the hall, I saw Mr Jeffrey go over to where Mr Allenby was sorting through his sheet music at the piano and bend down to whisper something in his ear. Mr Allenby's smug smile quickly faded and was replaced by a look of shock and then, right after that, fury.

The two of them left the hall together, Mr Allenby talking urgently in Mr Jeffrey's ear, like he was trying to convince him of something. Like he was trying to plead his case.

I slipped out of my chair and ducked backstage. I didn't really relish the thought of being in the midst of all the over-the-top actor camaraderie that I knew would be going on back there but I knew it wouldn't take long for the news of the email to filter back to Bert. I needed to get to her and reassure her that no one had taken it seriously.

As soon as I saw her, I realised she'd already heard. She was sitting in the corner on a sagging old armchair. She'd changed out of her costume but she was still wearing her Dorothea make-up. She looked a bit funny to be honest, her face all anxious and stressed under her bright pink cheeks and false eyelashes.

'Don't even give it a second thought,' Pippa was saying in her loud, honking voice. 'Don't let them get to you.'

'I just don't know why someone would do that . . .' Bert was saying in a small voice. 'And now everyone, *everyone*, is laughing and . . .'

I crouched down at Bert's feet and put my hand on her knee.

'Oh, Birdy,' she said. 'Did you see it? Is it really how they're saying? Do they think I propositioned Mr Allenby?'

I nodded slowly, a sympathetic smile on my face. ''Fraid so,' I said quietly.

She let out a long wail and covered her face with her hands.

'And you're sure you didn't send it yourself?' Pippa said. 'You know, as a joke or something?'

'Of course she didn't!' I snapped.

'All right,' Pippa huffed. 'I'm just trying to ascertain the facts.'

'Well thanks very much, Miss Marple, but we can do without your contribution.' I turned my attention back to Bert. 'Come on.' I gently pulled her hands away from her face. 'Let's get out of here. Let's go back to yours. It'll all be forgotten by tomorrow.'

I knew that was unlikely but I needed to say something. And I wanted to get her away from the sniggering and the whispering and away from bloody Pippa and her loud ascertaining.

Bert nodded and I helped her pack her bag and led her out of the backstage door, across the field and to the safety of her house.

'It's so weird, Birdy,' she said once we were safely in the den, a mug of tea resting in her lap. 'I just don't understand it.'

'There's no way you could've sent it when . . . when you were drunk or something?'

'Of course not!' She frowned, offended. 'I don't make a habit of getting drunk, you know. It was just at that one party I got carried away. And anyway, I *don't* like Mr Allenby so why would I say it, even if I was drunk?'

I didn't reply. I didn't have an answer.

'You saw the email,' she said. 'Was it even from my email address? Or was it a fake account?'

'It was from your account,' I said. 'Sorry.'

Bert narrowed her eyes and looked into the distance, thinking. 'So I've been hacked.'

'It looks like it . . .'

'Tell me again what it said,' she said, staring at me. 'Word for word.'

I recited the email again for what must've been the sixth time that afternoon and Bert winced.

'And why did they have to include that bit about the married man? It makes me look like such a . . . such a . . . harlot.'

'Yeah . . .' I said slowly. 'I was thinking about that. Did you, I mean, I'm not calling you a drunk or anything, but at Jac's party I know you were a bit . . . I mean, what I'm trying to say is, did you tell anyone about Richard?'

'No!' she said indignantly.

I was quiet for a moment. 'Are you sure? I mean, I know you'd . . . you'd had one or two too many, and I heard some boys saying . . . well, just saying you were a bit worse for wear.

Do you think there's any chance at all that something might have slipped out, anything at all, that could've given you away?'

'I don't think so . . .' Bert said, but she was chewing on her lip a bit. She looked pained now, rather than annoyed.

'But can you be totally certain?' I pushed gently.

Bert shook her head and looked down. 'No, I suppose I *can't* be one hundred per cent positively sure. I can be a bit of a . . . chatterbox, but I just . . .' She trailed off.

I sighed. Now we were getting somewhere. 'OK,' I said calmly. 'OK, so that means that anyone could've sent this really, couldn't they? I mean, there's not just the people at the party to think about. Any of them could have passed it on – I mean, you have to admit, it does sound like quite a good bit of gossip, doesn't it? Going out with a married man? It probably didn't take long to get round.'

I knew that Jac was still a perfectly plausible suspect – he'd been at the party after all and I didn't know what had happened that night – but I hadn't seen Bert with him since. If she hadn't given in to his pestering, there was still a good chance he was harbouring some kind of unrequited love thing – but I knew there was no need to mention him now, or to really talk about suspects at all. It didn't matter. The important thing wasn't giving Bert someone to blame. That wouldn't make her feel any better, not really. I just had to be there for her.

'Oh God!' Bert groaned, burying her head in her hands. 'I can never go back there, Birdy. My school career is over. I'm never leaving this room.'

I went over to her and put my arm around her shoulders. 'Come on,' I said, pulling her towards me. 'Come on. You're just going to have to wait this one out. It'll be old news in no time. We'll just have to battle through it. If I hear anyone saying anything I'll make sure I tell them what rubbish it all is. We'll shut the whole thing down together.'

Bert sighed. 'OK.' She looked up at me and gave me a weak smile. 'Thanks, Birdy. Thanks for believing me.'

'As if I wouldn't!' I said, smiling back.

Down in the hall as I got my things together, Bert was trying to persuade me to stay for dinner and I was just contemplating whether I could tell Nan I was still at school when Genevieve poked her head out of her studio.

'Actually, I think Frances should probably be getting home tonight,' she said.

I was a bit surprised but I just nodded and said, 'Yeah. I need to get back really.'

I was taken aback by Genevieve's comment. She seemed decidedly off, but I couldn't for the life of me think why. Looking back now I can't believe I didn't make the connection with the rather rude way Charlie shut the door in my face when I came to tell him about Bert and Jac. That was a bit off too. The signs were there, I suppose, that things weren't quite right, but I couldn't see them. Didn't want to see them. Instead, I figured it was just Genevieve's artistic temperament putting her in a bad mood. Maybe a customer hadn't liked their painting or something. But anyway, it actually felt like the right time to say my goodbyes. I felt like I'd had a successful few hours in the den. Bert seemed better. The worst of the crisis was over. My work was done, for now.

31

Back at school the following day, Bert was hauled into a meeting with Mr Hurst and Mr Jeffrey. She shot me a panicked look as she was led away and I must say I felt a bit worried too. What if they didn't believe Bert's story that her email had been hacked? Could you be expelled for sending that kind of message to a teacher?

But luckily when she came back she seemed relieved.

'It was OK,' she said. 'They weren't cross really. Well, Mr Allenby was a bit, because he was caught up in it all. And the embarrassing thing is, I still think a tiny part of him wonders if I did really send it. But Mr Jeffrey and Mr Hurst said it was obviously not my doing and that I should report anyone who teased me about it.'

Typical Allenby, I thought to myself, wanting to believe that someone really had a crush on him, that it wasn't all just some cruel prank.

'That's good,' I said. 'And see? It's blowing over already.' I gave her arm a reassuring squeeze and she smiled at me.

It wasn't all quite as plain sailing as that though, and over the next week or so, wherever we went, people would call things out or make childish comments. Mostly Bert dealt with it quite well I thought, usually by completely blanking whoever it was giving her a hard time. There were a few times when the teasing was a bit more persistent though and sometimes I had to step in and tell people to shut up. To be honest I knew it wouldn't really help that much, me wading in like that – in fact sometimes it just made it worse – but the important thing was that Bert knew she wasn't on her own. There's nothing worse than feeling alone when people are ganging up on you.

The good thing was the play was now in full swing as it embarked on its tour around the local area and that kept Bert busy. Talks of rehearsals and costumes were replaced with meetings about setting up venues and transport arrangements. Cast and crew usually had to leave last period a bit early to get to their performance location on time and the class would send them on their way with cheery waves and calls of 'break a leg'. These would usually be met with kind of grim smiles and serious nods from the actors, as if they were going off to fight for queen and country. Just a couple more weeks to get through, I told myself. Just a few more days. By mid-May, the play would be over and everyone's attention would turn to exams and then, more importantly, the summer holidays.

I usually dreaded the summer break – six weeks of nothingness stretching out before me, trapped in the house with Nan scrubbing and bleaching anything she could get her hands on and Granddad sitting in his chair, looking around the room in bewilderment, as if he was thinking, 'How did I end up here then?' This year though, I couldn't wait for the twenty-third of July to come around. Bert and I had big plans for the summer. Already we'd talked about hiring a rowing boat for the day and taking it down to the river for a picnic, barbecuing in her parents' garden, and there'd even been talk of a day trip down to Brighton. 'Let's do that in the summer!' had become our catchphrase and it felt to me as if the summer had taken on a kind of fairy-tale quality. It would be amazing. The weather would be perfect, Bert and I would see each other every day and school, Jac and Pippa and *An Outing to* bloody Oz would be long forgotten.

But then something happened. Something I honestly hadn't seen coming.

It was the day before the grand finale of the play. It was planned that there'd be a final big performance, back at school again, but this time attended by 'important members of the local community' including the mayor and people from a local TV station. Excitement was at fever pitch, not least because key members of the cast – including Pippa and Bert – were due to be giving televised interviews to some shiny-haired, blue-eyed woman from the BBC.

It was the start of second period – geography – and we were waiting for Mrs Hart to finish dealing with some boys who'd been caught fighting down the corridor. Bert and I were sitting at the front of the class and I was doing my best to look interested and supportive while Bert babbled on about whether she should look at the interviewer or straight down the camera and whether her hair looked best up or down. Suddenly Pippa came into the room and approached our desk looking preoccupied, maybe a bit anxious.

'Alberta,' she said. 'Have you got that list of answers we were jotting down, for the interview? I want to check I got everything.'

'Sure.' Bert nodded and heaved her bag onto the desk. She reached inside and pulled out her notebook, but as she did so a little wad of papers slipped out and scattered all over the floor. I looked down and straight away noticed that they were photos.

'Oops-a-daisy!' Pippa said, reaching down to start collecting them up, but as she turned one over she let out a little gasp.

A couple of other people looked down at the pile then too, and Matt Pereira laughed loudly.

'No way!' He reached down and picked one up. 'Nice tits, Alberta!'

Bert spun round and tried to snatch the photo from him but he held it above his head.

'Can I keep this?' He laughed and passed it behind him to Gary.

With that one roaming free around the classroom, we turned our attention to the rest of the pile. There were about four or five others, still scattered across the floor. I reached down and picked one up. The photo was of Bert. She'd obviously taken it herself in the mirror because you could see her holding her phone down near her hip. She was completely naked apart from a pair of little pink lacy pants and even they were almost see-through. I guessed that's what you'd call 'not leaving much to the imagination'. I stared at it for a moment then quickly placed it face down on the desk. I bent down to try to gather up the photos that were still on the floor but some of the boys had been quicker. There were now two or three pictures doing a tour of the classroom.

Bert just sat at her desk looking straight ahead. She didn't even try to grab the pictures back. She looked frozen. Then her face crumpled and she made a dash for the door.

I looked around at the classroom – Matt and Gary laughing loudly, Ella and Megan trying to hide their giggling behind their hands. For a moment I wondered if I should stay back to try to round up the loose photos but I didn't want Bert to think I'd just abandoned her when she was crying.

Pippa and I moved at the same time, both making towards the door to go after Bert. But I reached forward and pulled Pippa roughly back by the top of her arm. She turned and looked at me, surprised.

I glared at her. 'No,' I said in a voice that told her I wasn't going to be argued with. 'I'll go.'

I didn't hang around for a reply. I dashed out of the room, leaving Pippa and the others leaning out of the doorway, watching me go. As I jogged down the corridor, I heard Pippa bossily ordering everyone to hand back all the photos at once.

I eventually caught up with Bert in the toilets. She'd locked herself in a cubicle but I could hear her sobs.

'Bert,' I called gently, rattling the door. 'Come on, Bert, let me in.'

I heard the sound of the lock being opened and she stood in front of me, her eyes pink and her cheeks blotchy.

I pulled her into an awkward hug. She was too tall and I was too short for us to ever have a proper, fitting-together hug when we were standing up. I felt her tears soaking into my shoulder. She seemed to calm down a little and the wailing became hiccups and regular sniffs.

'Come on,' I said, leading her over to the sinks. I handed her a paper towel and she blew her nose loudly.

'Sorry,' she said in a small voice. 'It was just . . . such a shock.'

'What were you . . . I mean, why did you bring them to school, Bert? Those photos? Bit risky, don't you think?'

She spun round to face me. 'I didn't!' she said. 'Of course I didn't! Why would I?'

'I don't know,' I said, peering at her. 'I don't know, but then I guess . . . I'm not sure why you'd take them in the first place.'

Bert breathed out heavily. 'For Richard,' she said in a tiny voice. She leant against the sink, her head down. 'For him.' She was quiet for a moment then she looked up at me. 'He asked me to. Said he wanted something to keep with him because we couldn't be together as much as we'd like. I thought it was a good idea. I liked the idea of him thinking about me all the time . . . I thought it was . . . romantic, really. And then when he broke it off with me, I took more to send to him. Trying to win him back, I suppose . . .'

I frowned. 'Isn't that a bit . . .' I wasn't sure what word I was thinking of here. Slutty, maybe? Desperate? I decided the sentence was better left unfinished.

'I know,' Bert said quietly. 'I know. I don't know what I was thinking. And it's not as if it even worked. If anything it made everything worse. He threw them back in my face. Said he was insulted that I thought he was the kind of man who could be tempted into a relationship with a child by a few naughty pictures.'

Although, I thought to myself, he could hardly deny he was the type of man to be tempted into a relationship with a child at all and that was every bit as bad. I decided it probably wasn't the time to point this out.

We leant back on the sinks, our bums perched on the edge. Bert looked up at the ceiling and sighed.

'Someone put them in my bag, Birdy. Someone did this on purpose. Just like someone wrote that email on purpose. And printed it off on purpose. And passed it round the school on purpose. Do you think I should report it? I told them not to take it any further with the email because I didn't want any more fuss but now there's this too . . . Pippa's mum thinks I should tell someone. She said she'd do it herself in fact, if I wanted her to. She's on the PTA so they'd take her seriously.'

'Pippa's mum?' I asked, frowning. 'Vanessa? What's she got to do with it?'

I'd met Vanessa Brookman a few times. She was the adult version of her daughter – all busy-bodying and officious, always a key figure at any school fete, charity walk or sports match. It was no surprise that she'd offer to take charge in a situation like this, but I *was* surprised that she knew about it at all. When had Bert been talking to her? I raised this question now, taking care not to look as if I was getting distracted from the main issue here – the main issue being Bert's welfare.

'Oh, I've seen her quite a lot these past few months,' Bert said vaguely. 'You know, with the play and everything, I've had dinner at their place a few times. They're nice, the Brookmans. It turns out that our parents have a friend in common so they're talking about us all going to the Lake District in the summer . . .'

'Oh,' I said, frowning slightly. 'Right.'

We didn't say anything for a little while. The only sound was the dripping of a leaky tap and Bert's regular sniffing. I kept thinking about Bert and Pippa having dinner together, Bert chatting to Pippa's family around the dinner table. And that's when it came to me. It hit me like a slap but as soon as it had, everything was all so clear. The explanation for all this was obvious. So obvious, in fact, that I couldn't believe it'd only just come to me.

I'd been stupid, focusing all my attention on Jac. Silly, simple Jac. He wasn't a threat, not really. It was Pippa. Bossy, sneaky, *manipulative* Pippa. She'd stop at nothing to get what she wanted. She'd pride herself on it, in fact. It was classic keep-your-friends-close-but-your-enemies-closer stuff. All that sidling up to Bert, all that fawning and sucking up and dinners and holidays in the Lake District. That could all be written off. Bert would see that that didn't count for anything if, all along, all she'd been trying to do was get Bert out of the way – to break her emotionally, to humiliate her. It was all so obvious. It'd be hard for Bert to accept at first, but she'd have to. There was no way she could deny it.

I looked at her now as she wiped her nose with a paper towel, her cheeks damp and flushed.

I was going to have to break the news to her gently.

32

'What?' Bert said, looking at me. 'What are you thinking?'

I realised I hadn't said anything for a while – I'd been too busy thinking, the pieces slotting into place.

'Oh, nothing . . .' I said. 'It's nothing.'

I was deliberately making it sound like *not* nothing. I didn't want to go blurting out accusations, and for Bert to think I was going off on some deranged ramble. It hadn't been that long since I'd blamed Jac for all this, and you know what they say about crying wolf. I needed Bert to drag it out of me.

'Tell me,' she said. 'What is it?'

I sighed, and pushed myself off the sink. I paced over to the opposite wall of the toilets and leant back against it, my hands behind my back. 'OK,' I said with another sigh. 'But you're going to have to hear me out. Right to the end.'

Bert frowned. 'OK . . .'

'Think about Pippa,' I said.

'Pippa? What do you mean?'

'It makes sense. Think about it.'

Bert pulled a face. 'What, you think . . .? No. That's absurd.'

'It's not, Bert,' I said gently. 'Think about it. I mean, think about where all this started – with that graffiti on your locker. And when was that? A few days, maybe a week, after the whole Meadowrise thing. When you'd had the cheek to strop off in the middle of one of her big charity projects.'

'But that –' Bert began.

I cut her off. 'Just hear me out,' I said firmly.

She was quiet again.

'Then what happens next? You get that note. And again, look at the timing. Right after you got offered the part of Dorothea. The part *Pippa* wanted.'

Bert looked down. 'But I thought . . . I thought she took that rather well.'

'Yes, but you don't know what resentment was bubbling under the surface. That's the thing with people like Pippa, Bert. They don't explode. They don't wear their hearts on their sleeves. They brood. They play the long game.'

Bert's brow was furrowed but she didn't say anything.

I went on. 'So then everything goes quiet for a while – you and Pippa buddy up during rehearsals, she wins you over. But then, it's opening night. It's your big moment, time to go on stage after all your preparation, but just before you make your entrance, that email goes around and makes quite sure that everyone's more interested in your crush on Mr Allenby than your performance on stage.'

Bert sighed and closed her eyes for a moment. I could see she knew I was making sense. She had to admit it was a strong case.

'But then today . . . the photos . . . why?'

I thought for a moment. 'I don't know,' I admitted. 'I don't know for sure. But I think there's a good chance she's just trying to shake you up. Make sure you're a nervous wreck before tonight's performance, not to mention the TV interview. And remember, she was right there, wasn't she? It was her who appeared from nowhere and asked you for your notes, her who made you spill the whole pile of them right in front of everyone.'

Bert held a paper towel in her hand. She twisted it round and round, shredding it to pieces. 'Oh God,' she groaned, looking upwards. 'This is all my fault. I've been such an idiot.'

I went back over to Bert's side of the toilets. I put my arm around her and gave her a quick squeeze. 'Of course it's not your fault, silly. It's her. All her.'

Bert shook her head. 'No, I mean, I . . . I told her. About Richard.'

'Richard?' I said, turning to look Bert in the face. 'What did you tell her? And when?'

'Everything,' Bert wailed. 'I told her the whole lot. I can't remember when exactly, one evening at her house. After rehearsals.'

'So she knew before that email went round?'

Bert nodded forlornly.

I sighed. 'OK,' I said. 'OK. Well I guess you don't need me to tell you that you shouldn't have trusted her but at least . . . well at least one thing's clear. We've definitely got our culprit.'

'I knew it,' Bert said, shaking her head. 'I *knew* I hadn't been so drunk that I'd told people at the party. I would've remembered something like that.'

'Why didn't you tell me that you'd already told Pippa about Richard?' I asked. 'The day the email went round? It would've been obvious to me then that it was her. We could've ended this there and then.'

Bert just shrugged and stuck her chin out. 'Don't know,' she said sulkily. 'I just didn't ever think it would've been her. I thought she was . . . decent.' Bert looked away into the middle distance for a second but then she shook her head suddenly, like she was trying to snap herself out of her gloom. 'OK, so. Now what? We should speak to Mr Hurst about our concerns. Or Mr Jeffrey? I really don't want to get my parents involved though. They'd go mad if they knew I'd taken those photos. Do you think they'll keep it, you know, just between us?'

I shook my head. 'There's no point getting any of that lot involved. Teachers, I mean. Pippa's too . . . too clever. She knows how to play them. She'll wheedle her way out of it.'

'What, then?' Bert said, looking at me. 'What shall I do? Shall I confront her directly?'

'No,' I said firmly. 'You do nothing. Nothing at all. I want you to act like we don't know anything. Go back up there, act like you're feeling much better and ready to put the whole thing behind you. Be exactly the same with Pippa as before – be friendly as usual, make your normal plans. Leave her to me. I'll sort this out.'

I was rather impressed with myself at this point, how capable and in control I sounded. There was no way Bert could've known I had no idea what I was going to do, not really. I was sure I could work something out though.

Bert looked like she was going to argue or at least ask questions, but just then a couple of girls from our year came into the toilets. One of them had a packet of cigarettes and I

211

stared at them hoping they'd see they were interrupting and leave but they obviously weren't the type to be easily put off. One of them just gave me a little sneer and they headed into a cubicle together. I decided it was time to get going.

'Come on,' I said to Bert. 'Let's get back. When we get there, Mrs Hart and everyone else are going to want to know if you're OK, going to want to talk about it and all that, so just play it cool, OK? Shake them off. We need to do this my way.'

'Do what your way?' Bert said.

'You'll see,' I said confidently.

When we got back to geography, Pippa made a big show of giving the photos back to Bert.

'Here you go,' she said, looking at her earnestly. 'And don't worry, I got the lot.' She gave Bert a sympathetic smile as she handed them over.

Bert took them off her slightly hesitantly. I was worried she was going to crumble for a minute so I shot her a look that said, 'Be normal,' and she managed to break into a grateful smile and bury the naked pictures at the bottom of her bag.

Luckily, Mrs Hart is the impatient sort who doesn't have much time for children and their silly teenage dramas so was keen to press on with the lesson without further ado, which meant Bert's acting wasn't tested any more. I knew she wouldn't be able to keep up the normal act with Pippa for long though.

A plan was starting to form but I knew I needed to act quickly if it was going to work.

33

The operation began that evening. I insisted that we both went to Bert's house after school. That was important – I needed to make sure that her parents saw me arrive.

'What's going on?' she whined. 'Why do we need to be at my house? Why are you being so mysterious?'

I just shook my head. I didn't want Bert to get wind of anything and start flapping about and making a fuss, but I did need to make sure she understood her role.

'I need you to stay up here, in the den,' I told her. 'If your parents come up, say I'm in the loo or something. Whatever happens, today, later – I've been here the whole time, with you, OK? You'll know everything by the end of the day, I promise. You're just going to have to trust me for a bit.'

'Promise me you're not going to do anything that could get us into trouble.'

'Promise. I'm just going to talk to Pippa. That's all.' And I meant it.

'Then let me come. We'll have it out with her together.'

'No,' I said firmly. 'It'll work better if it's just me. She's too . . . rehearsed with you.'

With Bert in position and her role understood, the next phase of my plan was to make my way to the school hall without anyone seeing me. This wasn't exactly easy in full daylight, but it wasn't impossible either. I pulled my hood up to cover my face – that way even if anyone did notice a figure creeping around the back of the hall and in the stage door no one would be able to say with any certainty it was me. As it happened though, there wasn't anyone around as I got nearer school. As Bert had told me earlier, everyone involved in the play was having a 'well-deserved down day' ahead of the grand finale tomorrow.

I was a bit nervous as I pushed the stage door open. I'd carefully tracked conversations all morning and drilled Bert for all the details of people's movements and as far as I could tell, if everyone stuck to their plans, Pippa should be up there, backstage on her own, clearing a space and setting up chairs ready for the big TV interview. I just hoped that nothing had changed, that Pippa hadn't roped someone into helping her.

Pippa spun round when she heard the door open. I stepped onto the stage, taking a moment to check out my surroundings. Yes. Everything was as I'd hoped. We were alone.

'Oh, it's you,' Pippa said coolly, throwing me only a quick glance before she stood back and surveyed the furniture arrangement in front of her. 'What do you want?' Pippa might have turned on the charm for Bert but she was still as frosty as ever when we were on our own.

I didn't reply straight away. I just watched Pippa as she busied about, tidying costumes and props out of the way. I didn't have a script prepared. I was just going to have to play it by ear from here.

She picked up Bert's Dorothea costume from the floor and hung it on a hanger on the costume rail.

'It was a shame, wasn't it,' I said, perching on the arm of one of the lumpy old armchairs the old people sit on at the beginning of the play. 'About that email coming out. You know, just before the show and everything. Distracted people a bit, didn't it.'

Pippa hung her own costume on the rail – a long dress with daisies all over it, her orange wig hanging over one shoulder.

'Yes,' she said, her face grim. '*Such* a shame.'

'And the photos too,' I went on. 'Shame about that too. No one wants the whole class to see them naked.'

Pippa turned around and to look at me. 'No,' she said slowly. 'No they don't.'

She was staring at me now. I stared back. This was already a battle.

I flopped down in the chair, my legs dangling over the arm. The seat was lower than I'd thought it would be and I felt silly – like a rag doll, all folded in on itself. I didn't want to scramble back out though, and admit my mistake. That would look even sillier. I just had to style it out. I put my hands behind my head and leant back. That was better. The casual pose suited the conversation. Made me seem relaxed. In control.

'Bert's not like us, you know,' I said after a while.

'No. She's not.'

'She's . . . naive sometimes. Too trusting, don't you think?' I jerked my head upright so I was looking directly at Pippa, one eyebrow slightly raised.

Pippa stayed glued to the spot, watching me warily. I could tell she was trying to work out where this was going.

215

'What do you want?' she said eventually. Then she laughed suddenly. 'Seriously, Frances, you're such a *strange* little person. Always creeping around, trailing behind Bert. What do you *want*?'

She laughed again, her little stubby teeth and acres of gum all showing. I hated her so much at that moment. It was all I could do to stop myself rushing over there and punching her in her stupid face. I'd had enough of the mind games, the trying to psyche each other out. It was time to get to the point.

'Bert knows, Pippa. We know everything. We worked it out.' It was my turn to laugh now. 'You weren't exactly subtle. Never consider life as a career criminal.'

Pippa stared at me, her face blank. 'I don't know what you're talking about.'

'Oh for God's sake,' I said impatiently. I pushed myself out of my chair and stood up, facing her. 'You do realise that that's the exact line that every guilty person in history has come out with when they've been confronted? Couldn't you think of something a bit more original?'

Pippa just frowned. She wasn't really putting up a convincing defence so far. 'What?'

I sighed. 'Look, Pippa. We both know the truth now. There's no one else here. Just us. So can we skip all the boring denial stuff and get to the bit where we strike a bargain? Then we can both get out of here and get on with our day.'

'I honestly have no idea what you're talking about.'

I went around the back of the chairs where Pippa had left her bag – a light grey shoulder bag decorated with badges bearing various charitable slogans: 'Save the rainforest', 'Make cakes not war'. I held the bag up.

'That's mine,' Pippa said. 'Leave it.'

I ignored her. Instead, I unzipped the top.

'I said get off!' she said, making a lunge for it.

But I was too fast for her. I whipped the bag away from her and stood up on the arm of the chair, the bag high above my head. 'Oh I *bet* you don't want me to look. But why? That's the question. What have you got to hide?'

34

I didn't wait for her to reply. I opened the bag, turned it upside down and let the contents tumble to the floor. Then I jumped down from the chair and we both stared at the pile of books, scraps of paper, lip gloss and other debris that had fallen out. Pippa's face was pink, her eyes shining and her teeth gritted. I was careful to keep my expression cool. It wouldn't do to look too ferocious, too wild.

'Well, then,' I said, crouching down. 'What've we got here?'

I reached forward and picked up a little wodge of photos. There were about ten or twelve there I guessed, all bundled together with an elastic band.

'Photos, I see,' I said, holding them up. 'Holiday snaps, is it?' I flicked through. Exactly as I knew they would be, they were all of Bert. Bert in various states of undress. 'Oh!' I said, in mock surprise. 'Blimey. *Not* holiday snaps. Why have you got these in your bag, Pippa?'

'What?' she said. 'Give them here.'

I ignored her, still flicking through. There were a few of Bert with Richard there too, their faces pushed close together as they held the camera out in front of them.

'Oh, you found some of the man himself this time, did you?' I said. 'Well done. That'll help prove your point, won't it? People will *have* to believe her disgusting married-man affair once they see these.'

I tossed them down onto the pile and surveyed the scene again.

'What else have we got?' My eyes fell on an envelope. It wasn't hard to miss – it was bright pink and decorated with little hearts, drawn on in Biro. 'Mr Allenby', it said on the front. I picked it up. It was soft, stuffed full with something. I lifted the flap and pulled out a pair of lacy knickers. Quite possibly the same pink ones that Bert had on in the photos. As I tugged at them a little note fell out with them. I recognised the paper at once – it was the same graph paper that Bert's threatening note had been written on. And when I unfolded it, the little blocky handwriting was the same too. I read it out.

MR ALLENBY
KEEP THESE UNDER YOUR PILLOW,
LOVE ALBERTA

'What's this then, Pippa?' I asked lightly. 'Bert ask you to pass these on did she? Or was this the next step in your little plan? Your little scheme to ruin Bert's life? What were you going to do with them? Leave them on Allenby's desk?'

Pippa glared at me. 'You put that there,' she said, her teeth still bared like a little terrier ready for a fight. 'All of it.'

I'd expected this line of defence. Pippa was too, too predictable.

'OK,' I said in a sing-song voice. 'Let's go with that line of reasoning for a minute shall we? Let's say this is all just an elaborate set-up and you're completely innocent. Let's call Mr Jeffrey down here now. And Bert, let's get her in too. That's a good idea, because at the moment, she *sort of* thinks it was you, but she's not convinced. She doesn't *want* to believe that her dear friend Pippa has been going behind her back all this time. But if I bring her here, show her this, she won't have any choice.'

Pippa didn't say anything. I was still holding the knickers up but I felt silly waving them around like that so I tossed them back down on the pile. Pippa followed them with her eyes.

'*Or*, we can make a bargain,' I went on. 'That's why I came here, remember? To find you. To make a deal.'

'What deal?'

I went over to the corner of the stage and collected a metal wastepaper bin. Then I gathered up the photos, the knickers, the bright pink envelope, the whole lot of it, and I dropped it all into the bin, pushing it down nice and tight.

'In this bin is all the evidence of what you've been up to. I know what you've done and you know what you've done, but this is all the concrete proof. Sure, we can go through the long-winded process of calling Mr Jeffrey in here, getting Bert in, you denying it all, the formal investigation . . . blah blah blah. But how long will that take? Do you think they're going to let you go ahead with your big TV debut with this hanging over you? Do you really think Bert's going to cosy up to you now, when she knows what you've done?' I laughed suddenly. 'In fact, it'd be just like Bert to blurt the whole thing out on live TV.'

Pippa just looked at me. 'Sorry, so what's your point? I'm not really keeping up with this little charade. What exactly do you want, Frances?'

'I want you out of the way. Off the scene. Out of the picture.'

Pippa frowned, then looked down, into the bucket filled with photos. 'You want what?'

'I want you to leave Bert alone. I want you to stop hassling her, stop spending time with her at all. You're evil, Brookman. People like Bert are too good for people like you.'

Pippa rolled her eyes and sighed. 'God, Frances, you're so weird.'

I ignored her and neither of us spoke for a moment or two.

'For God's sake!' Pippa said, suddenly throwing her hands up. 'What will it take to make you – and all this,' she waved her hands towards the bin, 'just go away? To disappear and let me get on with things here?'

'Oh,' I said, 'that's easy. All I want is your word.'

'My word?' she repeated, one eyebrow raised. 'What word is that exactly?'

'I just want your word that you'll back off. You'll finish your little show tomorrow, and then you'll leave Bert alone. No more hanging around her, no more hassle.'

Of course, the idea that Pippa's word would ever mean anything to me – that I'd ever trust her to do what she'd said she would – was ridiculous, but that wasn't the point. I didn't care whether she promised to stay away from Bert or not. The important bit was the next bit. The bit where I took control.

'If you give me your word, I'll give you this,' I said, holding the bin up. 'And you can burn it. Burn it all. All the evidence – gone.'

I nodded towards a box of safety matches, sitting on top of the piano.

Pippa snorted. 'I'm not going to burn it!'

Of course I hadn't had long to put the plan together but as I'd been working through it, I'd assumed that Pippa would jump at the chance to destroy the evidence. It was all quite damning after all. My whole scheme rested on her taking me up on the offer and on her being caught in the act. I honestly hadn't anticipated her arguing at this point. I had to think on my feet.

'No?' I said, lightly. 'Well, well, well. What kind of friend does that make you? Here you are, with a whole pile of stuff that Bert would be horrified to know you have, and I'm offering you the chance to get rid of it, but you don't want to. You want to hold onto it. I've got to wonder why, Pippa. Either you want to use it for your evil campaign of terror or otherwise . . . otherwise you just want it for yourself.' I pulled my face into a disgusted grimace. 'I don't know which is worse.'

I reached over and took the matches from the piano. I held them out to her. 'Here,' I said. 'Do the right thing, Pippa. For once.'

'No!' she said, shaking her head. 'I'm not going to set fire to anything, you lunatic! Get Bert down here if you want. This stuff isn't proof of anything. There's nothing to prove I took those photos from Bert, nothing to prove I wrote that note. You've got nothing, Frances. Frances *Frankenstein*.'

I'd had enough of her by this point. I lost my cool. 'For God's sake!' I shouted. Then I roughly pulled the box of matches open and took one out. I struck it and it fizzed into life. I dropped it into the bin. It went out immediately.

Pippa laughed. 'So much for your towering inferno.'

I glared at her, then I took a couple of sheets of newspaper that were lying on the floor, screwed them into a ball and tossed them into the bin too.

'Hey!' Pippa said. 'That's a prop!'

'So buy another newspaper!' I yelled. I didn't care if I looked wild now. I felt wild.

I struck another match and dropped that one in. The newspaper caught straight away, and soon the photos were alight too, their edges curling, images of Bert and Richard warping into something quite hideous before our eyes.

'Happy now?' Pippa asked, one hand on her hip, the fire crackling next to us.

The fire seemed to catch whatever was in the bin and was burning away quite nicely. But it was then that I noticed Pippa's costume. The fabric belt of her daisy dress was dangling in the bin and the flames had started to crawl up it, towards her dress, towards her wig. Towards the whole costume rail.

'Oh yes,' I laughed, nodding towards the burning dress. 'Very happy.'

Pippa sprang into action. 'Shit!' she said, darting over to the other side of the stage and grabbing a blanket from a table. 'The costumes! Quick, help me put it out! The whole lot's going to go up!' She tossed the blanket onto the fire, I suppose in an effort to smother the flames, but the blanket just ended up catching fire too.

At this point the gathering smoke must've reached the hall's fire alarm because a piercingly shrill ringing noise surrounded us.

I laughed. 'How's that for a towering inferno?' I shouted over the noise.

I turned and headed for the stage door. It was time to make my exit. I slipped outside assuming that Pippa wouldn't be far behind – surely even saving the costumes for the stupid play wasn't worth hanging around in a flame-filled room, even Pippa would see that.

It was just as I was closing the door behind me that I heard the noise. It wasn't really a bang, more of a crack. Like a firework going off. I jumped.

And then I ran.

I didn't know she was going to end up dead. That wasn't part of the plan.

I'd planned to search Pippa's bag for the photos, the knickers, the note, all of it, then get her to try to torch the lot. The idea was that the smoke alarm would alert people to her little bonfire and when they came running, there she'd be, caught red-handed with a bucket of smouldering evidence. I knew just being caught with it wasn't enough. I wanted her to be caught *getting rid* of it. The unquestionable sign of guilt. Bert and I would report our suspicions about the identity of Bert's tormentor long before the rumours were out about what Pippa had been trying to burn, so when they sifted through the debris and found the traces of the photos, the charred knickers, all the rest, it'd fit together perfectly.

Pippa would probably be expelled, I thought. Both for the bullying and for starting a fire on school property. She'd protest her innocence but her explanation would sound half-baked. I have to admit, I have had doubts about the plan since that day but I hadn't had long to put things into action. It was the best I could come up with at short notice. I mean, it wasn't ideal that I ended up lighting the fire myself, for example. That wasn't the

35

I didn't know she was going to end up dead. That wasn't part of the plan.

I'd planned to search Pippa's bag for the photos, the knickers, the note, all of it, then get her to try to torch the lot. The idea was that the smoke alarm would alert people to her little bonfire and when they came running, there she'd be, caught red-handed with a bucket of smouldering evidence. I knew just being caught with it wasn't enough. I wanted her to be caught *getting rid* of it. The unquestionable sign of guilt. Bert and I would report our suspicions about the identity of Bert's tormentor long before the rumours were out about what Pippa had been trying to burn, so when they sifted through the debris and found the traces of the photos, the charred knickers, all the rest, it'd fit together perfectly.

Pippa would probably be expelled, I thought. Both for the bullying and for starting a fire on school property. She'd protest her innocence but her explanation would sound half-baked. I have to admit, I have had doubts about the plan since that day but I hadn't had long to put things into action. It was the best I could come up with at short notice. I mean, it wasn't ideal that I ended up lighting the fire myself, for example. That wasn't the plan. And I don't know for sure what she would've said about the whole episode or how convincing she would've been. I'd only just convinced Bert of her guilt. It wouldn't have taken much, I don't think, for her to be persuaded back to the other side. It was all a bit risky, I admit. But what choice did I have? This was Bert we were talking about. I had to do *something*.

Anyway, none of it mattered in the end. We never had to find out how good a plan it was because Pippa was dead. Obviously I never set out to kill her. Things weren't meant to get out of hand like that. I didn't know there was a half-empty spray-paint can in the bin. I didn't know that it was going to explode just as Pippa was leaning over the fire. I didn't know that Pippa's greasy hair was so full of hairspray and other gunk that she'd go up like a human candle. She died later that night. In a way I suppose it was for the best. She would've been horribly disfigured if she'd survived.

As I made my way back to Bert's I kept going over and over that time in the playground at St Paul's. All I'd wanted was one stupid chalk to play with. Was that too much to ask?

I was back at Bert's within ten minutes. I crept in the back door and up to the den. Bert was on her feet at once and peppering me with questions.

'What happened? What did Pippa say? Did she admit anything?'

I flopped down into the Egg. On the walk over I'd decided how much Bert needed to know. At this point, I hadn't realised the extent of Pippa's injuries so I decided I'd keep my version of events to what I'd planned to happen. I didn't want Bert to get in a panic.

I explained about the photos, the knickers – all the undeniable proof.

'My *knickers*,' Bert said, shaking her head in disbelief. 'When did she even get hold of them? God, when I think of all those times I let her in my bedroom . . . It must've been easy for her to root around, I suppose. To have a good rummage through my things . . .'

Bert did a little shudder and I felt myself do the same. It was the thought of Pippa hanging around Bert's house like that. In her bedroom. In the Egg too, I imagined. When had 'all those times' been exactly? No one had ever mentioned them to me.

I just shrugged. 'Didn't ask.'

Bert stared out into the middle of the den. 'God. So . . . she admitted everything . . . ?'

I nodded and sat down beside her. 'Yep.' I rubbed my face with my hand. I could smell the smoke. 'Pretty much.'

I gave Bert a minute to take this news in. I knew she hadn't fully accepted things, not until that point. I guess it was a hard thing to come to terms with, realising that even now she was still such an iffy judge of character. I knew it wasn't a time to be saying 'I told you so,' but I guess she was thinking it. I'd been right about Pippa all along.

Then I told Bert what had happened next, how Pippa had panicked and tried to persuade me to keep it all to myself.

'It was so desperate,' I said, laughing. 'The tactics she was trying – she was even offering to get me in on the TV interview. Said I could take your place, if I promised not to mention anything about what I'd found. Mental.' I laughed again and shook my head.

227

Then I told Bert how, in a last desperate attempt to cover up what she'd done, Pippa had frantically piled all the evidence into the bin and set fire to it. I explained that I'd made my exit at this point, that I hadn't wanted to be caught hanging about when the teachers came sniffing around to see what was burning.

'Yes,' Bert said seriously. 'Very sensible.' She leant forward and rested her chin on her palm. 'God,' she said again. 'I wonder what'll happen to her.'

We had a lovely dinner that evening – another takeaway. Charlie and Gen were busy so we were allowed to eat on our own, up in the den. Bert was a bit quiet. I figured she was worn out from the drama of the last few days. But I imagined she was relieved as well. It was all over at last. I was pretty pleased too. I'd done well, I thought. It hadn't gone exactly as I'd planned, but Pippa had been taught a lesson. Whatever happened to her now, whatever trouble she got in, Bert wouldn't go near her again.

The next morning, a text from Bert woke me up.

School's closed! Final show is cancelled! Come over.

I was slightly surprised – it seemed like a bit of an overreaction really, closing school and cancelling the final performance just because a few of the costumes had been singed – couldn't they just get hold of a few replacements? I was also dreading what Bert was going to be like – whining and wailing about missing out on her big TV moment. Still, I only had to get through today, I thought. After that we could say goodbye to the stupid show forever.

I didn't bother telling Nan about school being closed. No need to lumber myself with a bunch of questions about where I was going and what I was doing. I just put on my school uniform as normal and left the house, ditching my school jumper in favour of my blue Christmas one on the way to Bert's.

Bert opened the door. Her parents seemed to be sleeping late so we didn't have to deal with them, which I was glad about.

'Have you heard?' she said straight away.

I stepped past her into the hall. 'What do you mean? Only what you told me. School's closed.'

'There's been a *death*,' Bert said in a low, dramatic voice.

'What?'

But Bert just shook her head. 'Not here,' she whispered, looking up the stairs towards her parents' bedroom.

Once we were in the den, Bert dragged her laptop over.

'Look,' she said, perching it on her lap. 'I heard it on the radio first, but then I looked it up here. It's on the school website.'

I peered over her shoulder.

Urgent announcement:
School closed today (Thursday 16th May)
Due to a death on-site, Whistle Down Academy will be closed all day today. Further details to follow.
Check here for updates.

'See! A death!' Bert cried. 'Is it Pippa, do you think? I texted her, but got no reply. I was thinking, you don't think she'd do anything stupid, do you? Because she realised she'd been

229

caught . . .' She picked up her phone and tipped the screen to face her, but I snatched it away.

'Bert!' I said, trying to keep my voice down but not really succeeding. 'What are you doing texting her? After everything she's done?'

'I know, I know,' Bert said, reaching out to take her phone back. 'I just wanted to check she was alive! Do you think I should just ring her house?'

I sighed and sat down next to Bert. 'Of course she's alive,' I said. 'Pippa Brookman's hardly the type to top herself. It'll just be some alcoholic tramp who's crawled in to get warm and then choked on his own sick or something. At worst, it'll be some builder, doing work up high and falling. That kind of thing is always happening.'

'Really?' Bert said, looking down at her phone again. 'Do you think so?'

'Yeah,' I said. 'For sure. So let's . . . let's just enjoy a free day off!'

Then I remembered: I needed to be sensitive here. 'Oh, but your show!' I said, pulling my face into an expression of concern. 'The last performance cancelled. And your TV interview too. You must be so disappointed.'

Bert just shrugged and looked down. 'It's OK. It doesn't seem important now.'

We went out for the morning, killed a few hours down by the river, skimming stones and making daisy chains and doing other wholesome activities. I was having a hard time keeping Bert buoyed up; she kept mooning about, drifting off into her own thoughts. She must've checked her phone

230

at least twenty-five times. Then suddenly it started to ring. I jumped, and tried to get a look at the screen. I really thought it would be Pippa, phoning Bert to grovel, to persuade Bert to take her back.

'Oh, hi, Mum,' Bert said.

I breathed a sigh of relief.

'Just by the river. Yes. OK, but why? What's happened? OK. Yes. OK. Bye.'

Bert ended the call and looked up at me. 'That was Mum. She says I've got to come home. Something's happened. I don't know what.'

Charlie and Genevieve were sitting at the kitchen table with the laptop in front of them. As soon as we went in, Genevieve came over to us.

She put an arm around each of us. 'Come and sit down, girls.'

We let ourselves be led to the table and sat down side by side. Genevieve and Charlie sat opposite.

'I'm afraid there's been some bad news, from your school,' Genevieve said gently.

Neither of us said anything. We just kept looking at her.

'It's Pippa, darling.' Genevieve reached forward and held her daughter's hand. 'There's been an accident. She's . . . passed away.'

36

Blimey, I thought. Dead. Pippa's actually dead. I hadn't seen that coming. I mean I'd wished it often enough, but now . . . I wasn't sure what I felt.

I saw Bert swallow hard. 'Is it definitely . . . her? And she's definitely, definitely . . .'

She didn't finish the question but Charlie nodded. 'I'm afraid so, sweetheart.'

Genevieve spun the laptop round to face us. On the screen was the same page we'd looked at that morning, on the Whistle Down website.

Philippa Jane Brookman,
12th July 1998 – 15th May 2013

It is with the greatest regret that I have to announce the death of Pippa Brookman from Year Ten.

Pippa was one of our hardest-working pupils and well known for her selfless charity work. Most recently she'd been playing a key role in our project to raise awareness of the marginalisation of the elderly in our society. Our thoughts are with her family and friends at this terrible time. Details of memorial service and condolence book will follow.

Below this, in smaller print, a second paragraph added:

Pippa passed away after a tragic accident, out of school hours but on-site, and as such, a full investigation will be conducted. We thank you for your patience and understanding while this takes place. School will remain closed for the rest of this week.

On reading this my first thoughts were, Selfless? Hardly. Closely followed by, No school till Monday! But I knew that wasn't the kind of thing you were supposed to say out loud at times like these. At the moment, Bert had forgotten what Pippa was like, what she'd done to her. People always did that when someone died – got carried away, virtually turning them into a saint. I knew I'd just have to wait it out.

Genevieve came around our side of the table. She bent down and kissed the top of Bert's head. Then she put her hand on my shoulder and gave it a squeeze. It was nice.

'I'll get a card,' Genevieve said. 'And some flowers for her mother. Poor, *poor* Vanessa . . .'

She sat back down at the table.

'Have a quiet day today, girls,' she said. 'Look after each other.'

We hung about in the den for the afternoon, not doing anything or talking much. Bert put on some CD or other, some mournful-sounding music. It was peaceful up there. Hearing about Pippa had been a shock but I started to get used to the idea. Then I began to enjoy my own thoughts, having fantasies where school was cancelled forever, where I didn't have to go home. Where Bert and I stayed in the den every day, no one in the world but us.

Bert's phone kept ringing all day, but she didn't answer it. Once I caught sight of the screen. Jac.

'What's *he* doing ringing you?' I asked, trying hard to stop it sounding like an accusation.

Bert shrugged and cancelled the call. 'People just want to . . . talk. You know. Offer sympathy. They all knew I was friends with her.'

Around half past three, Charlie brought up a tray of lemonade and some thick slices of ginger cake.

'Keep the sugar up,' he said. 'It's good for shock.'

I thanked him and started to cram the delicious cake into my mouth. Bert nibbled at hers without much interest.

'There are some more details of . . . of what happened,' Charlie said as he turned to leave. 'Up on the *Echo*'s website. If it'll make you feel better to know, that is. Only look if you want to.'

Bert nodded and Charlie closed the door. Bert pulled the laptop over to us and flipped it up.

The story was on the website's front page.

Inspirational teen dies in bizarre backstage accident

I snorted, 'Inspirational!' But Bert shot me a sharp look so I was quiet while we read.

A Year Ten student at Whistle Down Academy has died on school premises after becoming engulfed by a fireball.

Philippa Brookman, 14, was making last-minute preparations backstage for the grand finale of the school's acclaimed *An Outing to Oz* production, created to help raise awareness of the struggles of the elderly, when for reasons that are currently unclear, a fire started in a metal wastepaper bin. A discarded aerosol can in the bin exploded with the heat, engulfing the tragic teen in a fireball. It is believed that Philippa had been trying to salvage show costumes and that this could've delayed her escape from the building.

Emergency services rushed to the scene but Philippa died of her injuries in hospital later that night, with her parents and brother at her bedside.

Mark Jeffrey, head teacher at Whistle Down Academy, has urged the public to respect the family's privacy. 'I would like to respectfully request that we don't intrude on the family's grief by speculating about the cause of the accident. A full investigation will be carried out in due course.'

Philippa's friends took to social networking sites to pay tribute to the youngster, described by many as 'a true angel'. There were also claims that Philippa had started the fire herself although these are currently unsubstantiated.

The article went on with more nauseating stuff about how wonderful Pippa was and everything she'd done 'for the community'.

'Hmm,' I said, closing the laptop. 'Don't mention anything about what a cow she could be though, do they?'

I tried a smile but Bert didn't return it.

'Don't,' she said, slightly irritably. She turned away from me.

Later that afternoon, when an invitation to dinner wasn't forthcoming, I headed home. I hadn't planned to tell Nan about Pippa or the accident or anything. I thought if I didn't mention that school was closed then I could head off as normal again tomorrow and have another full day with Bert, no questions asked. But Nan had found out all on her own.

'I've seen the paper,' she said as soon as I was in the door. 'About your school and that girl.'

'Oh,' I said. 'Yeah. That.'

'Did you know her? The girl?'

I shook my head. 'Not really. Just seen her around.'

'Stupid girl,' Nan said. 'Setting fire to herself.'

I nodded.

'Still, no school tomorrow then. Good. You can help me clean the oven.'

'OK.' I sighed and headed up to my room.

When I was in bed that evening, I texted Bert to let her know I wouldn't be able to go over tomorrow. We hadn't made a formal arrangement but I think it was generally understood that we'd be spending these bonus free days together. But it didn't matter anyway. Bert replied a few minutes later:

I'm going away tomorrow anyway. Parents taking me to my aunt's cottage in New Forest to get over things. Back Sunday night. See you on Monday.

I smiled at that text. 'To get over things.' God love Bert and her penchant for melodrama. Still, I thought, leave her to it. Things would be back to normal soon enough.

37

The next few days dragged, trapped in the house following a series of orders barked by Nan, both of us trying to ignore Granddad's nonsensical mutterings. I was actually relieved to get back to school on Monday.

I knew that people would be talking about Pippa of course, but I suppose I hadn't really anticipated quite how much fuss there would be. I've always found histrionics a bit annoying. I suppose I get it from Nan, but I find people making a drama and going over the top about things a bit embarrassing. As I made my way to our form room for registration I passed groups of people crying, arms around each other, or sitting alone on benches just staring forlornly into space. The corridor outside the hall was a carpet of flowers and teddy bears. I found it hard to believe that all these people could really have liked Pippa this much. In fact I'm sure some of the people dabbing at their eyes with tissues probably hadn't even spoken to her before. It annoyed me a bit really. I wondered if they'd still be crying if they knew her like I did. I just kept my head down and made my way to our tutor room ready to catch up with Bert and find out about her weekend in the New Forest.

But Bert wasn't there. I waited and waited for her to come bounding in the door but she never appeared.

I sent a text while I waited for first period to start:

Where are you?

She replied a few minutes later:

Still feeling shaken. Having a quiet day at home. See you tomorrow.

I rolled my eyes. I thought she was milking it a bit now, to be honest. And I was slightly irritated at her, leaving me to cope with all the drama on my own. I decided not to reply.

Mr Jeffrey did a special assembly for Pippa. I didn't go. I walked right down to the end of the field and sat in the trees where no one could see me. I suppose it was risky to draw attention to myself by not going, but I just couldn't bear the thought of it. Of sitting there while everyone spouted nonsense about how wonderful Pippa was, no doubt a huge photo of her massive moon face showing on the projector screen.

I don't think I spoke to a single person that day, except to answer a few questions in maths. Talk of Pippa was everywhere though.

'She must've been having a crafty fag, don't you think? Didn't stub it out properly.'

'Maybe it was an electrical thing . . . something must've just short-circuited or whatever.'

'God, what an awful way to go. Burnt alive.'

It was a bit annoying, I suppose, knowing what had happened but it not occurring to anyone to ask me for my theory, but really I knew it was a good thing that I was so invisible. I knew the sensible thing was for me to keep my head down for a few days.

Once it'd all come out – what Pippa had done, what she was trying to burn – then maybe I'd join in a bit more. I could tell them how I knew she was bad news all along. Hopefully by that point people would've got over the whole 'poor little dead girl' routine and they'd be ready to see her for who she really was.

At home that evening we'd just finished dinner and were sitting in the lounge when the doorbell rang. It made all three of us look up in surprise. The doorbell rang so rarely in our house I think all of us had forgotten what it sounded like. I got up to answer it.

There were two people on the doorstep, a man in a police uniform and a woman in a sensible trouser suit and long beige mac. Her hair was up in a tight bun and she looked a bit severe.

'Good evening,' the woman said. She flashed me a glimpse of an ID badge. 'I'm Detective Sergeant Dale and this is Police Constable Harding. Are you Frances Bird?'

'Uh, yeah,' I said, looking from the woman to the man and back again. The man seemed very young, I thought. He looked more like a teenager, dressed up in the police uniform for fun, than a real policeman.

'Are your mum and dad at home?' DS Dale asked.

I shook my head. 'My mum's dead.'

This seemed to throw her for a moment, which I suppose had been my intention. 'Ah. I see. Well, is there someone else?'

'My nan and granddad are here,' I said, gesturing to the living room. Right on cue, Nan emerged.

'Who is it?' she called. When she caught sight of the people on the doorstep she came over to join me in the doorway. 'Can we help you?' She peered at DS Dale and PC Harding suspiciously.

'We'd just like a quick word with Frances, please,' DS Dale said. 'It's with regards to an accident at her school.'

'That girl who set herself on fire?' Nan asked, still not showing any sign of letting them in.

DS Dale nodded. 'Philippa Brookman. Yes, that's right.'

'Well it's nothing to do with Frances, is it?' Nan snapped. 'She barely knew the girl.'

'It's just a few questions,' said DS Dale, her voice light and friendly. 'Shouldn't take too long. We're talking to everyone who might be able to help. We're just anxious that we get to the bottom of what happened.'

Nan hesitated for a moment but then she said, 'You'd better come in. Go in the kitchen.'

DS Dale said that Nan should stay with me while they talked to me and we all sat at the kitchen table. I wished Nan didn't have to be there. I wasn't sure what the police were going to say exactly but I knew it wouldn't take much for Nan to get snippy and blame me for something.

DS Dale did all of the talking. I wondered why PC Harding had bothered turning up at all to be honest. Maybe it was a work experience thing. She asked me a few general questions about how I knew Pippa and then she got onto the business of Wednesday night's fire.

'Can you tell me where you were at around five o'clock on Wednesday afternoon?'

I had to think about this for a moment. As far as Nan knew I was at school, in the library doing my homework, but then if anyone asked I'd planned to tell them I was at Bert's.

'I was at my friend Bert's,' I said eventually. 'Doing homework,' I added for Nan's benefit.

'Were you?' Nan said, looking at me. 'I thought you were in the library.'

'I was going to go to the library,' I said, 'but you can't really talk in there and it was a group project so we thought it'd be easier to just go back to Bert's and –'

'Sorry,' DS Dale said, interrupting and flipping through her notebook. 'Can I just confirm – you're talking about your classmate, Alberta Fitzroy-Black? You're saying that at around five o'clock on Wednesday the fifteenth of May, you were with her, at her parents' house?'

I nodded. 'Yeah,' I said. 'Alberta's. We were in her den. It's like her attic room.'

'And you were there the whole afternoon?'

'Yeah,' I said again. 'Right from the end of school until about eight o'clock. Maybe half past.'

DS Dale frowned. 'You're quite sure about that? You didn't pop out for anything?'

I squinted, pretending to think hard. 'Nope. I was with Bert the whole time.'

DS Dale put her notebook down and rested her pen on top. 'The thing is, Frances, according to our information, you left the Fitzroy-Blacks' at around four-thirty and didn't return until almost five-forty-five.'

I panicked. I searched my brain, trying to work out who could've seen me leave. I'd been so careful to pull my hood up the second I stepped outside the door. I hadn't seen anyone else the whole way to school, so whoever had spotted me must've been watching surreptitiously, through a window or something. I didn't have long to think. I needed to decide how to play this. I could either pretend that I had actually popped out, but just to run some innocent errand, not to go anywhere near Pippa or the school, or I could just deny everything. Tell them their witness had got it wrong. I decided the second option was safer. If I started changing my story now and 'remembering' new details like a trip to the shop or whatever I'd look guilty as hell.

I shook my head, being careful to make my expression look confused and not angry or defensive. 'No,' I said. 'That's not the case at all. I was in the house that whole time. Just ask Bert. She'll tell you. Your witness or whatever must be confusing me with someone else.'

DS Dale frowned again and shifted in her seat. She picked up her pen and clicked the button on the end. 'We did ask Alberta, Frances. And she told us that you left the house at four-thirty. And according to Alberta, you were heading to the school. To talk to Philippa Brookman.'

38

Everything seemed to go fuzzy for a moment. I felt like DS Dale
had set off a series of little bombs. It was Bert. She'd told them
I'd left the house. She'd told them I was heading to the school.

I shook my head. 'N-no,' I stammered. 'Bert wouldn't have
said that. You must've made a mistake. Misunderstood what
she was saying.'

DS Dale flicked through her notepad and stopped on a
page. She looked down and tapped it with her pen. 'Nope.' She
shook her head. 'No mistakes. Alberta was quite sure that you
left her at around four-thirty on Wednesday the fifteenth of
May and that you planned to meet Philippa Brookman on the
school premises. She said that you returned just over an hour
later, having had some kind of confrontation with Philippa.'

I just stared at DS Dale. I closed my eyes for a moment and
breathed out hard. The first thought was, *They're lying.* They're
just saying that Bert said that to make me crack, make me
change my story. But then I realised that that wasn't possible –
Bert was the only person who knew I was going to meet Pippa.
They couldn't have made it up from nowhere. Bert must have
said something. Bert. My best friend Bert.

I didn't have time to think about why Bert would have done it, to process how I felt about it. Part of me wanted to explode – I wanted to tell them that Bert was lying, tell them she was a girl who'd had a relationship with a married man, for God's sake, she was hardly an upstanding member of society. But I knew that that was risky. What if someone else had seen me and they backed her up? I needed to say something. I needed to be clear and reasonable. Whatever story I came out with next I was going to have to stick with, so it had to be convincing.

My first impulse was to think of somewhere I could've been going, some fictitious errand I was running to get supplies for our project or whatever, but I knew that could be hard to think up on the spot. That would bring a whole new selection of puzzle pieces into the mix – where I'd been going, who might've seen me, did I have a receipt, CCTV cameras along the route. I realised that my only sensible option here was to stick to something as near to the truth as possible. The thing I had to remember here was that I hadn't really done anything that wrong. I didn't go to the hall intending to burn the costumes. I definitely didn't go there intending to set Pippa on fire. I'd just gone to talk to her. To get her side of the story. That was exactly what I told the police now.

I told them how I'd confronted Pippa, how I'd found out what she'd been doing to Bert, how she'd panicked and tried to burn her own things. I told it all.

DS Dale listened without saying anything and without showing any emotion at all. She noted down the whole lot in her pad.

'What the bloody hell were you playing at?' Nan asked me. 'Why did you have to interfere?'

I looked down. 'She'd been bullying Bert,' I said. 'I had to stop her.'

A look passed between DS Dale and PC Harding. 'What I'm not quite clear on then,' DS Dale said, 'is why you didn't report what had happened straight away? Especially when you found out what had happened to Philippa? You knew there was an investigation, surely?'

I shrugged. 'Well, I knew I'd been the last person to see her alive. I just . . . just didn't want any hassle.'

'I see,' DS Dale said, clicking her pen again and closing her notepad. 'Right then. Thank you, Frances. I'm sure we'll have more questions as things progress but that's it for now.'

DS Dale and PC Harding stood up and Nan showed them out.

I barely listened as Nan launched into a tirade about lying to her and sneaking about and the stupidity of getting myself caught up in a police investigation. I just let it wash over me. What was really on my mind here was Bert. How could she have dropped me in it like that? *Why* would she? I was still holding out hope that there was some kind of explanation. It just couldn't be a simple case of betrayal. I just couldn't believe it.

I thought about texting Bert or calling her to have it out with her, but I decided it was a conversation that needed to be had face to face. I resolved to just act normally and do nothing until we got the chance to talk at school.

But when I got to school the next day, Bert still wasn't there. I texted her to ask her where she was as soon as registration had started and it was apparent she wasn't going to show up again. There was no reply.

As the day went on, I felt myself getting more and more agitated. Bert needed to get a grip. Why was she still moping around? I'd put up with her being a drama queen for long enough. Now she'd dropped me in it and I had the right to some answers.

In last period I sent her a text. I was careful to phrase it gently, although it took some effort:

How are you feeling? Can I come over?

This time I got a reply at least:

Better now thanks but helping Mum and Dad with chores tonight so think we'll just have to talk at school tomorrow.

I sighed. I didn't really buy the whole chores excuse, but then I was hardly surprised she was avoiding me. So she bloody well might, I thought, given what she'd done. I started to make my way home, but then suddenly the thought of another evening with Nan and Granddad in that silent house, Nan being even more snappy than ever, me stressing about what Bert had done, seemed too much to bear. I'd had enough. And even now, even though I was angry with Bert, I still missed her. We were never apart for this long. I just wanted to talk to her. I thought if we could just talk, we could sort everything out. There had to be some kind of explanation for what she'd said. I needed to find out what was going on.

I rang the doorbell and waited. No one came, so I tried the knocker. Still nothing. I stepped back and looked up at the house. The skylight in the den was slightly open and I could hear music drifting out. She obviously can't hear the bell up there, I thought.

I went around the back of the house. The back door was open as usual. I slipped inside and followed the music up the three flights of stairs to the den. I'd planned to use the chores she was supposedly helping her parents with as a pretext for my visit. I'd say I'd come to help out with whatever it was.

'Hello!' I called. I deliberately kept my voice light and cheery. I was determined not to go in there all guns blazing. I wanted to talk calmly, to sort this out and get things back on track. The last thing I wanted was to end up in a row with Bert. There'd been more than enough drama for one week.

I pushed the door open. 'It's only me! It's Birdy! I've come to lend a hand!'

I stood in the doorway and looked at them. It took me a couple of minutes to register what I was seeing, it was so unexpected. I think I kept my smile in place the whole time. I must've looked quite mad, come to think of it.

It was Bert, huddled in the corner of the Egg. And next to her, their legs entwined, her head on his shoulder, was Jac Dubois.

'Birdy!' Bert said, struggling to push herself upright. 'What are you doing here?'

I didn't answer the question, I just stared at them, looking from one to the other. Eventually, I said, 'I don't think he should be here. You're not allowed to see him, remember? Your dad said.'

Bert looked confused and maybe a little bit amused. 'What? Yes I am. Dad likes Jac actually.' Bert smiled at Jac in the most nauseating way and he returned the look. It was almost unbearable to witness. It was like I wasn't there.

'No,' I said slowly and clearly, like I was explaining something to a small child. 'You're not supposed to spend too much time with him. Your parents don't want you being harassed, after everything that happened with . . . you know. I was worried about you so I spoke to your dad myself and –'

I knew I was taking a risk, mentioning my little warning visit to Charlie, how I'd let him know what Jac had done at the party, but I was thinking on my feet. Desperate times, desperate measures, and all that. But Bert cut me off.

'Oh, Birdy . . .' she said, sighing and swinging her legs out of the chair. 'I know you came over telling Dad that Jac and I had been up to all sorts at that party – he told me straight away.'

'He didn't,' I said. 'He didn't!'

'He did, Birdy,' Bert said. 'It's OK. I don't mind. I know it's hard for you . . . it's always hard being the single one. I know you were just upset and feeling left out, that's why I didn't say anything. I didn't want to embarrass you.'

I couldn't think of anything to say for a minute. I just stood there, breathing hard. Staring at Jac's hand, resting on Bert's knee. Just casually sitting there, like it was the most natural thing in the world.

'But,' I said eventually, 'your dad phoned the school. Got Jac taken off the show. The seating plan . . . he was moved away from you.'

Bert looked at Jac and then to me, frowning. 'What? No he didn't. Dad wouldn't phone the school. That's not really his style.'

'Got kicked off the play 'cause of my shit maths grades,' Jac said, with a proud grin. 'All my own fault, that. They're still shit actually, so they shouldn't have bothered.'

'And I don't really see what the seating plan has to do with

249

anything,' Bert chipped in. 'That doesn't really add up does it? Who cares where we sit for the register? It only takes two minutes.'

'Would take more than that to keep me away,' Jac said, leaning forward and pulling Bert close to him. She collapsed in his arms, shrieking in mock protest. They giggled and then he leant down and kissed her forehead.

I didn't move. I could hear my pulse in my ears.

'Get off her,' I heard myself say. 'Get off her and get OUT.'

My voice started off quiet, but I shouted the word 'out'. It made them jump. They turned to look at me. The smiles disappeared from their faces.

'Birdy . . .' Bert began.

Suddenly I remembered something. I unzipped my bag. 'Here,' I said, hoping my voice wasn't giving away how desperate I was feeling. I reached in and pulled something out. 'I bought you a present.'

It was a little porcelain blackbird figurine I'd found a week ago at a craft fair outside the church. I'd bought it for Bert just after the Allenby email. I thought it'd cheer her up – a little reminder that I was still there for her, that I'd *always* be there for her, blackbirds forever. But then the whole naked photos and Pippa thing had erupted and there hadn't seemed a good time to give it to her. Now though, I was glad I was able to hand it over. She needed that reminder more than ever now.

'It's a blackbird,' I explained, holding it out to her.

But she didn't reach forward to take it. Instead she sighed. 'Oh, Birdy,' she said, closing her eyes for a second. 'You know, I think I've had just about enough of blackbirds for a while.'

Jac began to laugh. 'A blackbird? You're mental, you are.' He shook his head.

'Shut *up*,' I hissed.

'I've got a better idea,' Jac said, turning and looking at me through narrowed eyes. 'Why don't *you* shut up? Why don't *you* shut up and get out? Why are you here anyway? Why are you always hanging around, like some fucking poodle? She told you not to come.'

'I'm warning you,' I said, my voice low and dangerous again.

Jac laughed. 'Warning me? What are you going to do – set fire to my head?'

My eyes were on Bert then. She looked down. Guilty.

'Jac,' she said quietly. 'Don't.'

Jac wasn't going to be put off now though. 'Bert told me how you went to pay Pippa a visit. How she got one of your "warnings". Next thing we know she's gone up in flames.' He'd got out of the chair now and was standing facing me. 'What happened, Frances? What did you do to her?'

'Nothing,' I said. 'I did nothing.'

'Whatever,' he said. 'They'll find out soon enough. Then you'll be carted off to some asylum and we can all forget you ever existed.'

I think until this point I'd actually forgotten why I'd gone over there in the first place. I'd been so shocked to find Jac there that all the fire and police business had gone right out of my mind. But now it came back to me.

'You told them,' I said, turning to Bert now. 'You told the police I went to meet Pippa. Why did you do that, Bert? Why couldn't you just stick to our story?'

Bert didn't answer at once. She looked down into her lap. 'It just wasn't right to lie,' she said eventually. 'Pippa's *dead*, for God's sake. That's serious.'

'So?' I said, throwing my hands up. 'Who cares? Pippa was a cow, Bert. Can't you remember what she did to you? Don't tell me you've forgotten already?'

Bert sighed and looked upwards towards the skylight. She closed her eyes for a second. Then she opened them and looked at me again, her face completely blank.

'Maybe you should go now, Frances,' she said. Her voice was so cold suddenly. And the name – not Birdy. Frances.

'Birdy,' I said quietly. 'My name is *Birdy*.'

'Cuckoo, more like,' Jac said, sinking back down in the chair next to Bert. She burrowed into his shoulder like she was trying to hide.

The next bit is slightly blurred, in terms of memories. I remember being angry obviously. A raging fury. The kind that takes you over, makes you feel like you've got fire running through your veins. I remember there was a snow globe on the shelf. It was one of those ones that shows a summer scene – a palm tree and a hammock – but still with the white powdery snow. That made me even angrier. Who puts a fucking beach scene in a fucking snow globe for fuck's sake? I picked it up. And then I threw it.

Jac must've looked down momentarily, not seen it coming, because he didn't even duck. It hit him right on the top of the head.

'Argh!' he shouted. 'Bitch!'

'Frances!' Bert said, climbing out of the chair and coming

towards me. 'Stop. That. Now.' She was speaking firmly and clearly. It was horrible. Like she was talking to a toddler. Or a dog. 'Calm down. Go home. We'll talk tomorrow.'

'No,' I said. 'I'm staying. I'm spending the evening with you. Just the two of us.'

'No,' she said. 'I'm spending the evening with my boyfriend. Tomorrow, we'll –'

But she never got to tell me what we were going to do tomorrow, because I'd picked up the scissors from the shelf – they were the big, dressmaking kind – and in one quick, forceful movement, I'd lunged forward and stuck them into her.

You hear those stories, don't you, about people suddenly finding unknown strengths when they have to – lifting cars off babies and all sorts. It must've been like that because I don't remember it even being that difficult. There was no resistance really, the blade just sunk right in. Like cutting into a cheesecake. They were stuck right in her side, the scissors. They looked funny, poking out like that, the cheerful red and white spotted handle just perched there, suspended in mid-air.

Bert's knees buckled and she fell to the floor. Jac was all over her at once. Flapping, fussing. 'Bertie,' he kept saying. 'Bertie, Bertie, Bertie.'

He pulled the scissors out. That was stupid. You shouldn't take the plug out, I thought everyone knew that. That causes all sorts of mess. God, the blood! It was all over the place. They'll never get it out of the carpet. Served them right though. There, I thought. That's what I think of your precious evening with your precious 'boyfriend'.

Jac stared up at me, his face grey. 'You've killed her,' he said.

39

Of course, I hadn't actually killed her.

That was just Jac being a drama queen. No doubt he had visions of killing himself with the grief of it all, the two of them lying there together, beautiful pale corpses. A right little *Romeo and Juliet* scene.

Bert was whisked away in an ambulance. Spent a few days in intensive care, but she was well soon enough. They had to whip out one of her kidneys as it was too far gone, but I shouldn't think that matters much these days. Plenty of people manage with just the one.

I was so fed up with the whole thing by that point that when it came to the interviews I just told the police everything. I just let it all flow out, the whole exhausting story. I realised that I was just *sick* of being so unappreciated. I'd dedicated most of the year to Bert, to guiding her through, to taking care of her, to showing her what people could be like, and she'd repaid me by betraying me. By going behind my back with Jac, by ruining my alibi and reporting me to the police.

I tried to explain it to them all – to the detectives, the psychiatrists, the social workers – but I don't think I did a very good job because they just didn't seem to be getting it. They kept focusing on all the isolated incidents on their own and not seeing the bigger picture at all. I mean, I admit, if you just look at the scissor stabbing or the forged email or the naked photos on their own, then of course it looks bad, but I didn't just do them out of the blue, for no reason. They were all born out of the circumstances we were in at the time.

I admit that not everything went exactly as I'd thought it would that year, but then what they didn't seem to understand was that it wasn't *all* planned. They made out like it was some carefully constructed operation, each and every step plotted out months in advance – a 'systematic campaign of intimidation and manipulation', the judge called it – but really, that wasn't the case at all. I just dealt with things as they came up, doing whatever I thought needed to be done at the time.

It started with that graffiti on Bert's locker. I don't need to tell you I didn't have anything to do with that – as if I could have ever been responsible for such unbridled use of punctuation – but that didn't mean I wasn't pleased with its effect. I still have no idea who did scrawl that little message on Bert's locker – it was true what I'd said at the time, it could've been anyone. But it didn't matter. I saw how Bert reacted. Shocked, of course. Hurt. But when she'd got over it, when she'd bounced back, it was with a new wisdom. A new understanding of the world. An understanding that told her that she couldn't trust everyone around her, that not everyone liked her and not everyone would be nice to her, but that I – good, loyal Birdy – would always be there for her. Always ready to pick up the pieces.

It took more than one lesson though. People like Bert are flighty. Fickle. You saw what she was like for yourself – sworn off boys one minute, up to no good with Jac at a party the next, angry with Pippa one minute, planning minibreaks to the Lake District the next. She had such a short memory. When she got carried away again, when she got so caught up in the delight of being cast as the lead in that godawful play, I realised it was time for a reminder. Just something to make sure she remembered that even though the play might be exciting and she might be Little Miss Popular for now, there were no guarantees that everything was always going to be so rosy. And something that reminded her that I was still there, waiting for her, whatever happened.

The other bits – the Allenby email, the dodgy photos – there wasn't anything particularly meaningful about the timing of those really. I'd seen Bert's email account left open one evening and saw an opportunity. I knew how people would react to that email. I knew that would show Bert what people are like: judgemental, gossipy. And I hoped it would show her how important it was that she took care of her reputation. She couldn't just be getting drunk and cosying up to boys at parties. People in places like Whistle Down like to talk. I knew it wouldn't cause any lasting damage though. I knew it'd be just enough to show her just how supportive I could be, but I knew people wouldn't ever think it was really from her. I was clever you see – the last thing I wanted was for Allenby and Mr Jeffrey to think she'd actually sent the thing and get Bert expelled – so I put in those little spelling mistakes. Anyone who knows anything about Bert would know straight away that she wouldn't be caught dead writing 'wear' when she meant 'where'.

Those photos though, they took even me by surprise. I was definitely surprised when I found them, that's for sure. I mean, they weren't part of the plan at all really. I hadn't even meant for them to fall out in front of everyone like that. I just wanted Bert to find them when I was there, to see her squirm. I wanted her to explain herself. I was just so angry when I found them. I knew what had happened with Richard of course, but I suppose I'd chosen to block it out. Seeing them like that, together, it was like when she first told me all over again. And seeing Bert prostituting herself like that! I just couldn't believe it. Maybe I'd been hoping she'd tell me that they weren't for him at all. That she'd never given them to him. I suppose they scared me in a way. Why had she kept them? Was she still hung up on him? Or was she keeping them for someone else? I hated not knowing. I felt deceived. It just shook me up, really.

I do realise that some of what I did was hard for Bert at times. I didn't really enjoy those bits – seeing Bert looking so forlorn after her opening performance when she realised she was the talk of the school for all the wrong reasons, seeing her cry in the toilets knowing everyone had seen her practically naked – they were hard for me too. But people keep focusing on all the negative bits. It's like they've never heard of the end justifying the means. It wouldn't have worked at all if Bert hadn't felt a bit bad, a bit worried or embarrassed. How could I have taught her how nasty and immature everyone was if nothing had ever happened to get them to show their true colours? And how could I ever have shown her what a good friend I could be if everything was always plain sailing and she never needed me at all?

One idea they seemed to get a bit fixated on during the interviews was that I'd deliberately set out to frame Pippa, right from the beginning. I hadn't, of course. I barely gave her a second thought back then, when everything started. Again, I was just dealing with crises as they came up. Pippa was getting a bit too big for her boots as far as I could see and Bert was getting all too taken in by her. If I'd realised before that they were having dinner together and planning little summer holidays I might've stepped in sooner, but I didn't know about any of it until Bert told me that time in the toilet when she was crying about the photos. And at that point it just seemed like the perfect answer to everything – take Pippa down a couple of notches and at the same time show Bert that she could count on me to take care of things for her.

Planting the evidence in Pippa's bag was probably the trickiest bit of the whole operation. I admit, I did feel a little bit sly at that point. There was a lot to think about there. I'd kept all the photos I'd found so that was easy enough but I did feel a bit creepy sneaking a pair of Bert's pants out of her drawer when she wasn't looking. I was worried she was going to catch me with them actually. I mean, how awful would it have looked if Bert had found me smuggling a pair of her knickers under my jumper? She would've thought I was a right lunatic.

It wasn't just getting the evidence in the bag that I had to think about either. I had to make sure the stage was all set up ready – matches to hand, petrol-soaked rag packed in nice and tight at the bottom of the bin in case the fire needed a helping hand. I had to make sure it burnt for long enough, you see. I had to make sure it was still going when the teachers or fire brigade or whatever turned up. Wouldn't have been much good if the whole thing had fizzled out by then. I'd been in two minds about leaving the can of spray paint in the bin to be honest, but in the end I thought, why not? If it did explode, it might give Pippa a little fright, which would be amusing at least. I'd completely forgotten it by the time I went to meet Pippa actually. I definitely never planned for it to end up killing her. But then, thinking about it now, I'm not sure I would've been too concerned even if it had occurred to me. I probably would've thought it was worth a shot. Pippa really was a total pain in the bum, you know.

The court case was SO boring. You see these things on telly but you don't realise how slow they are in real life. And so full of people who think they're incredibly interesting and important. I mean, it wasn't the police and the judge that I minded so much – they seemed to have a bit of backbone about them at least – it was all the awful counsellors, psychologists, youth workers . . . they were the ones who really got on my nerves. So *earnest*, the lot of them. So smug.

The judge did come out with a bit of a corker at one point though – she said I 'exhibited a chilling lack of remorse'. I couldn't help but smile a bit then. *Seriously*, I thought, *is that the best you can do?* That line must've been used at least a thousand times by judges up and down the country; couldn't she think of something a bit more original? Although, I suppose she did add her own little twist because what she actually said was that my lack of remorse *would've* been chilling if it hadn't been for my 'obvious mental disturbance'. Honestly, these people are so rude sometimes.

So. Here I am. In this 'secure facility'. Not a prison, obviously. I'm too young for that. And too barmy, apparently. They like to make that point all the time: 'You're not here to be punished, Frances. You're here to be treated.'

'Wish you'd treat me to a pizza,' I replied the first time they said that, giving them a little grin. You know, to lighten the mood. Didn't grin back though, did she, that dour old doctor. Just stared at me, her head on one side. I don't know why I bother sometimes. They're such a humourless bunch in here.

Anyway, who knows how long they'll keep me here. Until I'm rehabilitated apparently, whatever that means. It could be worse I suppose. I don't mind sitting around in my room on my own. Wearing joggers all day and watching TV. Some people here make such a fuss about it, but then maybe their lives on the outside were a bit more enjoyable than mine. It's funny really, but for the first time in my life, I feel like I actually fit in quite well. Everyone's odd in here; I'm not even the worst. And everyone's on their own. There are a few desperate little cliques but no one really looks up to them. They're the weak ones. It's people like me, the lone wolves, who get the respect in this kind of place.

The therapy sessions are awful though. I can't wait to be rid of those. SO dull. Do you know they have whole sessions here where they teach you to control your breathing? Seriously. Not meaning to boast but I can do A-level maths problems without too much difficulty but here I am listening to some woman with bad eyeshadow teaching me how to breathe. And then there's all the constant talking things through as well. Do they really think that I'll suddenly start saying something different just as long as they ask me the same question often enough? I did make myself smile, actually, when I was writing the beginning of this, when I put that bit about how I used to want people to talk to me more. Careful what you wish for, eh? Anyway, that's why I've written it all out. It was their idea but I think it makes sense. Now if they want to know what happened – if they really want to know everything – then they can just read this. Then maybe they'll give the questions a rest for a few days.

Nan comes to see me every week. I don't enjoy the visits that much. She looks terrible these days, so old and tired. She was there every day of my trial. Up in the gallery, day after day, wearing her one smart jacket and the proper shoes that I know hurt her feet. I suppose that kind of thing wears a person out. And she's probably having to do everything at home now too, now I'm not there to help. Last week she told me she's thinking about putting Granddad in a home. Said she can't cope any more. I just nodded, but I'd wanted to reach out to her, to put my hand on hers. It'd shocked me, hearing her admit defeat like that. I wanted to say sorry then. They've been trying to get me to say sorry the whole time I've been here but Nan's the only person I really want to apologise to. She looked after me. She did her best for me and now I've left her on her own. I worry about Granddad too. I wonder if he misses me. Or Bridget. Whoever he thinks I am. Maybe he's too far gone now. Maybe he's forgotten I was ever there.

I expect you were imagining that Nan had gone mental at me when all this came out but actually she didn't. We've never talked about any of it really. She's never asked me why.

She had to bring me some things on my first night. Clothes and books and toothpaste. When she handed me the bag she just gave me this sort of smile and said, 'You'll be all right, you know.' It was nice that she seemed so sure. Nan can be a hard person to love but I do it anyway. Maybe she'd say the same about me.

Bert hasn't been in to see me once, if you can believe that. I'm sure she's out of hospital by now but I suppose her parents won't let her come. I saw them there, outside the courtroom, once. They gave me such a mean look. It was horrible – really cold, but full of pity too, and in a way that was worse. I suppose I shouldn't have let it get to me. They are lovely – Charlie and Gen – but they did have a bit of a superior air about them sometimes. They were always just a bit too satisfied with their perfect little family. With their wonderful Bertie.

That's been the really tough bit, of course. Not being able to see Bert. I haven't laid eyes on her since they carted her off on the stretcher and that really hurts. I suppose I would like to apologise to her too, really. Just for that last bit, I mean. For the scissors. There was no great plan there, I admit. I just lost my temper. But then, she and Jac were being really horrible to me so it's not like I wasn't provoked. I'm sure she can see that now.

I'm pretty sure Bert would like the chance to apologise to me too actually. It's all because of her that I'm here after all. If she hadn't grassed me up to the police they would never have known I was to blame for the fire. If she hadn't been so off with me in the den that day when I caught her with Jac I wouldn't have lost my temper and gone at her with the scissors. And I suppose, ultimately, if she hadn't been so erratic and changeable I wouldn't have been so constantly afraid she was going to leave me for Jac or Pippa or anyone else that came along, and then none of it would have happened at all. We'd probably still be OK now, still walking to school together, still going up the high street to look at the shops, still chatting in the Egg. Maybe I should've been more vigilant from the start, spotted what she was like and steered clear. I don't know. It's always easy to say, looking back, what you would've done differently, isn't it? In truth though, I don't know that I would've changed anything really. I certainly wouldn't have chosen not to meet Bert, not for anything.

Anyway, I've just got to keep my head down. Do my time. I'll be out soon enough. And I know that Bert will be waiting for me, ready to pick up where we left off. Maybe we can even get some of our plans back on track – the rowing-boat picnic for sure, maybe even that day trip to Brighton. Bert knows it would take more than a little row to get between us.

Because friends like us, like Bert and me, we'll always be together.

Acknowledgements

Acknowledgements

Thank you to my agent, Jo Williamson, to my editor, Emma Matthewson, and to everyone at Hot Key Books. All are much cleverer than me.

Thank you to James Dawson for the inspiration and the introduction.

Thank you to my mum for all the library trips. Thank you to my dad for doing the voices.

Thank you to Amber for the patience, the ideas, and for everything else.

Thank you for choosing a Hot Key book.

If you want to know more about our authors and what we publish, you can find us online.

You can start at our website

www.hotkeybooks.com

And you can also find us on:

We hope to see you soon!

Jess Vallance

Jess Vallance works as a freelance writer specialising in educational materials, and has written articles on everything from business accounting to embalming a body. Jess lives in Brighton. *Birdy* is her first novel. Follow Jess at www.jessvallance.com or on Twitter @JessVallance1.